C000205870

A Mu

Christmas

A Sanford 3rd Age
Club Mystery (#4)

David W. Robinson

CROOKED
CAT

Discover us online:
www.crookedcatbooks.com

Join us on facebook:
www.facebook.com/crookedcatbooks

Tweet a photo of yourself holding
this book to **@crookedcatbooks**
and something nice will happen.

About the Author

David Robinson is a Yorkshireman now living in Manchester. Driven by a huge, cynical sense of humour, he's been a writer for over thirty years having begun with magazine articles before moving on to novels and TV scripts.

He has little to do with his life other than write, as a consequence of which his output is prodigious. Thankfully most of it is never seen by the great reading public of the world.

He has worked closely with Crooked Cat Books since 2012, when The Filey Connection, the very first Sanford 3rd Age Club Mystery, was published.

Describing himself as the Doyen of Domestic Disasters he can be found blogging at **www.dwrob.com** and he appears frequently on video (written, produced and starring himself) dispensing his mocking humour at **www.youtube.com/ user/Dwrob96/videos**

By the same author

A Murder for Christmas

A Sanford 3rd Age Club Mystery (#4)

Chapter One

"The bus will be here in a few minutes, Uncle Joe," Christine said. "Now just go and enjoy yourself. We'll see to everything."

Joe Murray looked round his café and chewed at his lip. Half past eight, Saturday morning and already the place was heaving. The Lazy Luncheonette was busy every day of the week, thanks to the hands from the factories on the other side of Doncaster Road. Saturdays were normally quiet until 9:30–10:00 when the shoppers turned out in force, but this was not just any Saturday; this was Christmas Eve and the place was packed.

Haggard-looking men, irritable women, and excited children tucked into the festive fare on offer (some of it store-bought rather than home-produced). Tables were awash with cups, plates and cutlery, the Formica tops smeared with spilled tea, coffee and soft drinks. Half-eaten mince pies and slices of Christmas cake littered the place, and the general clatter and chatter was deafening.

Joe's casebooks, those booklets he produced detailing the mysteries and crimes he had solved, and which could normally be found racked neatly on shelves around the café, were now in the hands of customers, and he wondered irritably how many he would have to reprint after being smeared or dog-eared by grubby, infant mitts.

"It's one of the busiest days of the year," he complained to Christine. "I shouldn't be leaving you two alone."

"We'll cope," his nephew's wife assured him. She craned her head back into the kitchen. "Lee, will you tell him to stop worrying."

"Nothing to worry about, Uncle Joe," Lee called from

3

the kitchen and promptly dropped two plates on the tiled floor.

"Nothing to worry about, huh?" Joe whined. "How many is that this week, Lee?"

"He won't break any more," Christine promised. "We've got Thelma, my neighbour's mum, coming in at nine to help out. You've been planning this for months, so get your bags and get out before you miss the bus."

Joe reached to the floor for his suitcase. His fingers closed around the handle and he released it again, straightening up to look into Christine's amused eyes. "I'm only in Leeds. It's less than twenty miles away. I can be back in half an hour by taxi if I have to. Just promise me –"

Busy serving customers while trying to calm his worries, Christine laughed. "Pick up your case and clear off," she said, "and have a good time." She turned back to the customer. "What can I do you for, luv?"

Hands shaking, Joe collected his bag and stepped from behind the counter. He took two paces, stopped and turned around. "If anything goes wrong, you could ruin me."

The customer, a middle-aged woman wearing a heavy, quilted coat, glared at him. "If I don't get my toast soon, I'll bloody ruin you. Why don't you clear off and let the girl get on with it?"

Joe glowered back. "I have a reputation, you know."

"Yes," agreed the customer. "As a tight-fisted, miserable old sod. Do like the girl says. Clear off and give us all some peace."

With a grimace and matching growl, Joe stepped out into the bitter December morning.

Leaden cloud, heavy with snow, hung over Sanford. On the opposite side of the road, the factories stood dormant, their doors closed for the Christmas break. A hundred yards to the left, strung across the entrance to Doncaster Road Retail Park, fairy lights danced in the blustery air and a tall Christmas tree swayed in rhythm to the gusts. A long queue of cars stood at traffic lights, waiting to get into the mall, forcing through-traffic into the offside lane. There were thousands, maybe tens of thousands of people waiting to unload the weight in their wallets.

There were plenty of eateries in the mall, overpriced and over-hyped joints out to make a killing. Joe would benefit from the overspill and his coffers, too, would swell. When customers tired of paying exorbitant prices for plastic food, some would come to the Lazy Luncheonette to take in real, home-cooked fare (notwithstanding the mass-produced mince pies and cakes).

By straining his eyes to his right, he could see the Miners Arms half a mile away and on the car park, the coach where members of the Sanford Third Age Club would be boarding for their Christmas Weekend in Leeds. Joe would normally be there in his role of club chairman, ticking off the members' names as they arrived, but he'd arranged for Sheila and Brenda to deputise so that he could ensure everything at the Lazy Luncheonette was running smoothly before he left.

Wearing a thick winter coat, a scarf wrapped around his thin neck, flat cap covering his curly head of hair, Joe still shivered in the near-zero temperatures: a far cry from the warm September sunshine when he and his two assistants had first planned the jaunt.

Planning was Joe's forte. To his acute and logical brain, organising a three-day trip, arranging buses, booking hotels, was easier than guesstimating bread, bacon and pie requirements for a workman's café; a task he carried out every day of the week. The negotiating skills were similar. Grind the price down as low as you could before the supplier got ready to cut and run, but never skimp on quality. It was all meat and two veg' to him ... literally, in the case of the Lazy Luncheonette.

Joe had found himself painted into a corner by the reservations desk at the Regency Hotel in Leeds. The price was the price, and they would charge him for three days and nights even if he didn't show up until Christmas Day. At that point, Joe almost scotched the entire plan, but his two assistants were just as obdurate and refused to hear his business concerns.

"I can't not open on Christmas Eve," he told Sheila and Brenda. "It's one of the busiest days of the year. I'd lose a fortune."

Seated at the table nearest the counter, during a lull in morning trade, Sheila had said, "Lee can run the place." She immediately backed off as a stack of cups hit the tiled floor in the kitchen. "Christine can come in and run the place. Lee will do the cooking like he always does, and I'm sure you can get someone in casual to help out with the washing up."

"Oh, come on," Joe grumbled. "You guys have worked for me for five years or more. You know what it's like on Christmas Eve. Lee is a brilliant cook. He should be. I sent him to that fancy college, and taught him the best of the rest myself. But he couldn't run a marathon on a pushbike, and it'll need more than Christine and one other hand. I can't do it. I need to be here and I need you two here."

"And miss out on shopping in Leeds?" Brenda sounded convincingly shocked and winked at Sheila to show that she was winding Joe up. "I have plans for December twenty-fourth, Joe," she went on. "Me, you, a bottle of shampoo, and a secluded little room in a four star hotel, and –"

"Shampoo?" Joe cut her off. "You're gonna spend Christmas Eve washing your hair?"

"Yes," Brenda agreed. "In Bottinger."

"I think you mean Bollinger," Sheila corrected.

Ignoring their innate skill at delivering jocular misinformation to sidetrack him, Joe went on the attack. "Look, I'll tell you what I'll do," he offered. "We're only going to Leeds. It's half an hour on the motorway. We'll work here, shut the doors at half past two, give the place a quick clean down and I'll get Lee to run us to the Regency in my car."

Sheila's stern eye sent out a clear refusal. "Joe, you and Brenda and I are taking the day off. It's that simple. All you have to do is organise it."

Brenda came out in support of her best friend. "We want

a day in Leeds, then Christmas Day and Boxing Day filled with entertainment at the Regency. End of story."

Joe argued. Forced into a partial retreat, he made the booking but still argued. He spent three months applying pressure on his assistants, individually and jointly, but it was all to no avail.

And he had to admit that the Regency promised a good programme for the festive season. A disco on Christmas Eve, then breakfast, a traditional Christmas lunch and evening meal on the 25th, with live entertainment afternoon and evening, and to round off the weekend, a different but equally varied programme on Boxing Day. There would be no need for any of the guests to venture out of the Regency until they checked out after breakfast on the morning of the 27th. It was tempting. More than that, it was mouth-watering.

But it would mean leaving his precious Lazy Luncheonette in the hands of others for Christmas Eve and longer. Joe's final, desperate excuse that the factories would be open again on Tuesday the 27th fell flat.

"It's a public holiday," Sheila retorted. "Christmas Day falls on a Sunday."

Joe resigned himself to the inevitable. For the first time in living memory, the Lazy Luncheonette would be under the control of inexperienced family members on the busiest shopping day of the year. And with that depressing, almost frightening thought, Joe knew he could never enjoy the weekend.

In the distance, the bus pulled off the Miners Arms car park, into the queue of traffic, and Joe fulminated in silence.

Why couldn't these people see sense? Why couldn't they understand that business was business and took priority over everything?

Watching the bus crawl its way towards him, he understood that his obsession with the Lazy Luncheonette, his reluctance to leave the place, was a reflection on his sad life. Aside from the Sanford Third Age Club, his short writings on the mysteries, puzzles and crimes he had cracked in his 55 years, he had no life beyond the café. It had even been the deciding factor when Alison, his wife of less than 10 years, left him.

"I need more than a cheap diner and a skinflint husband," she had told him on the day the separation became official. Joe had watched her walk out of his life with something akin to sadness, then turned his attention to refurbishment work on the café.

As much as he recognised his failings, he could do nothing about it. The café was his business, his life. It was a virtual symbiosis. He was the driving force behind its success and it gave some focus to his life.

"Just a shame there won't be no one to leave it to other than loopy Lee," he muttered to himself as the bus drew nearer.

Christmas was the worst time of year. Divorced, no children, and aside from Brenda and Sheila, he had few people he could call real friends, so there was no one with whom he could enjoy Christmas, and even in the days when he had – during the years he and Alison were wed – he had never particularly liked the season. It got in the way of making money. He usually spent the day with Lee and Christine, and visited Sheila or Brenda or both on Boxing Day. And yet he never felt particularly lonely; not while he had the Lazy Luncheonette for company.

"So why am I shooting off to Leeds for three days to celebrate something I hate?" he muttered as the bus pulled into the kerb and the air-operated door slid open. Having no answer to the rhetorical question, Joe picked up his suitcase and waited for Keith, the driver.

Stopping like that did nothing to endear the bus driver or the Sanford Third Age Club to other road users and within seconds, horns were tooting.

"You do cause some trouble, Joe Murray," Keith Lowry, a veteran chauffeur of many STAC outings, chortled. He opened the side panel for Joe to drop his small suitcase into the luggage compartment. "Why couldn't you get on at the Miners like everyone else?"

"Gar." Joe's grumble summed up his feelings. Throwing his case into the luggage store, while the driver closed up again, he boarded the coach to a mixed chorus of greetings and complaints.

Sheila and Brenda had taken the front, nearside seats. Across the aisle from them, behind the driver, sat Mavis Barker, an empty seat beside her reserved for Joe. Settling in, he asked, "Everyone here?"

Sheila nodded. "All present and correct, sir. And good morning, Joe."

Alongside her, in the window seat, Brenda leaned forward and gave Joe a cheery wave. "Morning, maestro. In a Christmassy mood are you?"

Joe scowled.

To muted, derisive cheers, the bus pulled out from the kerb, Keith battling his way across to the outer lane where he could accelerate past the queue of traffic for the retail park.

Joe held out his hand across the aisle. "Gimme the microphone, Sheila."

"If what?"

Joe frowned. He was in no mood for lessons on saying please and thank you. "If you don't, I'll have to lean across you and take it and you're always complaining about people invading your personal space."

Sheila tutted. Brenda handed her the microphone and she passed it to Joe. "Good manners cost nothing, Joe."

"Then I'll buy as many as I can get hold of," he riposted and switched on the PA mike. Getting to his feet and turning to face his 70 or so charges, he said, "Morning everybody. Sorry about the slight delay, but I had to make sure my reserve crew didn't bankrupt me while I was away."

A few catcalls greeted his announcement.

"Bankrupt you, Joe?" laughed George Robson. "Rumour has it you supported the Bank of England in last year's downturn."

"Yeah, well I've told you before about listening to rumours. They're nothing but … er … rumours." Joe went

9

on, "All right, folks, here's the drill. We'll be at the Regency in Leeds in about thirty or forty minutes. You grab your luggage quick, and that way this bone-idle sod, Keith, can get his bus back to Sanford and take the rest of the weekend off, then you check in. Drop your luggage in your rooms and the rest of the day is yours. Don't forget, dinner is at seven thirty and the disco starts at nine."

Sat halfway down the bus on the nearside, Captain Les Tanner, looking his usual immaculate self in regimental blazer and tie, asked, "Are you running the disco, Murray?"

Joe shook his head and answered through the microphone. "We're not the only crowd in the hotel. Some mob called the Leodensian Historical Society are there, too, so the Regency have hired a pro DJ to entertain us."

Alongside Tanner, his open-secret lady friend, Sylvia Goodson, complained, "Yes, but he may play all this modern music. We want you to do the disco, Joe."

"Hey, don't blame me. I only made the arrangements and the Regency were insistent. No amateurs." He gave them all a wrinkled smile. "Mind you, by the time I've had a word with the DJ, he'll know that we don't care for anything later than Abba."

The announcement got Joe his first ragged cheer of the morning. Taking his seat again, he passed the microphone back to Sheila who handed it to Brenda who in turn hung it back on its clip above her.

***

Closing her mobile phone, Jennifer Hardy said, "Dennis is on the ground at Manchester Airport. He'll be here in about an hour."

Seated across from her in the grand lounge of the Regency Hotel, Tom Patterson, Chair of the Leodensian Historical Society, lifted his cup, little finger extended, and drank daintily. Putting the cup back on its saucer and replacing both on the table, he applied a judicious pout to his chubby, florid features and asked, "Why do you bother with him, Jennifer? He turns you down time and time again, yet you're still, shall we say, interested in him."

Jennifer crossed one knee over the other, exhibiting a broad expanse of her heavy calves. When they first became acquainted, almost 25 years previously, those calves had been shapely and alluring, exciting, Patterson decided. Back then, he too had been leaner, fitter, trimmer. Time, and the passing of the years, had taken its toll on both of them.

Not that Jennifer was unattractive, merely a little broader in the beam. The large bosom, which had been firm and titillating, now spread from shoulder to shoulder, and rested on the roll of her midriff, which likewise was a recent addition. The lean, hungry face, its high cheekbones and hazel eyes beckoning to admirers, had filled out with the first harbinger of an additional chin. The blonde hair now had a hint of white about it, but it still rained, in straight lines, framing her face.

And yet, for all that she was now in her early fifties, she had lost none of her allure.

She was over ten years his junior, and when he considered that age gap, so large when he was 35 and she 24, he knew that the last quarter century had been less kind to him than it had to Jennifer.

The death of his wife, three years back was, for him, the turning point and the start of a downward slide into middle-aged neglect; the early onset of his autumn years. When Eileen was alive, she had maintained the image that was him, insisted that he shave, put on a fresh shirt and clean underwear every day, keep himself fit and active.

"An image befitting a respected academic," she always said in that shrill voice of hers.

And Patterson had demurred. Not because he was a man easily dominated, but because he knew Eileen was right. In his world, the teaching of history at university level, appearance mattered as much as knowledge. It would be impossible for a man in his position to be taken seriously if he turned up at the university wearing a pair of gardening trousers and a frayed old cardigan. He had to look the part.

Eileen was gone, he reminded himself, taken too early by too much surgery to remove her tumours, and he had allowed the spirit that was the real Tom Patterson, subdued though it may have been, to go with her.

He needed a woman in his life, not only for the sake of love and companionship, but to re-ignite the man beneath.

The thought brought him full circle to Jennifer and the ex-pat, Dr Dennis Wright.

"We were very close," Jennifer was saying. "Especially while we worked on his manuscript." A hint of pleading burned in her hazel eyes. "He loved me, Tom. He still loves me. I'm sure of it. It's not me he rejects, but commitment."

Patterson sighed. "What is love if not commitment, Jennifer? He used you, and when he had no further use for you, he shunned you. Until he needed you again. Like now."

Jennifer lifted her cup and stared through the windows at the overcast morning. Lumbering clouds threatened sleet, if not snow, and the jovial illuminations of the Christmas tree standing outside Leeds Town Hall did little to lift the gloom. Patterson guessed she was reminiscing on the cloudless blue of Alabama skies, a universe away and a year in the past.

The interior of the Regency Hotel's lounge would not help, he surmised. The furnishings were new, but period designed to match the establishment's illusion of grandeur, and the wall lights were subdued to enhance the 'ageing' effect. Large screen TV sets mounted on the walls declared the Regency as a 21st century establishment, but the lighting might just as well have been generated by gas mantles from the turn of the 20th century. Christmas decorations festooned about the place merely added a little twinkle, lifting the sombre aura a few notches.

Jennifer turned her head slowly back to face him. "I know what I know, Tom. I'm not a child, and this was no mere infatuation. It was the real thing."

Patterson shrugged and sipped his tea again. "No one can lead your life for you, my dear, but I don't want to see you hurt again." He let out a long sigh. "You could have all the commitment you wanted right here."

Jennifer smiled, exhibiting fine, white teeth. "Dear Tom. You're very sweet, but you and I were never destined to be anything but the best of friends."

Patterson glanced around the room and concentrated on the bar where a short, rotund man argued with the staff over something. Patterson's lip curled in contempt. "I don't like your mixing with Dennis Wright," he said, "but rather him than Oliver Quinton."

Jennifer, too, looked across the room and Patterson was certain that she shuddered, much though she tried to hide it.

"I can't imagine what he's doing here," she said. "Well, I can, but I don't think it will do him any good."

"The Middleton Penny?" Patterson asked and Jennifer nodded. "You didn't invite him?"

Jennifer laughed. "Dear me, no. Whatever business I had with him was over weeks and months ago. He's a fanatic, Tom. Like Kirkland." She nodded in the direction of businessman Warren Kirkland, sat by the exit. "They're both obsessed with getting their greasy little hands on the penny." This time she made no effort to hide her shiver. "As long as he keeps his distance."

Jennifer drank her tea and stood up. Patterson's blood fired at the sight of her standing before him, attired in shin-length, brown leather boots and a dark skirt that finished just below the knee. "Now, if you'll excuse me, I have some shopping to do before I meet Dennis."

Patterson's eyebrows rose. "You're meeting him?"

"Sorry. Didn't I say? We're having lunch." She smiled again, more hungrily this time. "Prepare yourself for some exciting news this evening, Tom."

Putting her cup and saucer down, she strode off. Patterson watched her behind, broader than it used to be, but no less enticing, wiggle across the richly carpeted floor. As she neared the exit, Kirkland got quickly to his feet and intercepted her. She paused briefly to talk with him. Patterson had no idea what they were talking about, but Jennifer looked serious as she first nodded, and then firmly shook her head before leaving the room.

He sipped his tea again. "Exciting news, eh? We shall have to see, my love."

***

"The Leodensian Historical Society?" Brenda asked. "Who are they, Joe?"

Joe shrugged. "Search me. I assume they know all about Leodensians." He frowned. "What is a Leodensian, anyway? Some kind of lion?"

"A Leodensian is a resident of Leeds," Sheila told them. "Or more accurately, someone who was born in Leeds. The Leodensian Historical Society is precisely what its name suggests. A society of historians or history buffs, all of whom were born in Leeds."

"Where do you learn all this stuff?" Joe asked.

"I read a lot," Sheila admitted. "Books, not Wikipedia."

"I wish I had time to read," Brenda bemoaned. "Too busy partying."

"That's the spirit, Brenda," said Mavis.

Of the three women either side of him, Joe discounted Mavis as a friend except at those times when he needed an extra hand at the Lazy Luncheonette. At all other times, she was merely an acquaintance; a widow who, according to Joe, invested most of her time in the search for new men friends. Short of stature, plump, she had an appalling dress sense, which even now saw her clothed in a bright green winter coat and an equally lurid pair of red trousers. She reminded Joe of one of Santa's elves on an obesity kick.

Between the other two, Joe could never decide which was his closest friend, so he scored them equal. Both widows, known to the Sanford townsfolk as Joe's Harem, they were as chalk to cheese. Sheila was slender to the point of anorexia, Brenda was chunkier, without suffering the gross weight distortion of Mavis. Sheila was capable, intelligent and unflappable, Brenda was more outgoing, but emotional and more down to earth. If Joe had choice, he would have selected Sheila as a wife and Brenda as a mistress, but he did not have a choice. The two women were the best of friends, did everything together, and aside from Brenda's deliberate innuendo, they showed no romantic interest in him whatsoever.

Their attire for the journey highlighted the difference between them. Sheila, whose late husband had been a police inspector, wore a modest, beige jumper and black trousers, her feet clad in fur-lined, sensibly heeled boots. On the rack above her was a plain black, button-up coat. Next to it was a quilted anorak in less-livid red than Mavis' trousers, and Joe knew it belonged to Brenda. The woman herself sported a white blouse, through which her flowery bra could be seen, and a skirt in navy blue, which showed her calves above ankle boots with block heels. Not the warmest of attire for wandering the streets of Leeds on Christmas Eve, but more pleasing on the eye than Sheila's sombre-ish clothing.

Less than ten minutes after joining the motorway outside Sanford, Keith turned off onto the M1 for the last and most difficult leg into Leeds. As he did so, the first flecks of sleet began to hit the windscreen causing Joe to wonder how Brenda would get by in such thin clothing for the day.

He had dressed specifically for the weather, sporting a thick, crew-necked jumper and sturdy denims, with all-weather trainers on his feet. Comfortable enough to ensure he stayed warm no matter what the elements offered.

The bus dropped down the steep incline to the outskirts of the city, and over to the right, some miles away, Joe made out the vast spread of Cross Green wholesale markets. He recalled the days when he and his father had gone to those markets three times a week to buy potatoes and other vegetables, or meat for carving and cooking. That was in a time before daily deliveries from refrigerated vehicles became an option. It seemed to Joe that life was simpler back then.

"The rose coloured tint of nostalgia," Sheila said when he pointed the markets out and told them the tale. "Peter always said that policing was easier when he was a young patrol bobby than it was when he made inspector. I suppose the same is true of all of us."

"Maybe the Leodensians would like to research it," Brenda commented.

"Now that's a funny thing," Joe observed, changing the subject as abruptly as he had brought it up. "Why would a mob of history buffs choose to stay in a hotel in the city where they live?"

"Why are we going there?" Brenda returned. "It's less than twenty miles from Sanford. It's a change, Joe. That's all."

"There's also the point that not all of them live in Leeds," Sheila said, anxious not to openly disagree with either of her friends. "I'm sure some of them do, but I know for a fact that their members come from far and wide. One of them, Dennis Wright, teaches history in Birmingham, Alabama, but he was born in Leeds and obviously has a great affection for the city."

"He must have to drive all that way for a Christmas thrash."

"I said Birmingham, Alabama, Joe. You really should get your hearing checked."

Joe's eyebrows rose. He took out his tobacco tin and rolled a wire-thin cigarette.

"You can't smoke that on here," Mavis reminded him.

"I know, I know. I'm just getting it ready for when we get off the bus." He tucked the finished cigarette in the tin, closed it up and dropped it back in his pocket. Venting his irritation on Sheila and Brenda, he demanded, "Alabama?"

Sheila nodded. "I read about him in the Evening Post. He was born here, in Leeds, and moved to Leeds in Alabama when he was in his late twenties. Lived there ever since. Officially, he's an authority on old coins but he also knows plenty of the history of both cities; Alabama and West Yorkshire."

"Wait a minute," Joe interjected. "He lives in Leeds but teaches in Birmingham? I wouldn't like his petrol bill."

Sheila tutted. "Will you forget England and think Alabama. From Leeds, *Alabama*, to Birmingham, *Alabama* is about 18 miles. It's only like living in Sanford and working in Leeds."

"West Yorkshire or Alabama?" Brenda asked with a cheeky grin.

Sheila sighed. "Don't you start, too," she warned. "I can't see what's so complicated about it."

"It's Christmas Eve and you've taken me away from the Lazy Luncheonette," Joe grunted. "You can't expect my brain to be in high gear, too." He shook his head sadly. "I must have taken a wrong turn in life. I run a café and go nowhere; he looks into boring old cities and travels half way across the world for a Christmas party."

"It's worse than that, Joe." Brenda smiled wickedly. "He's happy and you're as miserable as ever."

Brenda's dig and Joe's responding grimace made Sheila giggle. More soberly, she went on, "He's not just here for Christmas. He's launching a book. *Missing Pennies*. It's all about old and rare coins that have gone missing. One chapter of it is concerned with the 1933 Middleton Penny."

"Nineteen thirty-three as in the year not the number? And Middleton here in Leeds, or somewhere on the outskirts of Scunthorpe, Alabama?"

"I don't think there is a Scunthorpe in Alabama," Sheila retorted.

Ignoring her sarcasm better than she had ignored his, he asked, "Who would want to read a book about pennies in Leeds?"

Sheila tutted and Brenda laughed derisively. "For someone obsessed with money you don't know a lot about it, do you, Joe?"

"I know I pay you two too much of it every week," he retorted. Concentrating on Sheila as the bus joined a long queue of traffic for the city centre, he asked, "So come on. What about these pennies."

She licked her lips and Joe sensed a lesson coming on. "There were only about seven George the Fifth pennies minted in 1933. No one's sure of the real number but the Royal Mint insists it was less than ten. Two of them were

17

installed in the foundations of churches here in Leeds. St Marys at Hawksworth Wood, Kirkstall, and St Cross in Middleton. The Middleton Penny was stolen sometime around 1970, and in order to prevent the other one befalling the same fate, the diocese had it removed from the church foundations and put into safe keeping in a bank. A few years later, it was sold at auction to raise funds for restoration work. No one's quite sure how much the missing penny is worth, but it's estimated to be in the region of £100,000. As I told you, Dennis Wright is an authority on the history of rare coins, and it was the Middleton Penny that got him started."

Passing the Brewery Wharf development on the final leg into the city centre, Joe observed, "He put together a career for tuppence."

Brenda laughed. "Jealous, Joe?"

Sheila joined in the ribbing. "Of course he's jealous. Even the Lazy Luncheonette cost more than tuppence."

Chapter Two

From the fourth floor of Debenhams, Joe gazed grumpily through the windows on the seething mass of people clogging Briggate. He shook his head in bewilderment. "What is wrong with these idiots?"

"I'm sorry. Were you talking to me?"

Joe turned his head to find a middle-aged woman sat right behind him. A blonde to white fringe settled above warm, hazel eyes, but there was nothing warm about the prim set of her small mouth.

"Sorry, luv," he replied. "I was talking to myself. My old man used to say it was the only way to get intelligent answers."

She did not even register his jest, but with a wincing frown, turned back to her male companion.

Joe's gaze passed quickly round the crowded cafeteria, and fell enviously on the long queue at the serving counter. He wished he had queues like that at the Lazy Luncheonette, but then, his place was so small that such popularity would see them lining up along Doncaster Road like they were waiting for tickets to a Neil Diamond concert, and most people wouldn't hang around outside that long. Not in the middle of December, anyway. Here the line stretched all the way back to the escalator and out into the cookshop. Somewhere in the midst of it were Sheila and Brenda.

It was 2:30. Having checked in at the Regency on The Headrow, they came out into the thronging streets just after 10:30. His two companions wanted photographs of Leeds Town Hall, a magnificent edifice with its grandiose columns and domed clock tower.

"After it was built, it became the model for buildings throughout the British Empire, and even Sir John Betjeman praised the building on TV during the early sixties," Sheila lectured them.

"You've also seen it a thousand times before," Joe complained as they stood before the stone lions guarding the grand entrance. "Why do you need your picture taken now?"

"It's a Grade One listed building," Sheila reminded him, "and it's also been listed as one of the top ten town halls in the country."

"It was a Victorian rip off," Joe declared, exhibiting some of his own knowledge of the place. "It was put up to show people how important the city believed it was, and most of those who were taxed to pay for it weren't even allowed to vote."

"Sounds a bit like the democracy at the Lazy Luncheonette to me," Brenda commented and posed with Sheila.

After Joe had taken the photograph, they ambled up The Headrow towards the shopping areas of Briggate. Light snow flecks fell and began to settle on the pedestrianised streets, but the threat of the weather did nothing to quell the shoppers' determination. Every store they visited was full to the gunnels.

Trailing his two friends through the packed streets, his mind on anything but shopping, his arms beginning to fill with their purchases, Joe rang the Lazy Luncheonette several times to make sure everything was fine, and each time he received an irritated response from Christine.

"We're chocabloc, Uncle Joe, and I'm busy. Please stop ringing."

Wandering further through the city, they tackled Kirkgate Market and found it more like the New York Stock Exchange on a busy day. By 12 noon, jostled, pushed, having fought his way through huge crowds, Joe could feel his temper on the verge of snapping, so the two women took him into the General Elliot, opposite the market, for a calming beer.

Even here, getting to the bar was like fighting through a rugby scrum.

"We could have done with Lee," Brenda said when she and Sheila finally secured a half of bitter for Joe and spirits for themselves. "You need a prop forward like him to get attention."

"So how did you manage?" Joe asked with an eye on her cleavage. "Did you show off your finer assets?"

Brenda took his jibe in good part and waggled her bosom at him. "Oh, Joe, if only you knew how much fun you're missing."

Twenty minutes later, they stepped out into the thronging streets again, the women tackling their shopping with apparently indefatigable energy, Joe trudging miserably after them, laden with carrier bags, mostly containing goods Sheila and Brenda had bought and which they could no longer carry.

"You're using me as a bloody pack mule," he grumbled.

"And we have a nice bag of hay for you in the stables at the Regency," Brenda teased.

By two o'clock, even the women had begun to flag.

"Time for din-din," Brenda said.

"I thought you'd never get round to it," Joe whined. Of the mass of goods he carried, his purchases were limited to small bottles of eau-de-toilette, one each for Sheila, Brenda and Christine, a bottle of after-shave lotion for Lee and a selection box of chocolates for his great-nephew, Danny. He had also bought tobacco for himself and a couple of disposable lighters.

"That's me spent up for Christmas," he had declared when he came out of the tobacconist's.

They tried several cafés on Vicar Lane and Boar Lane before turning back up Briggate and eventually deciding on Debenhams.

"You get us a table, Joe," Sheila had suggested, "and Brenda and I will queue up."

It was non-starter. The queue was so long that the

management were refusing to allow anyone through to the tables until they were served.

"Leave it to me," Joe told them, and doubled up convincingly as if he were struggling to breathe and walk.

Taking his cue, Sheila went into negotiation with the manager. "Excuse me. I'm sorry to be a nuisance, but my friend is disabled, and he's suffering a little. Would it be possible for him to sit while I queue up for him?"

The manager took instant pity on them, and agreed to make an exception in Joe's case. Under the envious eyes of some in the queue, he took their mound of purchases, and helped Joe through the multitude to a table by the window, where he now sat, resting his aching bones, waiting for his two companions, with only a grumpy old woman behind and her male companion for company.

Even through the noise of the café, the sound of the Salvation Army playing *Oh Come All Ye Faithful* out in the street still reached his ears. The pavements heaved with people, one or two Santas stood in shop doorways welcoming customers, and those same doorways were packed with slow-moving whirlpools of humanity fighting their way in or out. And yet there did not appear to be much friction. It was as if everyone had taken on the seasonal air of peace and goodwill. Despite the comparatively early hour, the Christmas lights were on, dispelling the overcast gloom and bringing a feeling of good cheer to the retail revellers.

All except Joe. He passed the 20 minutes or so waiting for Sheila and Brenda by ringing the Lazy Luncheonette and hassling Christine (again) until she tired of his whining and cut the connection.

For want of something to occupy his mind, he checked the queue again and the pangs of hunger grew in his belly. At least Sheila and Brenda were almost at the checkout.

"All I'm asking is that you give me what I've earned. What I have a right to expect."

Listening to the woman sat behind him, Joe was almost relieved to know that he was not the only one in a foul mood. Recalling the way she had spoken to him, he half turned in his seat, and demanded, "Are you talking to me?"

She glowered first at her companion, a tanned, stocky man whom Joe guessed to be in his fifties, and then at Joe. "Mind your own bloody business."

It was for moments like that Joe treasured his high threshold of embarrassment and sheer neck. He feared nothing and no one, and if rudeness was the order of the day, he was more than capable of matching it.

"You know when people wish you a merry Christmas?" he asked. "Are they being sarcastic?" He cast a glance at the tanned man sat opposite her. "And you should do yourself a favour, pal. Suicide. It's cheaper than divorce."

"Thanks for the advice," the man replied with a vague smile, "but we're not married." The accent sounded strange. American, but not quite American. British, possibly, with an American drawl. Or maybe Dutch. Their accent could often be confused with English and American.

"Sensible," said Joe, and returned to people-watching through the windows and around the café.

His exchange with the bad tempered woman had not made them the centre of attention (the café was too busy for most people to notice) but one man appeared to be taking an interest. Sat several tables away, his bearded features serene and composed, a pristine white shirt and dark tie showing beneath the folds of his dark, quilted coat, his eyes stared directly at Joe ... no. Not at Joe, but at the table behind him where the couple had settled into a more muted debate. There was no emotion in the beard's face. He simply watched intently, almost as if he were waiting to see the outcome of the argument.

"Dear me, what a to-do." Sheila's voice brought him back into the cafeteria.

Dismissing the couple and their observer as none of his business, relieved at the thought of food on the horizon, Joe helped unload her tray of teapots, cups, saucers, and cakes. Behind her, Brenda waited with three hot meals.

"It's like Debenhams at Christmas." Sheila smiled. "Are

you feeling a little better, Joe?"

"No. And I won't until January fourth."

Sheila removed her tray and sat opposite Joe while Brenda placed hers on the table. "You're all right with fish and chips, aren't you Joe?" Brenda asked. "Only we figured you wouldn't want a steak and kidney pie cos you sell 'em all week."

"Whatever it is, it won't be a patch on the Lazy Luncheonette," Joe replied, lifting two plates from the tray and placing one in front of Sheila.

With Brenda's tray unloaded, she sat alongside Joe and prepared to tuck in.

"It's absolutely nuts out there," Joe said, chewing through a mouthful of battered cod. He nodded at the scene out in the street. "Next year I'm going to Lundy Island."

"Lundy?" Brenda asked. "I thought that was a shipping forecast thingy."

"It's an island in the Bristol Channel," Sheila explained. "It's where people who don't like Christmas can go." She chewed delicately on her fish. "I think Joe would be in excellent company there. In fact, he could open a new branch…"

"Please your damned self. You know what happens next."

Having snapped at her male companion, the woman behind Joe jolted her chair backwards to stand up, knocking it into Joe. He was about to protest, but Brenda got in first.

Turning and craning her neck backwards, she gazed sympathetically into the woman's eyes. "Is everything all right?"

"Get out of my way, you fat cow," barked the woman and barged past Brenda to storm from the cafeteria.

"Hey!" Joe half rose.

Brenda stopped him. "It doesn't matter, Joe."

"She ought to learn some manners."

"You'll have to forgive her, ma'am," said the man. "She's a little highly strung."

"She should be," Joe commented. "About six feet off the

24

ground."

"Let it go, Joe," Brenda urged. "We're here to enjoy ourselves."

"Joe is enjoying himself." Sheila pointed out. "He loves a good argument, don't you, dear?"

"I don't like bad manners," he pressed, "and if you'd have let me I'd have given her both barrels."

Putting down her knife and fork, Brenda huddled up to him. "I'm ready for both barrels, Joe, whenever you want to give them me."

The two women laughed and Joe scowled. Looking around for another direction to vent his anger, he noticed the beard hurrying towards the escalators. "If there's nothing going on there," he muttered, "I'll give everyone a free meat pie on Wednesday."

***

Please your damned self. You know what happens next.

Jennifer's last words to Dennis Wright echoed around her head as she hurried along the icy pavements of The Headrow, every slippery step fuelled by a fury she had not known in years. The last time she had been so angry was when she learned of her ex-husband's affair with a colleague.

Paradoxically, Dennis' rejection hurt more than her husband's. She had been married for nearly 25 years, and despite her own shortcomings, she was shattered when it came to an abrupt and adulterous end. She had known Dennis since her university days, when they were constant companions. It was a relationship that petered out naturally as they went their separate ways, and contact became limited to occasional correspondence. Even that stopped when Dennis moved from West Yorkshire to Alabama, but it had been granted a fresh lease of life when they both became members of the LHS. They had finally met again during the summer before last, when she flew to Alabama to work with him for three months. Not only work. The fires that had burned so strongly back in the 1970s, were re-ignited and those 13 weeks in Alabama were some of the most passionate she could recall.

Logic dictated that the wreckage of her marriage should have been more painful, but it was not. Or was it simply that she had had time to get over the divorce? It was, after all, five years in the past, whereas her steamy affair with Dennis had come to an end only when she flew back to the UK.

Such questions, she knew, served no practical purpose. She was hurting more than she could ever recall and that was all that mattered. Snapping at the threesome on the table behind her was proof, as if she needed any, of her pain. But she couldn't help it.

For two hours she and Dennis had wandered the streets of Leeds, shopping, talking, reminiscing, Jennifer taking photographs – Dennis even agreed to appear on one with her, and they had press-ganged a passer-by into taking the picture for them. And then they had gone into Debenhams for lunch and for over an hour, when he wasn't queuing for refills of tea and coffee, she had pressed him on the subject of *them*. Jennifer was due to accompany him on his book signing tour, which would begin here in Leeds on the 28th. It would finish in London in February, and Jennifer's main aim was persuading him to take her back to the United States, let them begin a new life together. Dennis steadfastly refused to even consider it.

At first the rejection had been mild, almost flattering.

"You're an exciting woman, Jennifer," he had told her. "Seductive and inventive, the best lover I've known, but you don't want to waste that on a tedious life with a boring academic."

"I don't care what you do for a living," she had replied. "I'm a boring academic too, remember. It's what we do, Dennis, you and I, together, after five o'clock when the classrooms are locked and we're alone."

"My work is my life," had been his only reply.

As the time wore on and she became increasingly desperate and demanding, so his patience wore thin.

"Don't you get it?" he growled. "I don't want you, I don't want anyone. I just want to be alone."

"There's someone else, isn't there?" The cliché made her cringe, but having persuaded herself that it was the truth, it still hurt.

"No there is not, and there never will be," he replied.

And from there the argument went downhill all the way to the final threats.

"If you won't agree, I swear I'll make you sorry."

"Do whatever you want," he invited coldly. "I don't care."

The sullen disinterest sent her storming from the café out into the snowy streets, with her final words ringing, she imagined, in his ears and bouncing around her head. *Please your damned self. You know what happens next.* After all she had done on his behalf, too.

She charged her way through the crowded store, not knowing, not caring how many people she pushed out of her way, how many sour glances she drew from others. Out in Briggate, she shouldered aside a charity collector dressed as Santa and continued her blind, raging rush through the streets towards the Regency.

Reaching The Headrow, outside Dorothy Perkins, she glanced back down Briggate and for a brief instant she would swear she saw Warren Kirkland ducking into Starbucks on the corner of Thornton's Arcade. The idea that he might have been following them incensed her even more, and for a moment she thought about making her way back to Starbucks, finding him and giving him a piece of her mind, too.

The wind pushed icy sleet into her face, slapping her cheeks as hard as Dennis' rejection had done, and she forgot about Kirkland.

How dare he make such a fool of her? Hadn't he had everything he wanted in Alabama? Were her demands for some return on that physical, emotional investment, so expensive? Hadn't she done even more for him since she came back to Britain? Wasn't that worth the price she asked.

Charging into the hotel, she snapped at the reception clerk. "Two-oh-seven." No 'please', and when the red-haired woman handed it over there was no 'thank you' either. Jennifer snatched the credit card-sized, electronic key and hurried to the lift. A couple of minutes later, she emerged onto the dull red carpets of the second floor and almost ran along the corridor to her room. As she reached it, Tom Patterson emerged from 208.

He took one look at her and concern etched itself into his malleable features. "Are you all right, Jennifer?"

"Yes, dammit. Just leave me alone."

Tom appeared taken aback. "I'm sorry. I was only trying to be a good neighbour."

His acquiescence brought some perspective to Jennifer. She forced herself to calm down and heaved a sigh of regret. "I'm sorry, Tom. It's been a trying afternoon."

"Dennis?" he asked, and she nodded. "I did try to tell you."

Jennifer pushed open her door and stepped in.

Tom stood on the threshold. "Is there anything I can do to help?"

With a backward jerk of the head, she invited him in and closed the door behind him.

Patterson seated himself at the escritoire overlooking Park Row and its blocks of solicitors' and accountants' offices. Jennifer opened the mini bar and pulled out a miniature Armagnac. She raised her eyebrows at Patterson and he shook his head.

Snapping the screw cap from the bottle, she drank straight from it. "By God, that is so good." She sneered at his owlish stare. "I feel like getting drunk."

"Drowning your sorrows?" Patterson asked.

"Probably," she reported.

"It won't help, Jennifer. It won't make the problem go away. It'll still be there tomorrow when you sober up. You have to come to terms with it now."

She took another slug from the bottle. "What do you know about it?" Her words came out dripping with scorn.

"I know how it feels to be rejected," he said, his voice as placid as hers was angry. "And I know what it feels like to lose someone." A little sigh. "I may be Mr Boring, but that doesn't mean I'm totally devoid of emotion."

"Especially when it comes to old maps." Jennifer's senses cleared. "Oh, I'm sorry, Tom. Here I am taking it all out on you and you've never been anything other than one of my best friends."

A little shrug this time. "Friends are there to lend a listening ear."

She nodded and finished the bottle. Tossing it to one side, she sat on the bed and leaned back on the mattress, her arms straight out and behind, causing her chest to thrust out and her skirt to ride up above the knee. "He has someone else," she announced. "He won't admit it, naturally, but I know it. I tried everything." Tears of self-pity welled in her eyes. "Even threats to expose him for what he really is. A cheat. No good. He wouldn't budge."

"Jennifer…"

"Well I'll show him," she growled, cutting Patterson off. "I'll show him just what I can do. By the time I'm through his current little tramp won't want to know him." The tears dried as quickly as they had begun. "You just watch me."

***

Joe, Sheila and Brenda came out of Debenhams just after 3:30 and already the fading light of afternoon had turned to dusk. Over to the west, beyond the cloud, they could see a hint of red in the sky as the sun dipped to the horizon. The sleet had turned to light snow, some of the street traders, almost sold out, were packing away their wares, ready to call it a day. Many shoppers were making their way from Briggate through to the bus stops on Vicar Lane and Boar Lane.

By common consent, the three companions made their way along the streets leading west off Briggate.

Joe called into WH Smiths and came out again twenty

29

seconds later. "Like an asylum in there," he grumbled.

"What is it you want, Joe?" Sheila asked.

"Never you mind," he retorted, and cut down a side street towards Commercial Street.

"He's buying gifts for us, Sheila," Brenda remarked. "A copy of Catering Weekly for me and Meat Pies Monthly for you."

Joe allowed them the joke at his expense and nipped into Clinton Cards. A few minutes later, he emerged with a carrier bag containing a roll of wrapping paper and several small cards.

"Have you seen the prices they charge? Extortion. That's what it is. Christmas Eve, they know you don't have time to go anywhere else, so they rip your arm off."

"Whining again, Joe?" Sheila asked.

"The airline industry has a joke about Joe, you know," Brenda said. "How do you know Joe Murray arrives by plane? The engines stop but the whining goes on."

The two women laughed again. Joe scowled.

"Lighten up, Joe," Sheila urged. "It's Christmas."

"Christmas?" Joe growled. "Peppermints."

"You mean humbug," Sheila corrected him.

"I don't like humbugs."

They wandered along the streets, early evening descending rapidly, the snowflakes increasing in size and density, and the crowds thinning even if they were still thronging the streets. Turning up Albion Street, where more shops awaited their attention, they stopped outside Waterstone's, and while Joe and Brenda peered at the window display, Sheila hurried inside.

"What's she after now?" Joe asked.

Brenda pointed to a stack of books and a large, freestanding poster beside it. *Historian Dr Dennis Wright of the University of Alabama will be here on Wednesday December 28th, signing copies of his new book, Missing Pennies.*

The cover of the book showed two old pennies, the obverse engraved with the head of George V, and on the reverse, the traditional figure of Britannia, holding her shield and trident.

The poster also carried a head and shoulder image of the author and Joe recognised him immediately. "Hey, that's the guy who was arguing on the table behind us in Debenhams."

Brenda nodded. "I'll bet Sheila recognised him, too, and that's why she's gone in the shop. She'll be buying a copy of his book."

"Why? Just cos she's seen him in a café?"

Brenda laughed. "You're forgetting, Joe, he's a member of the Leodensian wossnames. He'll be staying at the Regency. Sheila will probably look for him in the bar and get him to sign her book."

Joe harrumphed. "She never buys copies of my books."

"Mainly because she was involved in the cases. Besides, you don't sell them. You keep them on the shelf at the Lazy Luncheonette. You're even funny about customers reading them."

"I do sell them." Joe argued. "As e-books."

"And one day, when you're dead, some publisher will come along and pay Lee a fortune for the rights. You should be putting them out there, proper, Joe. They're good reading."

Sheila came out of the shop and ended the debate.

"*Missing Pennies*?" Brenda asked.

"Yes. I thought I'd ask Dr Wright to sign it at the hotel."

Brenda gave Joe a superior smile as they walked on.

"You do realise he was with that harridan sat behind Joe in Debenhams?" Sheila asked.

"We were just talking about it," Joe told her as they turned into a fierce north-westerly wind whipping along The Headrow. "Imagine that, huh? He flies all the way from America into a bloody snowstorm and gets pinned down by a virago. Not his lucky day, is it?"

Joe pulled his cap lower over his forehead, Sheila and Brenda turned their faces to the side, away from the driven snow.

"The way the weather's going on, we'll be lucky to get home on Tuesday."

"Don't say that, Brenda," Joe pleaded. "I feel bad enough leaving the Lazy Luncheonette today without worrying about getting back to open up on Wednesday."

They neared the Regency and across the road, the dome of the town hall was almost lost to the increasing blizzard.

They stood waiting for the lights to change at the top of Park Row so they could cross, and Joe's attention was caught by a refuse vehicle emerging from the narrow entrance alongside the hotel.

"You're fascinated with rubbish, Joe," Brenda commented.

"Just thinking how criminal it is," he told her. "We throw hundreds and thousands of tons of garbage away every year, and some of it is still good, you know." The vehicle drew away from the hotel, down towards City Square. "How much serviceable gear is crushed up in the back of that truck right now? And when it comes to food … oh. Don't get me started."

"It has to be disposed of, Joe," Sheila argued as they crossed the street. "Once it reaches its sell-by date, it's useless."

"But it isn't," he protested. "That sell-by date is usually weeks, sometimes months before the stuff will really begin to go off. I tell you, it's criminal."

"Shut up moaning and let's get in," Brenda urged and hurried up the brief steps into the grand entrance of the Regency.

Despite its name, it was one of the city's newest hotels, but for all that it looked like an office block from the outside, no expense had been spared on the interior. Pink marble abounded on the reception counter and the tops of occasional tables. Styled chairs, Regency, naturally, stood around the area, the gold braiding contrasting sharply with the scarlet upholstery. Potted plants, everything from rubber plants to aspidistra, grew in an orderly fashion in various ornamental planters, and even the frame around the menu of the Regency Grill boasted aesthetically pleasing scrolls in gold leaf.

Dressed in a smart, pale blue uniform jacket, completely at odds with her shock of red hair, the receptionist appeared at her most imperious when the three companions approached.

"Good afternoon, sir, madam, madam."

"Rooms three-oh-two and three-oh-six, please," Sheila asked.

The clerk handed over their electronic keys with a welcoming smile but Joe noticed a hint of snootiness in her eyes when he took his key. "Cold out there," Joe complained.

"It's the north-easterly winds, sir," replied the clerk.

"Yeah? I would have sworn it was the snow."

Leaving the receptionist flummoxed, Joe followed his friends to the lift.

"Dinner at seven thirty," Joe reminded them when they stepped into the car.

"Shall we meet at seven and have a drink first?" Sheila suggested.

Brenda agreed and Joe nodded. A minute later, they parted company on the third floor, Joe letting himself into room 306, the women disappearing into 302.

Ensconced in his room with the lights on, Joe made himself a cup of tea, and then sat at the escritoire beneath the window, staring out into the late afternoon gloom. It was just after four and already the street lamps lit the way along The Headrow, the gay profusion of colour from the town hall Christmas tree and lights adding to the seasonal feel. It did nothing to cheer him up. He could see the driving snow highlighted in the lamps, the white sheen whipping across the streets, and already blurring the lines of the traffic lanes.

He hated this time of year, he hated this weather. Snow, low temperatures and early sunset kept people indoors – people and their wallets. Snow made it almost impossible to keep the tiled floor of the Lazy Luncheonette clean and ice-free. Low temperatures meant turning up the heating to keep the customers warm, and the short days meant keeping the lights on all day. This time of year, it was expense after expense after expense.

People milled in the streets. Long queues formed at bus stops and taxi ranks. The city was going into that lull between the shops closing and the commencement of genuine revelry. In an hour or two, those pavements would be packed with drinkers crawling from pub to pub and even the snow would not keep them in. Across The Headrow, a clutch of young men and women were snowballing each other. Joe could not hear their laughter but he sensed it and the thought annoyed him. They were enjoying life in a way that he never had, not even when he was their age. To him life meant work and earning; it was all it had ever meant.

Reaching into his bags, Joe took out his netbook computer, set it on the escritoire and switched it on. While waiting for it to boot up, he plugged the mains extension into a wall socket and took some slight pleasure from the thought of using the Regency's electricity to charge up the netbook's batteries.

Joe considered the small but powerful computer one of his best friends. Even at school, getting on for half a century ago, he had loved to write, but these days the scrawl that passed for his handwriting was illegible to most people, and often to himself. The word processing software on this machine was a godsend. It permitted him to keep notes, diaries, journals, and accounts of his cases in a form that was not only legible but printable, too. The range of small books on the shelves of the Lazy Luncheonette, all of them true tales of his past investigations, would not have been possible without the computer or an investment he would not have been prepared to make. Thanks to modern technology, he could produce quality copies cheaply, and give his customers something to read while they enjoyed their food.

Opening up the software, typing in '24/12 – Leeds' as a heading, he reflected that computers were the only thing about him that could be described as modern. Every other aspect of his life was lodged firmly back in the 1970s.

He spent an hour on an account of the afternoon, from leaving the Regency, through the nightmare of shopping in the city centre, to lunch and the vicious woman behind them, to picking up the wrapping paper and the cards and Sheila buying a copy of *Missing Pennies* before the snow arrived in force. At 5:30, he shut the netbook down, tucked it back in its case, and locked the whole lot in the wardrobe. He spent another thirty minutes wrapping the gifts he had bought in Leeds, then took a shower and promised himself a nap before dinner.

"Christmas," he said to the ornate ceiling as he lay on the bed. "Humbug."

Scrooge had chickened out in the end, he thought as his eyes closed and he drifted into sleep. "The silly old sod fell for the supposed magic."

It was not a mistake Joe Murray would ever make.

Chapter Three

While Joe waited for his drinks at the bar, a short, tubby man came alongside him. Dressed in a dark pinstripe and a pale blue shirt open at the collar, his greasy hair was slicked back from his forehead, and his piggy eyes stared out from beneath fat lids. His expression was mean and determined, his cheeks flushed with hypertension, arms spread slightly away from his chest as if they were packed with muscle. Patent leather shoes shone with the gleam of either high polish or synthetic gloss, Joe did not know which.

He rattled his glass on the bar. "Hey. How about some service here?"

The barman, working alone and busy tallying up Joe's bill and change, glanced across. "I'll be with you in a moment, Mr Quinton."

"I'm a regular here, you know. I expect better than this."

Joe took his change and checked it. With an apologetic smile at Joe, the barman moved along to attend to the offensive newcomer.

"Red wine. And fill the bloody glass up."

"Yes, sir."

Joe could resist the temptation no longer. "You wanna learn to chill out, pal," he said. "You'll live longer."

The tubby one glowered. "Is that a threat?"

"No. An observation," Joe replied. "Your blood pressure's already sky high, and getting yourself worked up over waiting an extra minute or two won't help."

The other glared at him and was about to say something when the beard from Debenhams arrived at the bar. Ignoring Joe, he addressed the greasy-haired one. "Shooting your mouth off again, Quinton?"

"Sod off, Kirkland."

"I could say the same to you," Kirkland retorted. "You won't get it, so why don't you just get on a bus and go back to your little hovel in, where is it, Rotherham?"

Joe had been about to return to his table, but he paused to watch the argument develop. Even from these early skirmishes, it was clear that the two men had no love for each other. Kirkland had made Rotherham sound like an insult, and the blaze in Quinton's eyes said it had been taken as one.

"You wanna play hardball, Kirkland, and you'll end up mashed. I can buy you out twice over."

"We'll see about that, won't we?"

The barman interrupted proceedings and Joe returned to his companions.

"Trouble at t' mill?" Brenda asked taking a glass of Campari from him.

Joe settled into a seat between them. "Noisy little joker at the bar," Joe replied. "Had a pop at the barman, then me, and now he's arguing with some suit with a beard.

"That noisy little joker is Oliver Quinton," Sheila said. "And the suit with the beard is Warren Kirkland."

Joe took a swallow of his bitter and savoured the bite on his tongue. "Can't get quality ale like that anywhere south of Wakefield," he declared. Putting down his glass, he asked, "Who is Oliver Quinton and who is Warren Kirkland?"

"Quinton is a self-made millionaire from Sheffield," Sheila said. "Bit of a wheeler dealer, so they say. Kirkland is a management consultant. Comes from Northampton. They're both coin collectors."

"Coin collectors?" Joe asked. "Here, this weekend, with Dennis Wright in town promoting his book on missing coppers? Didn't I always say there's no such thing as coincidence? How do you know all this?"

"I told you earlier, I read a lot." Sheila giggled at Joe's irritation. "They featured in one of the Sunday tabloids a few months back. Some argument over rare coins. And I think you're right, Joe. With one of the world's leading authorities on coins staying here, I don't think their presence is a coincidence."

"I know the greaseball is an arrogant little swine," Brenda said. "I bumped into him coming out of the lift when we first got here this morning, and he had the cheek to tell me to watch where I was going."

"Judging by the way he spoke to the barman, that sounds about right," Joe commented.

Brenda took another gulp of Campari. "One thing's for sure, if he starts with me again, he'll end up head down in the fish tank."

"Best place for him, too," Joe agreed.

Taking another sip, smacking her lips in anticipation, Brenda said, "The food here is supposed to be the very best. I'm hoping so."

"You're a slave to your appetites," Joe complained.

"Better that than a slave to money," Brenda countered, and huddled up to Joe. "What say you forget all about the price of a pork pie for the evening? We can boogie the night away in the disco, then boogie some more back at your place."

Joe's scowl told her everything. "If that's the mood you're in, Brenda, why don't you go chat up George Robson?"

"Too late," Sheila said with a gaze that directed their eyes across the lounge. "Our Romeo looks like he's already set up for the evening."

Across the vast lounge, George sat at a table with Jennifer Hardy, the pair exchanging a laugh.

"He was never one to waste time." Brenda's observation carried the conviction of insider knowledge.

Joe frowned again. "I hope he knows what he's doing."

The two women queried with raised eyebrows and Joe tutted.

"Don't you people ever take notice of what's going on around you? That's the woman who jammed her chair into my back in Debenhams, and then slagged Brenda off."

Sheila studied the couple more intently. "You know, I do believe you're right."

***

"She's obsessive," Dennis Wright said. "Obsessed with me. And look at her now. Flaunting herself with that guy. Why? To make me jealous?"

He gestured to the dance floor where Jennifer was glued to a male companion, the pair moving slowly to Matt Monro's *Walk Away*.

Turning his back on them, Wright faced the bar, picked up his glass and sipped at the whiskey sour with approval. "Not often you can find a European barman who can get the balance of bourbon, lemon juice and sugar just right." He turned to his right and rested his left elbow on the bar. "Enough of my woes, how are you, Tom?"

Patterson, who throughout dinner and afterwards, had been watching Jennifer with the bulky, handsome man, one of the Sanford Third Age Club people, dragged his attention back and smiled up at Wright. "Oh as usual, Dennis," he said. "Old maps and charts. Nothing spectacular, but it pays the bills and keeps me out of trouble." He sipped at his scotch. "I'm not in your league."

Wright's laughed dripped with scorn. "My league? Come off it, Tom. American hype from a true blue Englishman doesn't wash. Anyway, right now, my league is brokesville. Or very near."

"Sorry, Dennis. I don't follow you."

"No, I'm sorry, Tom. I'm just having a good old Yorkshire moan. You'd think thirty years of living in the USA would have knocked it out of me, but it's still there, buried way down and it comes to the surface now and again."

Patterson was completely lost by the debate and elected for silence. He had no doubt that Wright would make his meaning apparent.

"Money, Tom, money," Wright went on. "We all pretend

to hate it, but we can't get ahead without it. That's particularly true in America."

The fog created by the eclectic discussion cleared slightly. "I think I understand. Expensive divorce?"

"What? Oh, yeah. Just a little. Then I got involved in a real estate deal on the Keys: Florida. I dropped a packet on that."

Patterson had read of the incident, but it seemed diplomatic to project sympathetic ignorance. "Oh dear. I am sorry."

"I'll survive," Wright responded. "I may be down but I'm not out. Not yet. When I get the History Chair at Alabama…" He laughed. "*If* I get the History Chair at Alabama, I'll pick up again."

Wright gazed absently across the dance floor again. Patterson followed the longing eyes to Jennifer Hardy, now apparently welded to the man with whom she danced, her body pressed close to him, her lips near to his ear.

"She doesn't understand," Wright said. "She can't see the big picture because she doesn't have the 3-D glasses."

"Jennifer?" When Wright nodded, Patterson went on, "I spoke to her earlier. She was very upset at your, er, rejection. Very angry."

"She'll get over it."

"She made veiled threats, Dennis. I don't know what hold she has over you, but it sounded to me as if she were threatening to make it public."

Wright laughed and looked down on his chairman. "Hot air, Tom, hot air. She won't say a word to anyone about anything."

***

"You're the chair of the Sanford Third Age Club?" Patterson asked. "I fulfil the same function for the Leodensian Historical Society."

Joe sipped at a half of bitter. "Yeah? But yours is just a mob of old fuddy-duddies, ain't it?"

Patterson laughed, his 60-something face creasing into a sea of wrinkles from his bald forehead down to his several chins. "I may be an old fuddy-duddy, Joe, but may I remind you that it was you who asked the DJ to play a good dash of 70s music. My crowd would have been quite happy with Westlife and The Spice Girls."

Seated at the bar with Patterson, Joe took a look around the ballroom. The dance floor was packed with members of both societies, jiggling around to Slade and *Merry Xmas Everybody*. A bit obvious, Joe thought, and he felt sure that the DJ, a 35-year old local man by the unlikely name of Nate Immacyoulate, would follow up with Greg Lake's *I Believe in Father Christmas* and then Johnny Mathis singing *When a Child Is Born*. Later on, he would no doubt find room for Paul McCartney's *Mull of Kintyre,* and Joe could guarantee Wizzard's *I Wish It Could Be Christmas Everyday* putting in an appearance before midnight.

Even allowing for Christmas, Joe's playlist would have been more varied. He'd have dropped in several 60's tracks, and more exciting, less seasonal numbers from the 70s.

Trying desperately to throw off his earlier depression, which he recognised as symptomatic of his solitary and celibate existence, he made an effort to enjoy the evening. Dinner had been a carvery where he could choose his own menu and he had settled for topside of beef with roast and minted potatoes, fresh carrots and a small range of green vegetables, with a slice of lemon meringue doused in cream for dessert. He confessed to his two companions that the food was excellent.

"Me and Lee could do it as good," he concluded, "but there's no call for it at the Lazy Luncheonette."

Dinner proved to be a leisurely affair and it was almost 8:30 before they left the elegant dining room for the spectacular ballroom, its polished dance floor gleaming in the light of many chandeliers, the rich carpeting of the surrounding area soft and yielding under tired feet.

Joe's companions had dressed for a party. Brenda turned out in a knee-length dress of bright red, cut low at the top, augmented by red high-heels. Slightly more conservative, Sheila had nevertheless let her metaphorical hair down in a voluminous pale cream blouse offset by a dark skirt, and she, too, wore heels, but not as lethal as Brenda's. Joe had opted for his customary conservatism and comfort. Light grey trousers and a short sleeve shirt, his feet snug in a pair of black leather loafers.

Settling at a table near the exit, Joe bought them drinks and the two women chattered excitedly as the lounge began to fill up. By the time Nate Immacyoulate, the DJ, started his show, the place was humming.

The first number out of the hat was from Girls Aloud and that set Joe's teeth on edge. "Where the hell does he get a name like Nate Immacyoulate?" he grumbled.

"It's a stage name, Joe," Sheila said.

"You'll probably find that his real name is Nathan Bickerdike," Brenda suggested. Shortly after the Girls Aloud track ended, Joe made for the stage and had a quiet word in Nate's ear. He came away with a firm promise that the "old folks will be catered for, man."

"That's passive," Joe complained as he left the stage. "He shoulda said he'll cater for the old folks." The full meaning of Nate's words struck Joe and he turned back. "They're not old," he shouted. "They're mature."

But the music of Take That drowned out his words and Nate did not hear him.

While Sheila and Brenda kept up a steady banter between themselves and others seated around them, Joe spent much of the next hour assessing the crowd, particularly the LHS section of it. He guessed there were about 80 of them, slightly outnumbering the STAC contingent. The ill-tempered woman from Debenhams was dancing with George, and Joe was not surprised to see Dennis Wright over by the bar (Sheila had wasted no time in buttonholing him for his autograph). But if Wright was no surprise, Joe was intrigued to see Warren, the beard, Kirkland, and Oliver, greasy hair, Quinton taking an interest in George and the Dragon Lady.

He pointed it out to Sheila.

"Dennis told me all about her when he autographed my book," she said. "Her name is Jennifer Hardy and she's one of the leading lights of the LHS."

"Yeah?" Joe asked, raising his voice over the sound of Jedward. "What's her specialist field? Losing the plot in public?"

"Judging by the way she's latched onto George, I'd say it was trapping off," Brenda commented and Joe followed her envious stare to where their STAC friend had gone into a clinch with the woman.

"Well, George always did have a silver tongue when it came to women," Joe commented.

Brenda smacked her lips. "He has more than a silver tongue, believe me."

Her cheeks colouring, Sheila giggled at the innuendo and Joe permitted himself a grimacing smile. Brenda's amorous adventures were almost as legendary as George's.

Eventually bored with the women and the chatter and the persistent good wishes of the STAC members, he ambled over to the bar where Tom Patterson introduced himself.

"Joe Murray," Joe said shaking hands, and it was at that point that Patterson displayed astonishment at the name.

"So you're the famous Joe Murray," he went on after his comment on the LHS preferring The Spice Girls.

"Well, the Lazy Luncheonette does well, but I'd hardly call it famous. It's well known in Sanford."

"It's not your business I'm talking about, Joe," said Patterson, "but you. Rumour has it you're one of the best detectives in Yorkshire."

Joe smiled modestly. "I make a hobby of puzzles, mysteries, and I pride myself on my powers of observation."

Patterson reflected the smile. "You're too modest. I read the reports of the way you proved your nephew innocent of murder, and the manner in which you cornered three people in Filey who had killed a man. Let's try an experiment, Joe. What can you tell about me by just looking at me?"

Joe almost said, 'You're a boring, half drunken idiot,' but he checked himself. "I don't play games," he said. He scanned the room in time to see Dennis Wright and Oliver Quinton arguing. Wright must have said something final, because Quinton, his face blazing with anger, stomped away, looking around the room. On the dance floor, Kirkland was moving alone, alongside George Robson and Jennifer Hardy, and her face looked as mean as Dennis Wright's.

"Oh come on, Joe. If you're that good, you must be able to make some kind of assessment just by looking me over."

Patterson's words brought Joe back to the bar. He sighed and scanned the LHS man up and down. It was the barest of glances, but he took in the stained fingers, the wedding ring, a florid complexion, the threadbare Paisley tie, and a straining button at the waistband of his sombre suit trousers.

"Not much," he said, "and nothing you'd like to hear."

"Oh, come on, old boy," Patterson insisted. "You're a detective and I'm really fascinated by your claimed powers of observation and deduction."

Mentally Joe added another item to his list. "All right. You smoke too much, you probably drink too much, too, and you're widowed."

Patterson's mouth fell open. "I, er, well, good lord." He glanced at the brown stains on his fingers. "Nicotine. That's how you knew I smoked too much."

Joe nodded. "One cigarette is too many, and you're hearing that from a man who rolls his own and has done for forty years."

"And drink?" Patterson asked.

"You're holding a glass of spirit, but look at your complexion. It's glowing like a traffic light on stop. Could be high blood pressure, but it's more likely to be a boozer's blush."

Patterson shook his head in bewilderment. "Fair enough. Those I understand, but how did you guess I'm a widower?"

Joe indicated the waistband of Patterson's trousers, where the button hung by a long, stretched thread. "You

44

called me, old boy. That tells me you were privately educated and it means you come from well-to-do stock. You probably chose your wife carefully, and such women are particular. For them, appearance matters. No wife like that would allow her husband to be seen in public with his button hanging off. She could be long-term ill, bedridden, hospitalised, but even so, she would insist on you turning out as you should be turned out. It means, Tom, that your good lady is no longer a factor in your life. She's deceased."

Patterson smiled and applauded. "Very good and very accurate. But how do you know I'm not simply single or divorced."

"You're wearing a wedding ring." Joe indicated the gold band on Patterson's left hand. "Most bachelors won't wear one because it puts other women off. Men who are divorced tend to throw the wedding ring in a box and leave it in the attic because they don't want to be reminded of a relationship gone sour. That's where mine is. Only a man who had a stable marriage and who had lost his wife would continue to wear the wedding ring." He raised his eyebrows. "How long?"

"Three years," Patterson said. "And it doesn't get any easier."

"I wouldn't know," Joe said. "My wife walked out on me ten years ago, and I don't miss her at all."

Patterson shook his head in amazement. "That is tremendous, Joe. You deduced all that from such tiny clues."

"It's all about attention to detail," Joe said. He turned from the bar and looked out across the crowded dance floor. His eye caught George Robson and Jennifer Hardy smooching to Judy Garland's rendition of *Have Yourself a Merry Little Christmas*.

He saw Oliver Quinton struggle his way through the crowded floor to reach the couple. Quinton must have said something because the next moment, Jennifer broke her clinch with George and turned on him. Joe wished he could lip-read; he would give his eyeteeth to know what she was

45

saying. The argument went on for a good minute and at one stage, Jennifer took a pace towards Quinton whose body language spelled fear to Joe. As Quinton backed off from Jennifer, George took her arm, trying to persuade her to let it drop. At first she shrugged him off, but eventually she calmed down and while Quinton skulked off the floor, George and Jennifer went back to their smooch.

"That woman of yours attracts a lot of attention and she certainly has a hell of a temper on her," Joe said. "She had an argument with Warren Kirkland two minutes ago and she's just ripped Oliver Quinton to pieces but look at her with George. She's practically glued to him. Now what's that all about? Trying to make Dennis Wright or Quinton or Kirkland jealous?"

Patterson, too, had been watching the scene. "Jennifer? She's not my woman."

Joe caught the inflection in Patterson's voice. "She belongs to your crowd."

"And how do you mean she has a temper?" Patterson asked, ignoring Joe's last remark. "I've known her for 28 years and I've never found her anything but charming."

Joe felt the inner glow again. Patterson was too easy to read. "Even though she turned you down?" he asked.

Patterson blushed. "How did you know?"

"It was what you said." Joe grinned. "See, if you've known someone that long, you'd usually say something like, 'I've known her for twenty-five years or more,' but you were very specific. Twenty-eight years, you said. That usually means it's someone special to you." He took a swallow from his glass and smiled again.

"That's very perceptive, Joe."

"It's the way I am," Joe replied without a trace of modesty. Putting the glass on the bar, he asked, "You've known her all that time and never seen her snap? She tore a real strip off Wright in Debenhams this afternoon."

Patterson pursed his lips. "Dennis told me. It's unusual. They normally get on very well."

Joe laughed aloud. "Well obviously *he* turned *her* down

46

this time, huh?" His gaze travelled further round to where Dennis Wright was talking with other members of the LHS. "Talking of Wright, he must be sure of making some money to travel this far with his book."

Patterson nodded. "He's likely to need it, too. Poor chap's having a rough old time of it."

Joe raised his eyebrows. "A Brit living in America? Most of our ex-pats do well over there."

"Wright's lived there a long time, Joe. Long enough to become established in academic circles, but he dabbled in a real estate deal which went wrong."

"Burned his fingers?"

Patterson laughed. "Burned? It was like the fire that wrecked Leeds market back in seventy-five. Not a lot left after the flames had died down. Rumour has it he lost almost everything on the deal. He's twice divorced, too. God only knows what kind of alimony he's paying out."

"No wonder he didn't want Jennifer Hardy climbing into his bed."

***

The smooth voice of Judy Garland faded along with the backing music, and George Robson prised himself away from Jennifer.

Many men would consider George lucky, but he dismissed the argument every time he heard it. His success with women had nothing to do with luck and everything to do with charm.

Aged 55, he looked ten years younger. He kept himself fit, thanks to his job and a couple of sessions a week in the gym at Sanford Sports Centre. He was good looking, still had a full head of hair, even if he did touch it up now and then to hide the grey, and his smooth, languorous voice had a soothing, persuasive effect on everyone – particularly women.

Many of his peers would describe him as a Lothario, but that was unfair. He wasn't simply racking up a string of bedfellows. Some of the women he had dated since his divorce had become steady girlfriends, with odd relationships lasting months at a time. Always, however, he moved on, especially when a woman began dragging him to furniture stores and hinting how well a particular piece would look in a shared home. George Robson was not interested in remarrying; merely having a good time. And STAC outings, like this one, provided him with the perfect opportunity to indulge his playfulness without the danger of deeper involvement. He and Jennifer would share a bed tonight, tomorrow, probably Monday, too, and over breakfast on Tuesday, they would make the usual overtures of her visiting him in Sanford or him coming over to Leeds, but it would all amount to nothing. He would go home, so would she and if they ever saw each other again, it would only be by chance.

George didn't mind. It was the way he preferred things.

Coming off the dance floor, heading for the bar, he spotted Joe Murray talking to one of Jennifer's colleagues, with Sheila Riley and Brenda Jump bearing down on them. He'd always felt Joe could take leaf out of his book. Get out of that café and live a little.

"Come on, Jennifer. I'll introduce you to Joe and his crowd."

She leaned tipsily into him, chuckling. "I'm quite happy tripping the light fantastic with the Director of Leisure Services."

George laughed. "Tell me what it's all about."

She echoed the laughter. "It's just a way of putting those two in their place. That's all."

He wagged a jocularly disapproving finger at her. "No. There's more to it than that. I know there is."

She huddled close to him and nuzzled his neck. "Come on, George. Do it for me. I promise you'll get what you want."

He grinned. "We'll see. Now come on. Let's meet Joe."

Jennifer pulled a face. "Do I have to?"

"Oh yes," he assured her. "Everyone should meet Joe

48

Murray at least once in their life. He confirms the theory that there's always someone worse off than you."

She baulked again. "Only if you promise to do it for me? It'll only take a minute."

George sighed and laughed. "All right. Come on. Meet Joe."

Judy Garland faded and couples began to leave the dance floor. Joe caught sight of Sheila and Brenda coming towards him and, at the same time, he noticed Patterson's eyes follow George and Jennifer to the bar.

"There you are, Joe," Sheila said. "We wondered where you'd got to."

"Just having a drink and a natter," Joe responded. "Ladies, this is Tom Patterson, Chair of the Leodensian Historical Society. Tom, these two chickens are my partners in crime, Sheila Riley and Brenda Jump, respectively the Membership Secretary and Treasurer of the Sanford Third Age Club."

Patterson shook hands with both women, and the three fell into immediate and animated conversation. Joe collected his drink and was about to return to his table, leave them to it, when George and Jennifer Hardy blocked his way. She was dressed casually yet smartly in a low cut top and short skirt. Around her neck, a gold chain gleamed in the flashing disco lights. Joe studied the pendant, which read MDCCMMLVIII.

"Jennifer," George said, "this is the famous Joe Murray. Joe, you miserable old sod, have you met Jennifer Hardy?"

Joe scowled. "We've met."

She smiled drunkenly, showing even, white teeth. "Have we? I don't think so."

"Debenhams earlier today. You were in a bad mood." Her features became more serious as she racked her drunken memory, and for a moment Joe thought she was about to apologise. He headed her off. "That date doesn't make any sense," he said, waving his glass at her pendant.

Jennifer giggled. "It does if you take out a couple of

initials."

Joe gazed at the necklace, his agile mind computing the necessary subtractions. He had the answer in under five seconds. "Oh right. I get it. Take out two ems and you have 1758. The year of your birth or the time of day someone gave you the necklace?"

"Told you he was a cynical old git, didn't I?" George chuckled.

Giggling again, Jennifer announced, "It's the year of the Middleton Light Railway, Mr Murray. The world's first commercial railway, used to carry coal from Broom Colliery to the canals near Meadow Lane, right here in Leeds." She smiled, revelling in her superiority. "I'm a historian. Tom must have told you. The Middleton Light Railway is my specialist area of study. And the two ems are for Matthew Murray. Your namesake, and the man who built the first steam engine to run on the railway."

"You know your stuff," Joe said, disdain pouring through his words. "But you really ought to do a bit less specialising and pick up some manners in the time you free up. Excuse me." He walked off, ignoring her gawping face and George's fury.

"Joe," George called after him.

Nearby, Sheila, Brenda and Patterson stared after his retreating back.

Still ignoring the anger he had caused, Joe crossed the dance floor where a few couples were jiving around to Elvis Presley's *Blue Suede Shoes*, and returned to the table, and while he walked he was conscious of Jennifer Hardy's and George Robson's livid stares on him, and of both Sheila and Brenda hurrying after him.

"Joe," Sheila scolded, "that was very rude."

"And what she said to Brenda in Debenhams wasn't?" Joe snapped.

"Of course it was," Brenda agreed, "but you don't deal with that kind of behaviour by retaliating. You rise above it. I have and her insult was aimed at me."

"Gar." Joe waved their arguments away with an irritable

sweep of his hand. He dug into his pockets, came out with his tobacco tin and began to roll a cigarette.

"You can't smoke –"

He cut Sheila off. "I know I can't smoke it in here, for God's sake. What is it with everyone? Do you think I'm living in the past just because I'm from the past?"

Sheila tutted and turned away. Brenda settled alongside him and put a friendly arm around his shoulder. "What is it, Joe? What's wrong?"

He ran his tongue along the gummed edge of the cigarette paper and completed the roll-up. "It's this whole thing," he barked, tucking the cigarette in his shirt pocket. "Christmas. I don't like it in Sanford and it's worse here. At least when I'm home, I can be miserable on my own. Now for crying out loud, just let me be."

He jumped to his feet, fished into his pocket for his cigarette lighter, fought his way from the table and hurried out of the room, turning right to the main entrance.

Once outside, he was greeted by a freezing wind whipping at his face. He did not feel it. All he could feel was boiling anger. He jammed the cigarette between his lips and struck the flint wheel on his Zippo lighter. A bright fire erupted between his cupped hands. He pulled on the smoke, and drew it deep into his lungs, letting it out with an angry hiss.

A group of young people walked past. "Merry Christmas, pops," one called to him.

"Bugger off," Joe grumbled and pulled at his cigarette again.

The snow came down heavier, the wind seemed colder and he began to shiver. With the sensation came the first hint of self-recrimination.

"Serves you right," he said to himself. "You're a nasty old sod, Joe Murray."

He knew he would have to apologise to Sheila when he returned to the ballroom. Not only Sheila, but Jennifer Hardy too, unless she was so drunk that she could see no further than George Robson's charms.

51

Thoughts of George tumbled through his agile mind. The same age as Joe, they were friends in the schoolyard four decades back and they had a lot in common. A gardener for Sanford council, his situation was similar to Joe's inasmuch as his wife had left him almost ten years previously. Unlike Joe, George did not brood on his return to bachelorhood. Instead, he lived a fairly full life, enjoying a startling reputation with the ladies. Joe did not know where Jennifer Hardy would be sleeping tonight, but it was odds on George would be alongside her. The man simply revelled in life, whereas Joe did not. Unless he was presented with a puzzle or working at his business, he was surly and zero fun to be with.

And yet, even though Joe recognised his failings, they were like his passion for the Lazy Luncheonette; he could do nothing about it. No amount of persuading himself that he was having a good time would make him enjoy the evening, and no amount of telling himself that he loved Christmas would make him do so.

Give him a robbery, a murder, put him on the dais as a DJ or behind the counter at the Lazy Luncheonette and he was the life and soul of the party. But drop him in an alien environment like the Regency and he was the Grinch personified.

He took a final drag on the cigarette and stubbed it out on the wall before throwing the butt into a waste bin. From somewhere to his left came the sound of church bells pealing, calling the faithful to prayers before Midnight Mass. Joe wondered where his own faith had gone.

"To the Canary Islands," he muttered, turning back into the hotel, "along with Alison."

The crowd on the dance floor was moving to Greg Lake when he arrived at the table. Sheila and Brenda were somewhere amongst them, and he could see George and Jennifer in another clinch.

"If he doesn't have that one saddled before morning, I'll serve minestrone for breakfast a week on Monday."

Shivering as his body came back up to normal operating

temperature, he finished off his drink and made for the bar, where he stood with Patterson again.

"Gimme a pint of bitter, a gin and it, easy on the it, and a Campari and soda," he ordered, then spoke to Patterson. "What are you having?"

"Kind of you, Joe. I'll have a scotch and ginger."

With a nod to the barman, Joe concentrated on Patterson. "Whenever I buy a round of drinks, it's guilt," he explained. "I was a bit rough with your lady friend." He laughed nervously. "Let's hope she's too drunk to remember, huh?"

"Jennifer? Drunk? Not likely, old boy. Likes the odd glass of wine, but hardly touches the stuff otherwise." Patterson tapped his head. "Can't take alcohol, see."

The barman delivered the drinks and Joe handed over the money. "Cheers," he said to Patterson. "She seemed pretty drunk when she and George came over here."

"Had a glass of wine at dinner," Patterson confirmed. "That's enough to set her off."

Joe chuckled to himself. "Maybe George won't get so lucky tonight, then."

"She actually said you were right," Patterson told him. "After you'd gone. She told me how badly she behaved this afternoon."

"That doesn't cut much ice with Sheila and Brenda," Joe said, "and they'll give me both barrels before the night's out."

With the last chords of *I Believe In Father Christmas* ringing round the ballroom, the crowd on the dance floor began to disperse again and Joe picked up his drinks.

"And talking of Sheila and Brenda, if you'll excuse me, Tom, I have some more grovelling to do."

"Of course, Joe, and if I don't see you again, Merry Christmas."

Joe scowled and just as quickly smiled. "Yeah. Likewise, I'm sure."

***

53

The knock on the door was timid, but audible. Switching on her bedside light, Jennifer checked her travel clock. 3:30 a.m. Who on earth could be knocking at this time of night? George? She hoped not. He had left her satisfied but thoroughly exhausted, and she needed rest, not more excitement.

She slid from beneath the sheets and checked her appearance in the full-length wardrobe mirror, ensuring her black nightie, designed to conceal as much as it revealed, was fulfilling the former role, and padded across the carpet to the door. She pressed her eye to the viewer, recognised the face and slipped back the lock.

Opening the door, she yawned. "Do you know what time it is?"

"I couldn't sleep for thinking about you." He held forward a bottle of house red. "Merry Christmas."

Jennifer sighed. After her earlier exertions, all she wanted was sleep, not Christmas partying in the early hours, and she certainly did not want any more physical attention.

His face appeared like a puppy keen to curry favour with its mistress.

"Just a small one, then. But no more." She turned back into the room. He followed her and closed the door behind him. "I know it's Christmas but…"

She never finished what she was going to say. Blinding pain shot through her skull accompanied by a loud shattering of glass. The floor rushed up to meet her. The aroma of inexpensive wine filled her nostrils, red fluid spattered across the carpet. Somewhere in the depths of what remained of her consciousness, she realised that some of that liquid was blood – her blood. Her hands clawed at the hard fibre of the carpet, trying to find a purchase, trying to drag herself away from him.

The shattered remnants of the bottle lay around her head. The lights began to dim as she drifted to eternal sleep. The last thing she saw was the contents of her handbag spilling out around her.

Chapter Four

Detective Constable Isaac Barrett yawned. "You'll have to excuse me, Mr Glenn. The last thing I expected in the early hours of Christmas morning was a murder."

The Regency's night duty manager, Andy Glenn, still white faced and shaking, smiled weakly. "I understand, constable."

In his early forties, tall and balding prematurely, Glenn looked every inch the hotel manager, if anyone wanted Barrett's opinion. Smartly turned out in a company-issued pinstripe, with a clashing, pale blue waistcoat, he had that air of haughtiness about him redolent of 4-star fusspots.

Barrett felt himself to be exactly the opposite. A graduate of Leeds University, not yet thirty, it was incumbent upon him to be as neatly attired as Glenn, but he had to pay for his own suits, and as a consequence, they fitted better. Like Glenn, he too had procedures to which he must adhere, but there was none of the prim, prissiness about them such as was attached to Glenn's duties. Barrett was a cop. It was his job to ask awkward questions and carry on asking them until he arrived at satisfactory answers.

Running a hand through his head of untidy, black hair, the constable checked the notes he had made in his pocketbook. "So let me run through this again. You were called about half past three by the gentleman in the next room, Mr Patterson, after he heard a disturbance, and you couldn't get an answer when you knocked on the door."

Glenn agreed with a nod. "You have to understand my job requires a great deal of discretion. Even when confronted with Mr Patterson's concerns, I could not simply barge into an occupied room."

"Obviously. Wouldn't do to walk in on a lover's tiff only to find that they were making it up in the time-honoured fashion, would it?" Barrett chuckled.

Glenn took the innuendo more seriously. "That, constable, is precisely why I have to be discreet."

Barrett read through the account again. "So you knocked, got no answer and then used your pass key?"

Glenn took the digital key from his pocket and held it up. It was about the size and shape of a credit card, coloured a rich red and emblazoned with the Regency's logo. "Every room has its own key, programmed to the lock, but this one will open any room in the building."

"And when you opened it," Barrett said with complete disinterest in the technology of the key, "you found the lady on the carpet, dead?"

Glenn shook his head. "I found the lady as she is. I didn't know she was dead. I just assumed she was. It was obvious that she'd been attacked, she wasn't moving and I feared the worst, but I did not touch anything in the room."

"You didn't think to check her pulse?"

The manager shuddered. "I could never bring myself to touch any person or animal that was, er…"

"Dead or, shall we say, apparently dead?" Barrett suggested, and the duty manager nodded. "What are the chances of someone getting hold of a pass key like yours?"

"Very slim," Glenn replied. "We insist that guests do not take them out of the building, but hand them in at reception when they go out. Obviously, some do take them, but…"

He trailed off lamely and Barrett made another note. "So it's unlikely that someone just let themselves in? Mrs Hardy would have answered the door to him … or her."

"Very likely."

Again, Barrett made notes. "How many staff do you have on duty, Mr Glenn?"

"Perhaps a dozen," the manager replied. "I'm usually manning reception, we have a couple of kitchen porters on duty, and the rest are maintenance staff. They busy themselves all over the building carrying out work such as…" Glenn paused, his eyes raised. "Changing light bulbs, for example. It's work we don't want them doing during the day. As long as a job is minor, and doesn't present a danger to the guests, we leave it for the night crew."

Barrett nodded. "And did any of your staff report anything unusual?"

"No. Nothing at all."

Barrett folded his pocketbook away. "All right, Mr Glenn, you can go back to your duties. This room will be sealed until Scientific Support are through and my boss, Chief Inspector Dockerty says it can be used again."

With the look of someone relieved to be away from the situation, Glenn turned and hurried along the corridor to the lifts.

With a wry, dismissive smile, Barrett knocked on the door of room 208, and presently a worried Tom Patterson opened it. Despite the early hour, he was already dressed, wearing a plain white shirt and dark trousers.

Barrett showed his warrant card. "Good morning, sir. Detective Constable Barrett, West Yorkshire CID. It is Mr Patterson, isn't it?" The older man nodded and Barrett asked, "May we speak in private, sir?"

Patterson stood back and let the policeman into the room. Barrett noticed that it was pristine, not a thing out of place, and he surmised that, like Glenn, this was a man in whom tidiness was a habit. A plain tie and jacket hung on the wardrobe door, and on the escritoire, a laptop computer glowed, its screen filled with text.

"A disturbed night," Patterson said. "I thought I might as well do a little work in the interim."

"Of course, sir," Barrett replied while Patterson shut down the computer.

The historian sat at the escritoire, and Barrett perched on the edge of the mattress, noticing that the bed, too, had been made. He checked his watch and made a note of the time in his pocketbook and with a smile of reassurance to Patterson, he said, "I understand you raised the alarm, sir."

Patterson nodded. "I had a couple drinks in the bar last

night and, well, you know, at my age..." He trailed off and looked pointedly towards the bathroom.

"I understand, Mr Patterson," Barrett said. "Please go on."

"I was awake, and I heard voices from next door. Then there was this awful, er, crash of glass shattering against wood, or what sounded like wood. I was scared half to death, I don't mind admitting. After that, all I heard was Jennifer's door closing a moment later. When I finished my business in the bathroom, I went out and knocked and I couldn't get an answer. I knocked several times. You have to try to keep the noise down at this time of night, but I was worried, so I contacted the night manager and told him of my concerns."

"And he came up to see what was going on."

Patterson chewed his lip. "Yes. And he took his damned time about it, too."

"You were aware of the time, were you, sir?" Barrett asked.

"It was just before three thirty when I woke up," Patterson said. "Everything happened within the space of a few minutes, but it was a quarter to four before I heard the manager knocking on Jennifer's door, and it was another few minutes before he knocked on my door and told me how he had found her."

"Discretion, sir," Barrett explained, utilising Glenn's excuse. "He did not want to go barging in there and find the lady *in flagrante delicto*, as it were."

Patterson snorted. "Jennifer? What kind of woman do you think she was, constable?"

"I notice that you use her forename, sir, so you must know her well."

"I do." Patterson smiled weakly. "We're both historians, and we both teach at the university. She was one of the longest serving members of the Leodensian Historical Society, and a close, personal friend."

Pedantically wondering what kind of close friend there could be other than a personal one, Barrett asked, "She wasn't, shall we say, the gadabout type, then?"

"Oh, good lord, no." Patterson appeared quite shocked by the question. "Obviously, she had relationships. Don't we all? She's been divorced some five years as I understand it, but she has the occasional, er, dinner date. But that doesn't make her a..." He trailed off unable to verbalise his thoughts.

"Quite, sir. May I ask, do you know where Mrs Hardy spent the evening?"

"In the bar downstairs. Along with the rest of us, and that crowd from Sanford."

Barrett checked his notes again and the information Andy Glenn had given him on the hotel guest list. "That would be the Sanford Third Age Club?"

Patterson nodded. "That's them. I was chatting with their chairman, grumpy chap by the name of Joe Murray. That would have been about 10:30-ish. At the time, Jennifer was dancing with one of the Sanford number. Man by the name of George Robson, if I have it right. He's the Director of Leisure Services in Sanford, from all I understand. They came across and Jennifer introduced him, then that Murray tore a real strip off her. Apparently they had met earlier in the day quite by chance and had a bit of an argument."

Barrett made a note. "Mr Murray was angry, sir?"

"Very angry. And very rude to Jennifer. His colleagues explained that he's a naturally ill-tempered sort, but Jennifer admitted she had behaved quite badly earlier in the day."

"I see, sir." Barrett made more notes. "And after the bar closed?"

Patterson shrugged. "I really don't know. She left with Robson, and that is as much as I can tell you... oh." Almost as he was about to speak, Patterson clammed up.

"Go on, sir."

"No. One doesn't like to say."

The CID man sighed. "Mr Patterson, someone has killed your neighbour, a lady you claim was a close friend and colleague. For now, we're treating it as murder. The best chance we have of catching the killer is to move quickly and early. You must give me whatever information you have in order for our inquiries to proceed. Now please tell me what's on your mind."

Patterson sucked in his breath and let it out with a sigh. "I'm sure it's nothing, but Dr Dennis Wright is in the hotel. He's one of our members from the University of Alabama. He recently published a book and he's over here to promote it. Jennifer was in Alabama last year, helping him with the research and manuscript preparation. They had a, er, liaison. You understand?"

"Perfectly, sir."

"Jennifer," Patterson went on, "was half convinced that she and Wright would get together again while he was here, in Leeds, but I spoke to her yesterday afternoon, and he had rejected her. She was quite angry about it, and Murray, the chap from the Sanford club, told me there had been a bit of an argument between Jennifer and Dr Wright in Debenhams some time earlier in the day. That was why Jennifer was so rude to Murray."

Ignoring the comment on Joe, Barrett asked, "Enough of an argument to turn this American into a killer?"

"That's not for me to say," Patterson argued, "but one would hardly consider Dennis Wright a murderer. He told me last night that he considered Jennifer obsessive, but he didn't appear unduly worried or angry about her persistence."

Barrett made a note. "Is there anything else you can tell me, Mr Patterson?"

The academic shook his head. "Nothing."

Barrett closed his pocketbook and put it away. As an afterthought, he took it out again. "Do you know if Mrs Hardy had any family, sir?"

Patterson nodded. "She had children. Let's see, Jennifer was about 52, so they would be in their late twenties now. I'm afraid I don't have any contact details, but they may be in her diary. Failing that, you'd have to come to the university on Wednesday in order to get them."

"All right, Mr Patterson, that's all for now, but my boss,

Chief Inspector Dockerty may want to speak to you when he gets here." Barrett put his notebook away again. "In the meantime, I wonder if I could ask a favour. We need someone to identify the body. Could you oblige?"

Patterson shook visibly. "Must I?"

"It would help, sir."

With great reluctance, Patterson nodded and Barrett stood to lead the way out. "When Scientific Support are through, Mr Patterson, we'd also be grateful if you could take whatever personal effects we're allowed to let go."

"That's no problem," Patterson assured him.

***

The clock read just after five when Detective Chief Inspector Raymond Dockerty arrived at the hotel to be greeted by Barrett. Travelling up to the second floor in the lift, the junior man briefed Dockerty on events so far.

Coming up to the age of 50, stout, square shouldered, his dark hair thinning on the crown, Dockerty's reputation for thoroughness was matched only by his reputation for speaking his mind and not caring who heard. A long-serving detective with an impressive arrest record, it was often said that the only things preventing his promotion to Superintendent were his love of detailed investigation and his propensity for treading on delicate toes.

"Who have you interviewed so far?" he asked when Barrett had run through his initial report.

"No one, sir. It is still quite early."

"I'm up," said the Chief Inspector, "and I see no reason why these bone idle buggers should be still sleeping when I'm not. And I certainly see no reason why a murderer should be snoring his head off, whether it's Christmas Day or Judgement Day. Give me those two names again."

The lift stopped and the doors soughed open. Coming out into the corridor, leading the way to room 207, Barrett consulted his pocketbook. "Dr Dennis Wright and Mr George Robson. Wright is on this floor, room 204, opposite the woman, and Robson is on the next floor, room 319."

"What do Scientific Support have to say?"

"Nothing too detailed, sir," Barrett reported, "but you wouldn't expect it yet. They're keen to get her away to the mortuary. At the moment, all they're saying is she was struck from behind. A single blow to the back of the head with a bottle of wine. Cheap house slop, looking at the label."

"I'm not remotely interested in your love of fine wine, Barrett," Dockerty grumbled. "I wouldn't know the difference between Sainsbury's red and a bottle of vinegar. Stick to the facts, lad."

"Yes, sir. As part of the general Christmas thing, the hotel handed out a 75-centilitre bottle of wine, and a box of Belgian chocolates, to every guest at last night's disco. The bottle which killed the woman was probably one of those, but we'd need to check the details on the label and compare it to the hotel records to confirm that."

"If it's cheap stuff as you insist, they're unlikely to have kept a record of who got which bottle." Dockerty paused outside room 207. "How many guests staying here?"

"One hundred and fifty-nine, sir. Seventy-one are from the Sanford Third Age Club, and a further eighty-six are with the Leodensian Historical Society. There are two guests not associated with either organisation or each other: Warren Kirkland and Oliver Quinton."

"That second one rings a bell," Dockerty ruminated.

"Lottery winner, sir." Barrett beamed in the light of his own efficiency. "I had records run a check on him. Dropped a half share of a large jackpot some years ago, and now spends his time and money chasing rare coins. Kirkland is a businessman from the Midlands. He's a coin collector, too."

Dockerty nodded. "So discount one dead woman, and we have one hundred and fifty-eight suspects." Dockerty hunched his shoulders. "I want every one of them interviewed, so I'll address them at breakfast. After we're through here, you get onto the station and have some manpower shipped in for the interviews." He nodded at the door. "All right, Barrett, let's see her." The constable pushed open the door and allowed his chief in first.

Forensic officers, dressed in antiseptic white, all-in-one, coveralls, busied themselves around the room, dusting furniture and fittings for fingerprints, one taking photographs, the fourth man labelling sample bottles.

Jennifer Hardy lay where she had fallen, her outstretched right hand close to a scrap of paper on which was a drawing. A deep welt had opened in the back of her head, and the surrounding carpet lay covered in a mixture of blood and wine. Her upturned handbag lay slightly out of reach of her hand, and the contents were spread in the immediate vicinity. Lower down, her knee-length, black nightie had ridden up exposing her buttocks.

"Morning, Doc," the Chief Inspector greeted the fourth officer currently labelling sample bottles. "Can you tell me anything?"

"Very little. I can confirm what the reports say. She died an hour or more ago as a result of a blow to the head. I'll know more when I've done the post mortem."

"Today?"

The doctor sighed. "It is Christmas, Dockerty."

"I'll be sure and let the killer know that when I have him." Dockerty's eyes narrowed. "I want the post mortem result ASAP." He looked down at the woman. "Tasty for her age. Had she had sex?"

"I don't know," the doctor replied, and when Dockerty scowled, he said, "I haven't been allowed to move her. We were waiting for the senior officer to arrive and see her *in situ*."

Dockerty ignored the irritation. "Well, the senior officer's seen her now, so you can take her." He aimed his next order at the forensic officer nearest Jennifer's head. "You. Get those items photographed," he gestured at the contents of Jennifer's handbag, "then bag them up and give me that scrap of paper." He turned to his assistant. "Have you checked the mobile?"

"Not yet, sir."

"Then do it, lad. I want to know who she's spoken to in the last week or two, right up to her death."

"Yes, sir." Barrett pulled on forensic gloves and made to pick up the phone.

Dockerty stopped him. "After the photographer's got all his snaps." Barrett straightened up and Dockerty said, "Right, sonny Jim. Let's talk to the management and find ourselves an office where we can interview this Patterson bloke, and the other one. Doc, as soon as you can tell me anything, you ring me. Come on, Barrett."

At 6:15, a bleary-eyed George Robson entered the manager's office at the rear of reception accompanied by Detective Constable Barrett, and found himself confronted by the businesslike Dockerty.

"Sit down, Mr Robson," the Chief Inspector ordered after introducing himself.

George did as he was told, and Barrett took a seat to his right, opened his pocketbook and poised his pen, ready to take notes. Dockerty sat opposite, with several evidence bags at his elbow.

"Right, sir, I need to ask you some questions, and I would appreciate honest answers. May I ask where you were at three thirty this morning?"

"In bed."

"Alone?"

George nodded. "And asleep. What's all this about?"

"All in good time, sir. You were pretty friendly with a lady named Jennifer Hardy in the bar last night."

George nodded. "That's not a crime, is it? She's over twenty-one, so am I, and we're both unattached."

"Did you escort that lady back to her room?"

"Yes. And I don't think that's a crime, either."

"It isn't," Dockerty assured him. "Did you and Mrs Hardy have sex?"

George bristled. "Mind your own bloody business."

"We'll establish whether or not it's my business shortly, sir." Dockerty consulted his notes. "According to Mr

64

Thomas Patterson, Chair of the Leodensian Historical Society, you introduced yourself as the Director of Leisure Services for Sanford Borough Council. According to our inquiries, you are, in fact, a gardener for Sanford Borough Council."

George blushed and grinned. "Yeah, well, Jennifer asked me to play the part. See, she was taking the mick with two guys who'd been annoying her in the bar."

Barrett made hurried notes. "Which two, er, guys, Mr Robson?"

George shrugged his heavy shoulders. "I dunno their names. One was a small, fat bloke with greasy hair, the other was well dressed and had a beard."

"And they'd been annoying her?" Dockerty asked.

"Yep. I think they'd been hitting on her, y'know? She asked me to put on this big show so she could give 'em the brush off."

"And you didn't mind?"

"I was on a promise," George replied. "What did I care?"

Owlish stares greeted his reply and George went on the defensive.

"It was a white lie, for God's sake. She asked me to tell it and I agreed cos I was trying to get into her pants."

"And did you, sir?" Barrett asked.

"I've told you once, that's nowt to do with you."

Dockerty reached into a buff folder and withdrew a seal-easy evidence bag containing a single scrap of paper. "Have a look at that, Mr Robson, and tell me what you think it means."

George drew the bag towards him.

It was a drawing like nothing he had ever seen in his life. Two horizontal lines, curved, one up, one down, and next to it a circle at the top of a cross. Done in heavy, black pencil, it was scrawly, ill-defined, as if the artist had been shaking while drawing it.

George handed it back and shrugged.

"You have nothing to say about it, Mr Robson?" Dockerty persisted.

"What would you expect me to say?" George demanded. "I'm a gardener, not a blooming archaeologist."

Dockerty put the drawing to one side. "Jennifer Hardy drew that," he said, "just before she died."

George's heartbeat increased. He began to tremble and suddenly felt weak. "What?"

"Mrs Hardy was murdered, Mr Robson, at three thirty this morning. Now I will ask you again, did you have sex with the lady last night."

George took a long time answering, as if the implications of the situation were just beginning to sink in. "Yes. Yes I did," George snapped.

Dockerty ignored him. "Or did she refuse and faced with her refusal, did you lose your temper and hit her on the head with a bottle of hotel wine?"

George's head spun. A vision of the carpet spinning up to meet him filled his head. Fighting it down, he yelled. "No. I didn't hurt her. We went back to her room after the disco finished, about one this morning. We had a drink from her mini-bar, she took a photograph of me with the camera on her phone, and then we got it on. I left her at two, and she was fine then. I went back to my room and straight to bed."

Pulling on forensic gloves, Dockerty dug into the evidence bags at his elbow and came out with Jennifer's mobile phone. It took a few moments for him to work his way through the menus, but when he turned it to face George, there was a photograph on the screen; a photograph of himself smiling into the lens. It was a half body portrait, from head to waist, his hands held forward , holding a CD case in his hands, just as Jennifer had asked him.

"Is that the photograph you mean, Mr Robson?"

George reached for the phone. Dockerty stopped him.

"Don't touch it, sir. We don't want to get any more of your fingerprints on it than we may find already. Can you confirm that this is the photograph Jennifer Hardy took of you last night?"

George nodded. "Yes. Yes it is."

"Did Mrs Hardy say why she wanted the photograph, sir?" the Chief Inspector asked.

George's heartbeat had settled a little. "Julio Iglesias," he said, pointing to the CD. "He was one of her favourites, and all she said to me was, she wanted a picture of her two favourite men of the moment. She was gonna use it to wind those two men up. I thought, whatever turns you on, chicken, and I posed for her." George took in their disbelieving eyes. "It was what she wanted. That's all I know."

Dockerty switched the phone off and put it back in the evidence bag. And what happened after that, Mr Robson?"

"I just told you. I did as Jennifer asked, and then we, er, you know, got down to it.

"But we have only your word for that, Mr Robson, and based on the evidence of this drawing, I'm inclined not to believe you."

"For God's sake, man –"

"I think she asked you to leave," Dockerty pressed on. "I think you pressured her, she insisted, and threatened to call the police. I think you picked up that CD and that is when she took the photograph. I think she then warned you to get out, but instead you took a bottle of the house wine the hotel had given to every guest, and hit her with it."

"This is nuts."

"George Robson, I'm arresting you on suspicion of murder. Constable Barrett will caution you, and you'll be taken to the station for further questioning."

Chapter Five

When Joe rose at eight, it was to the sound of church bells pealing into the still, quiet air. He rolled from his bed and crossed to the window, parted the vertical blinds a few inches and looked out on streets covered in a white shroud. The snow had stopped but it was Sunday, December 25th and in common with the rest of the Christian world, the gritter drivers had not yet turned out.

The Christmas card scene, the town hall and art gallery festooned with decorations, augmented by the overnight snow, appealed to the child in him. It was as if the magic of Christmas, so long buried in a lifetime of business concerns and work, had suddenly reappeared. But when he tried to tell himself he was excited, his inner self did not marry up to the feeling.

He had made his peace with Sheila and Brenda before the clock struck midnight, and at the appointed hour, he handed their gifts over, to receive a bottle of aftershave from Sheila, a shower kit from Brenda, and a kiss on the cheek from each of them.

There was more celebration in the crowded lounge before the DJ ended his show at half past midnight, and even then there were many 'season's greetings' to be exchanged with both STAC and LHS members and it was almost one before the room began to clear.

Walking out with his two companions, Joe spotted Tom Patterson leaving with Dennis Wright, the latter dividing his attention between Patterson and the sight of Jennifer Hardy arm in arm with George Robson. Wright was not the only one interested in them, either. Approaching the exit from opposite ends and sides of the room, Kirkland and Quinton were both intent on her and George.

Joe noticed that several people were carrying bags emblazoned with the hotel logo. Then he noticed that everyone had them and it stung.

"So what happened to my goodies?" he growled.

"I have them here," Sheila said, handing over his carrier. "I think you'd gone to the little boys' room when the staff handed them out. Either that or you were skulking outside with a cigarette."

"I do not skulk," he reproved her. Peering into the bag, he found a 75cl bottle of house red and a small box of luxury chocolates. "Remind me to give them to you two tomorrow," he said.

"Ungrateful swine," Brenda giggled.

"Joe doesn't drink wine, do you, dear?" Sheila teased.

"Wine is for toffs," he grunted. "Give me brown ale every time. And who eats fancy chocolates like that?"

"Brenda," Sheila replied.

"Me," Brenda echoed.

"Well you can have 'em. I'll settle for a steak and kidney pie at the Lazy Luncheonette on Wednesday."

He escorted his lady friends back to their room, bid them both as fond a 'goodnight' as he could muster, and then retired to his own room where he switched on his netbook and wrote a brief account of the evening. Half an hour later, he settled into bed and switched off the lights.

As usual, an evening of drinking had seen him out of bed several times during the night to visit the bathroom. On one such occasion, he thought he heard the sound of police sirens close by, but decided that there was nothing unusual about that in wintry conditions on a night of unrivalled revelry. "More likely an ambulance than the cops," he muttered as he climbed back into bed.

Coming down in the lift at 8:45, when it stopped at the second floor to pick up more passengers, Joe felt certain he had seen a uniformed police officer standing outside a room door further along the landing, but the doors closed, the lift carried on down to the ground floor, and he thought no more of it. If he had known any of the passengers in the lift, he may have asked, but they were all members of the LHS and he knew none of them.

It was only when he made the dining room and found several uniformed officers in attendance that the matter began to coalesce in his mind. After helping himself to bacon, eggs and two slices of toast from the buffet, he took a seat between Brenda and Sheila, his mind filled with questions.

"What's going on?"

"I don't know," Brenda replied through a mouthful of corn flakes, "but it must be serious. When Sheila and I came down the stairs, there were plain clothes men all over the second floor, and I saw others coming in wearing white overalls."

"Scientific Support," Sheila said. "Front line scene of crime officers, dressed so that they don't contaminate any evidence."

Joe's tired eyes brightened. "Maybe a bit of excitement, eh? Could be that they'll need some … hang on a minute. What were you doing coming down the stairs? You're not that much into exercise, either of you."

"The razor mind is beginning to sharpen," Sheila said.

"We waited ages for the lift and it never came," Brenda explained, "and in the end we decided to hike down the stairs. That's when we saw them."

"Hmm." Joe chewed on a piece of cold bacon and grimaced, but behind the scowl, the eyes burned as bright as ever. "Major crime, obviously. They're gonna need some help."

"Forget it, Joe," Sheila warned. "You're not in Sanford now, and the big city police will not take kindly to your interference."

"Interference, my eye. Assistance is what you mean. And old Talbot in Hull was glad of me, wasn't he?" He swallowed the bacon and washed it down with a mouthful of lukewarm tea. "What these places know about genuine catering, I forgot before I left school," he grumbled, and began work on the eggs with a notable lack of gusto. "Second floor, you say? The LHS mob are staying there." Joe looked around the room for signs of Tom Patterson, and could not see him. Still smarting from Sheila's last words, he went on, "My reputation as a detective spreads further than Sanford, you know."

"So does your reputation as a cook," Brenda chuckled. "The last report I read described the Lazy Luncheonette as a place to avoid if you don't want…"

She trailed off. Andy Glenn, a man she recognised as the night duty manager, entered the dining hall accompanied by a tall, stout individual clad in a heavy overcoat.

"What's going on now?" Sheila asked.

Joe shushed her as the newcomer put himself in a position where everyone could see him, and raised his voice above the hubbub. "Ladies and gentlemen, could I have your attention please."

Silence fell over the cavernous room and all eyes turned to him.

"Thank you. I'm Detective Chief Inspector Dockerty, of West Yorkshire CID. I'm sorry to interrupt your meal, but I have some disturbing news to impart. During the early hours of this morning, there was an incident in room 207. A woman was attacked and died of her injuries. We have already arrested a man concerning the incident, but we now have to take statements from you all."

Someone near the front asked Dockerty a question, which neither Joe nor his two friends caught. Dockerty listened politely, nodding his head as if confirming he understood.

At length, he raised his voice across the room again. "We do appreciate that it is Christmas Day and that you've all paid a lot of money for your stay here. We will inconvenience you as little as possible and hopefully, we'll be through by mid afternoon. In the meantime, if any of you are churchgoers and you wish to attend Christmas service, please let one of my officers know so they can arrange to see you later in the day. But we must insist that even if you know nothing about the night's events, you do not leave the area until we have taken a statement from you."

The dining room became an instant den of concerned chatter. Dockerty consulted briefly with Glenn and then raised his voice again. "Is Mr Joseph Murray here, please?"

He had been Joe Murray for so many years that it took him a second or two to recognise his full name. In the silence that followed, surprised at having been called out, Joe stood, self-consciously aware that all eyes were on him. *Strange*, he thought. *It doesn't bother me when I'm deejaying.*

Aloud, he announced. "I'm Joe Murray."

"Thank you, Mr Murray. I wonder if I could speak with you now, sir?"

Joe frowned and glanced down at his plate and the unpalatable food. Being the centre of attention did not stop the rumble of irritation in his blood. "I'm in the middle of breakfast," he protested.

Dockerty sighed. "We have a lot to get through, Mr Murray, and I need to speak to you urgently. I'm sure the Regency will ensure there is fresh food left for you, and it won't take longer than a few minutes."

Joe scraped back his chair. "Look after my plate," he told Sheila and Brenda, and left the table.

The policeman led him from the dining room through to reception and showed him into a back office, where Barrett sat to one side of the desk making notes in a file.

"This is Detective Constable Barrett, Mr Murray."

Joe and the younger man exchanged nods of greeting. Barrett brought a chair for Joe and placed it opposite the one Dockerty approached.

"Please sit down, sir."

Taking the chair, while Dockerty removed his overcoat, revealing an ill-fitting, baggy business suit beneath, Joe concentrated on the view through the window of the Regency's rear yard where crates and barrels could be seen stacked high alongside large capacity bins, everything covered in a thick coating of snow. The bins were obviously already full, and black, plastic refuse bags were stacked up around it. Up above, the sky was as grey and grim as it had been the previous day and Joe guessed it would snow again before the day was out. How much evidence would that snow cover?

Barrett opened his pocketbook, ready to take notes as his boss went into the interview.

"I won't keep you long, Mr Murray," Dockerty assured him. "I understand you're the organiser for the party from Sanford."

"I'm Chair of the club and I organise all our outings."

"Thank you. May I ask, then, do you know a man named George Robson?"

Joe nodded. "George? Sure. He's one of my members."

The younger man consulted his notebook. "That's the Sanford Third Age Club, is it, sir?"

"That's right. Listen, if something's happened to George…"

"In a moment, Mr Murray," Dockerty cut in. "Did you see Mr Robson last night?"

Joe nodded. "He was in the bar with everyone else. Will you just tell me what's happened?"

"All in good time, sir. Can you confirm that Mr Robson was, shall we say, overtly friendly with Mrs Jennifer Hardy in the bar last night?"

Joe tutted. "If you mean did George hit on that bad-tempered tramp from the LHS, then yes. But that's George. He's a bugger with the women. Now are you gonna tell me what's going on?"

But Dockerty would not be moved. "Do you know whether Mr Robson went back to Mrs Hardy's room last night?"

Tired of the circumlocution, Joe went on the attack. "Ours is the Sanford Third Age Club. Get that? Third age. It means every member must be over the age of fifty. In other words, Dockerty, they're mature adults, not children. It's none of my business whether George went back to her room last night. And I don't see where it's any of yours, either."

"But it is, Mr Murray," Dockerty declared. "At three thirty this morning, another guest reported muttered voices coming from Mrs Hardy's room, and what sounded like a bottle smashed against a piece of furniture. When the duty manager, Andrew Glenn, knocked, he got no answer, so he used his pass key to let himself in. He found Mrs Hardy on the floor, dead. She'd been hit on the back of the head with a bottle of wine. One of the complimentary bottles the hotel gave out to all the guests last night. The smashed pieces were all around her."

Joe's colour drained. His shoulders slumped and he sat back in the chair, stunned. "Hell's bells. And you think George did it?"

"I arrived at four thirty this morning, sir," Barrett explained, "and after Mr Glenn, the first person I spoke to was Thomas Patterson, Chair of the Leodensian Historical Society. He told us that Mrs Hardy had been, er," his ears coloured, "canoodling – Mr Patterson's word, not mine – with George Robson in the bar last night."

Joe grimaced. "Do you have a problem with the word canoodling, sonny? Maybe you should speak to your mum."

Barrett's cheeks coloured, too, and Joe concentrated on the senior man.

"I've known George Robson since we were both kids. Fifty years. He may be a charmer with the ladies, but he's no killer."

"I think differently, Mr Murray," Dockerty responded. "For example, can you explain why George Robson would introduce himself as the Director of Leisure Services at Sanford Borough Council?"

Joe almost sniggered, but caught himself in time. "So George told her a few porkies? What's the big deal. He was trying to get her knickers off."

"I think so, too, Mr Murray," Dockerty declared, "but Robson told us that Mrs Hardy had asked him to pose as the Director of Leisure Services. When we asked why, he couldn't satisfactorily explain it. I think Robson accompanied Mrs Hardy back to her room, tried his luck, she said no, he got angry, there was an argument, and he killed her."

"And what does George say?" Joe demanded.

"He admits he went back to her room, but he says they had sex and he left. That is all he says. The next thing he knew was when Ike, here, woke him up."

"Ike?"

Dockerty jerked a thumb at Barrett.

"It's short for Isaac." Barrett sounded apologetic.

"You poor sod," Joe commiserated. "Forget what I said about asking your mum. Any woman who could saddle a child with a name like that wouldn't understand canoodling."

"Can we leave my mother out of this, sir?"

"If my mother had named me like that, I'd have left her out of my life for good," Joe commented with a wry smile. He rounded on Dockerty. "Have you confirmed whether George had sex with her?"

"Not yet, sir, no," the Chief Inspector admitted. "We should get the post mortem report later today."

"Then without knowing, why did you arrest George?"

"His story was not particularly convincing and he cannot account for his movements between two, which is when he says he left Mrs Hardy, and three thirty five, which we have temporarily established as the time of death based on the noises heard by Mr Patterson in the next room. For now, Robson has been arrested on suspicion and taken to the police station for questioning."

"That's crazy," Joe said. "I can't account for my movements between two and half past three this morning." His face screwed up in a scowl. "Actually, I can. I was rushing to the lavatory most of the time. Too much to drink." He glowered at Dockerty. "But you only have my word for that. Are you going to arrest me?"

"You don't have a motive for killing her, sir," Barrett observed.

"Oh yes I do. We had a set to in Debenhams yesterday afternoon. She was arguing with some guy called Dennis

75

Wright and she knocked me in the back. She was intolerant and abusive. I gave her a mouthful about it in the bar last night. I've a damned sight more motive for killing her than George had, especially if he'd already had his legover."

"That's as may be, Mr Murray, but your fingerprints are not all over her room."

"And George's are?"

The Chief Inspector nodded. "We found his prints on the toilet flush handle, on a brandy glass, and in several other places."

"But not on the bottle?" Joe asked.

"The pieces have been taken away for reconstruction and analysis," Barrett said. "Once they've completed the jigsaw puzzle, we'll know."

"I'm telling you now, you have the wrong man," Joe asserted. "George Robson wouldn't hurt a fly, never mind a woman."

"We have the testimony of the woman herself," Dockerty insisted.

Joe's brow creased. "According to what you just told me, the night manager found her dead. Are you saying she was actually alive when you got to her?"

"No, but before she was killed, she took a photograph of your friend, which confirms he was in the room, and as she lay dying, she scrawled something out on a piece of paper. It told us all we needed to know. Especially when Robson told us of his womanising habits."

Dockerty's smug complacency began to get to Joe. "May I see this note?" he asked.

"No, you may not."

Joe got to his feet. "I'm giving you fair warning. George has the best detective in Sanford to prove him innocent."

Young Barrett frowned. "The best detective in Sanford? Who?"

Joe pointed to his own chest. "Me."

"Sit down, Mr Murray." The Chief Inspector sighed. "Ike may not have heard of you, but I have. Let me give you fair warning. You're not in Sanford now … or Hull, and I'm not as tolerant as Terry Cummins or your local bobbies. You will keep your nose out."

"Even if it means letting the real killer escape while you hound an innocent man?" Joe challenged. "I don't think so. You may not like me, Dockerty, but you're stuck with me and I will exercise my right to help clear my friend's name."

With an angry grunt, Dockerty snatched the file from under Barrett's forearms, reached into it and withdrew a scrap of paper and a sheet of printed A4. The scrap, Joe noticed, was in a seal-easy evidence bag.

"Take a look at that, Mr finest detective in Sanford."

Taking his seat again, Joe dragged the evidence bag across the desk and studied the note inside. It contained the simplified, scrawled drawing Dockerty had shown to George earlier.

"In order to make life easier for everyone, we reproduced it on a computer," Dockerty went on as he passed the A4 sheet across to Joe.

It was the same drawing but very much tidier.

"Now what do you make of that?"

While Joe, lips pursed, studied the two drawings, Dockerty took out Jennifer's phone. At length, Joe shook his head and looked up. "You tell me what you make of it."

"Simple," Dockerty went on as he worked through the phone's menu. "Remember the woman was dying, and she probably knew it. That's why the original drawing is so poor. The two horizontal, curved lines represent a man and woman having sexual intercourse. The stick figure represents a woman, Mrs Hardy herself. She was telling us that the man who wanted sex with her was the man who took her life. That man was George Robson." The Chief Inspector glared defiance. "Well?"

"Seems a bit of a wild conclusion to me," Joe replied. "I mean, if she was trying to implicate a man, why not draw the figure for Mars? A circle with an arrow pointing up and to the right. It's not much harder to produce."

"If you look at her original drawing, you'll see that the curved lines have small, er, nodules on the end. They could conceivably represent sperm."

Joe nodded. "They could also represent badly drawn coal tongs."

"They don't meet in the middle," Dockerty pointed out.

"And if they're sperm, they're travelling in opposite directions," Joe argued. "Are they trying to get in or out, or did they just get lost in the condom?"

Dockerty tutted. "I did say she was dying, Mr Murray. She probably realised she hadn't much time left."

"And if she was dying, her brain won't have been working right, so this will never stand up in court," Joe argued.

"I don't say that it will," Dockerty agreed. "We can bring it in as corroborative evidence once forensics give us everything else." With the phone displaying the photograph of George, Dockerty laid it down facing Joe. "We also have this."

Joe almost picked it up, but checked himself. "Give me a pair of forensic gloves, will you?"

Barrett obliged, Joe slipped them on and picked the phone up. After studying the photograph closely, he handed it back to Dockerty. "Odd picture. Why is he holding a

78

CD?"

"He claims Mrs Hardy asked him to pose that way," Dockerty replied. "We don't think it to be true. We believe he had been pressuring Mrs Hardy into bed, she refused, the argument began to get heated, he just happened to be holding the CD when she took the picture to warn him that she would use it to prove he was there. If you look closely at it, you'll see the escritoire that is common to all rooms at the Regency, in the background."

"That doesn't make a lot of sense, Dockerty. George is smiling. He doesn't look particularly threatening."

"I insist that our explanation makes more sense than his."

As the Chief Inspector was about to put the phone back into the evidence bag, Joe reached for it. Puzzled, the two police officers waited while Joe fished through the menus. Eventually, a gleam of satisfaction in his eyes, Joe laid it on the desk.

The photograph had gone and in its place, was a menu detailing the photograph file type, size and more importantly, date and time it was taken.

"Look at that," Joe said. "Taken on the 25th at 0122. Just turned twenty past one in the morning. She and George left the bar at about one, along with the rest of us. This picture was taken within minutes of getting back to her room. You yourself admitted that the time of death was about 3:35. What the hell was going on for those two and a quarter hours? She takes a picture warning him to get out at twenty past one, and he finally loses his rag two and a bit hours later? Get real. Whatever this photograph means, it doesn't mean she was trying to get rid of him."

Barrett looked away and Dockerty coughed to hide his embarrassment. "All the same, Robson's story remains suspicious."

Handing the phone back, Joe drummed his fingers on the desktop. "I suppose you won't let me get a look at the room?"

"Out of the question," Dockerty declared.

Handing back the two items, staring into Dockerty's

fierce eyes, Joe softened his approach. "Look, Dockerty, I'm not after letting George off the hook for no good reason. If he did it, he did it, and he should pay, but don't let your professional pride stand in the way of genuine assistance. I am very skilled at seeing things others miss, and by 'others' I include the police. I just did, didn't I? Check with Detective Sergeant Gemma Craddock of Sanford CID. I can bring you other references to my skills, too, people way above Terry Cummins; the Assistant Chief Constable, for instance."

"I'm aware of your contacts, Mr Murray," Dockerty responded. "Now let me tell you something about me. I have a reputation for being my own man. I don't care if you're *sleeping with* the Assistant Chief Constable, I will not allow you to interfere with my investigation."

"I wasn't thinking of interfering." Joe backed off another step. "All I'm asking is you keep me informed of where you're at, and I swear that if I come across anything, I will bring you up to speed on it. For instance, you must have taken pictures of the crime scene. What's to say that I won't see something you didn't?"

"Of course we have and I doubt very much that you will be able to spot anything I haven't already seen. Those photographs may be introduced as evidence, and I will not, therefore, allow you to see them." Dockerty, too, backed off on his hard line stance, but not as far as Joe. "We appreciate whatever help we can get, Mr Murray. I'd be grateful if you kept us informed of anything you may learn."

"You're not easy to work with, are you? I mean, I already worked two things out, didn't I?"

"The photograph and what else, Mr Murray?"

"If George had already had his oats, why would he kill the woman? He's not married, she couldn't blackmail him, so why?"

"Maybe he wanted seconds," Barrett said.

Joe snorted. "Ike, at your age, I'll bet George would have come back for seconds, possibly thirds, but he's in his mid-fifties. He may still be a bit of a ram, but he's no stallion.

80

Not anymore."

"Mr Murray…"

Joe went on before the Chief Inspector could get any further. "And that drawing. Did you show it to George?"

"We did," Dockerty agreed.

"And what did he have to say about it?"

"He said he couldn't make head nor tail of it because he's – I quote – 'a gardener, not a blooming archaeologist'," Barrett reported, reading from his pocketbook.

"He's also thick as a brick," Joe ventured. "If you asked an archaeologist about those signs, he'd put completely the wrong interpretation on them." He stared at the two police officers. "Just the way you have."

"And what do you mean by that?" Dockerty demanded.

Joe pointed to the stick figure. "That is the astrological symbol for the planet Venus. Astronomers use it too. It's also the internationally recognised symbol for a female."

"Which is exactly what I said." Dockerty remained smugly triumphant.

"I know you did. But it's the other lines I'd query. See, I print my own little books." Joe smiled modestly. "Details of my successful cases. Now, back in the days before the internet, when I first looked into the possibility, I was told I would need to learn about printer's galley proofs and correction marks. Jennifer's drawing isn't strictly accurate, but those curves remind me of an author's rough note on transposing words."

Both officers frowned. "Come again," Barrett said.

With an irritated cluck, Joe took the officer's notebook and wrote his name, surname first, then drew curved arrows pointing in opposite directions above and below it.

Murray Joe

"You see, if someone had printed my name like that and I wanted it the right way round, that is how I would let the printer know, and that is exactly what the drawing found near Jennifer Hardy looks like to me."

"Well, I disagree," Dockerty said. "There are probably dozens of different interpretations we could put on it, depending on your point of view. To me it indicates something to do with sex, and that points the finger straight at George Robson."

"If that spells sex to you, Dockerty, you should spend more time with your wife. Either that or find yourself a bit on the side."

Chapter Six

"George? A killer? That's absurd."

Joe nodded his agreement with Sheila's assertion.

"Bloody crazy is what it is," Brenda growled. She bounced to her feet. "Well, I'll put 'em right. They'll let him go when I'm through with them."

Half an hour had passed since Joe's interview with the police, and they had moved from the dining room to the lounge where many people sat in cliques. There was only one topic for discussion and as if to reinforce it, the police sat at half a dozen tables under the windows furthest from the bar, taking statements from individuals.

Of his two friends, Brenda, as usual, had dressed more outrageously, wearing a bright red, knitted sweater, festooned with reindeer and Christmas tree motifs. It was also a size too small and stressed her finer points: both of them. Sheila, meantime, looked as demure as ever in a navy blue jumper and trousers.

And it was Sheila who called a halt to Brenda's bullheadedness. "What are you going to tell them?"

Brenda maintained her defiance. "I'll tell them George spent the night with me and can't have done it."

"But that's a lie. You were asleep in our room all night," Sheila reminded her best friend.

"So what?" Brenda challenged. "They can't prove that."

"Sheila's right, Brenda, so sit down and wait until you're called," Joe ordered. "And when they do call you, tell them the truth. You know nothing."

"So we leave poor George to suffer?"

"No, we don't," Joe assured her. "What you do is listen to me. For a start off, George has already admitted he was with Jennifer Hardy, so there's no point trying to lie him out of jail from that angle. We know George hasn't killed her, but we only know it intellectually. We can't prove it. We have to prove he's innocent and based on the thin evidence the cops have gathered, that won't be easy. Their interpretation of that drawing is the only thing they have on George, but trying to shake them is like trying to get a hungry Rottweiler away from your waste food bins."

"The simplest way is to find the real killer," Sheila ventured. "Just like we did in Chester."

"It's not the simple way," Joe argued. "It's the only way, and it won't be easy. It happened in the early hours of the morning. Who was out and about? No one. Who saw anything? No one. The only real information the cops have is from Tom Patterson, in the next room, the guy what raised the alarm."

"So what can we do?"

"We can get logical. Tom heard the bottle being smashed. Apparently, he said it sounded like it was smashed against a piece of furniture, but that's exactly what anyone would think. What he actually heard was the bottle smashing against her head."

Brenda cringed. "Joe. Please."

"Hey," he urged, "get real on this. Murder isn't pleasant. No matter how the killer moves his victim to the next world, it's nasty. But this method begs a few questions, doesn't it?"

"Does it?" Brenda asked.

Sheila smiled. "I sense a Joe Murray analysis coming on, and I'm quite ready to pull it apart. Go on, Joe."

He sat forward, closing in on them so no one could overhear. "Brenda, you're the expert on bed-hopping. Suppose –"

"I beg your pardon." Brenda's interruption was loud enough to be heard across the room. Aware that she was suddenly the centre of everyone's attention, including the police's, she toned it down. "You make me sound like a tart."

Joe huffed out his breath. "All right. Let's say you're

84

more experienced at relationships than Sheila and me. Suppose someone came knocking on your door carrying a bottle of wine? What would you think?"

"That he was after bed-hopping with me."

Sheila laughed. "How very succinctly put, Brenda." More soberly, she went on, "The problem is, Joe, that it's exactly what the police will think George was up to."

"I know that. But even if you lose your temper, why hit the woman with the bottle? It's noisy and messy. The wine won't just have been all over the floor, but over the killer, too. See? If you're going to lose it, you strangle the poor sow. It's much quieter and less messy."

"If he's angry, he won't have been thinking straight, Joe," Brenda objected.

"All right, so maybe it was a spur of the moment thing, but what caused him to lose his temper?" Joe pressed on before they could try to answer. "I saw him and Jennifer Hardy walking out of the ballroom at one o'clock. The police have established the time of death at just after three thirty. What were she and George doing for that two and a half hours?"

Brenda chuckled. "I've yet to meet a man who can make it last half an hour, never mind two and a half."

"My point precisely," Joe agreed. "Yet the cops are working on the theory that he killed her because she turned him down. It doesn't take two and a half hours to say no to someone. Even someone as persistent as George."

"This is all circumstantial, Joe," Sheila argued. "It is entirely possible for George to have spent two and a half hours talking with Jennifer, and he may have made several attempts to seduce her. She may finally have said something like, 'you can try all you like, George, but you're not going to get what you want,' at which point, he may have lost his temper and killed her."

"Whose side are you on?" Joe demanded.

Sheila shrugged. "I'm simply stating facts. I don't believe George killed her any more than you do, and I said so just a few moments ago."

Joe stared around the room, seeking inspiration. Tom Patterson had just entered and sat with some of his people. He looked tired and despondent.

Joe returned to his two companions. "The killer still has to get the hell out of the room, and he has to lock the door. Dockerty told me the night manager had to use the pass key to let himself in."

Sheila shook her head. "Wrong again, Joe. The doors lock automatically from the outside when you close them."

"Do they?" Joe appeared startled. "Yeah. Course they do." He dragged the discussion back where it should be. "No matter. He's killed her. He's covered in wine and possibly blood. Patterson has heard the fuss and he's called the night manager. Our killer needs to get away. He legs it. But where to?"

"His room, presumably," Sheila said.

Joe nodded. "Which is where?"

"If it was George, it was on the third floor," Brenda said.

"Correct, and that is exactly why it isn't George." He could see the puzzlement in their eyes. "Think about it. He's coming out of the room, he's in a hell of a mess, soaked in wine and stuff, maybe even blood. At all costs, he dare not meet anyone else. He doesn't know the night manager is on his way up, but it's a risk he daren't take anyway, so he goes straight to his room. He wouldn't use the lift because he has no way of knowing whether there's anyone in it until it stops and the doors open. He would have to use the stairs, but again, he doesn't know if there's anyone about and he can't know until he reaches the next floor up. If no one, particularly the night crew, saw anyone, the simplest, most logical explanation is that the killer's room was on the second floor, not the third."

"That's an assumption, Joe, not an explanation," Sheila told him. "And did any member of the night crew see anything or anyone?"

"I dunno and Dockerty probably won't tell me … but young Ike might." He grinned wolfishly and took out his tobacco tin.

"Oh, Joe, you can't –"

"If you're gonna tell me I can't smoke this in here, don't bother."

Brenda fumed. "I wasn't going to say anything about smoking. I was going to tell you, you can't leave the hotel. The police won't let you."

Joe rolled his cigarette with practised ease. "They're letting the bible bashers go to church, so they can let me out the front door for a cigarette."

Sheila clucked. "Really, Joe. Bible bashers? They're devout Christians."

Joe shrugged. "I don't have a problem with church," he admitted, "except when they come round rattling the charity box." He tucked the cigarette in his shirt pocket, and abruptly changed the subject. "And that drawing doesn't make sense, either."

"You mean the police interpretation of it?"

Joe shook his head. "No, I mean the whole thing, and that includes Dockerty's interpretation of it."

"All right," Sheila asked, "what is it that doesn't make sense?"

Joe fiddled with his Zippo lighter. "Put yourself in Jennifer Hardy's position. Someone has just lamped her with a bottle of wine. She's dazed, dying, in terrible pain. And the first thing she does is draw a crazy diagram that is wide open to several interpretations. Does that make sense? Why not scrawl out the killer's name or even his initials?"

"Maybe she didn't know his name," Brenda suggested.

Joe snorted and Sheila giggled.

"Brenda, this woman was well educated; a bit of class totty, not Sanford rough. She would have at least known with whom she was having the pleasure."

"That's not what I meant," Brenda objected. "And if you call me a bit of Sanford rough again, I'll be the next one arrested for murder." She took a moment to calm down. "Someone may just have knocked on her door at random. There are plenty of nutters around who do that sort of thing."

Joe considered the possibility and dismissed it with a shake of the head. "No. She knew who it was, all right. She turned her back on him."

"How do you know?" Sheila asked.

"Dockerty told me. She was hit on the back of the skull. That means she had turned away from the attacker, and you don't turn your back on nutters. Besides, if she didn't know him, what was the point of the drawing? No, this whole thing just doesn't add up." His eye roamed the lounge again and fell on Tom Patterson sat with a few of his members. Joe stood. "I'll be back in a while."

He crossed the room, nodding to Les Tanner, Sylvia Goodson, and Alec and Julia Staines, all of whom were sitting together. Arriving at a group of chairs occupied by LHS members, he tapped Patterson on the shoulder.

"Morning, Tom. I'm sorry to hear about Jennifer."

"So are we all, Joe. What a terrible thing to happen."

"One of your crowd was arrested, I believe," said an elderly man wearing a pristine shirt and tie beneath a dinner jacket.

Taking him to be an academic, Joe said, "Yeah, well, you know what we ex-miners are like. Thugs, the lot of us." Leaving the other man gawping, he said to Patterson, "Could I have a word, Tom?"

"Of course, Joe."

Patterson got to his feet and leaving the LHS assembly at the table, the two men ambled across to the shuttered bar.

"This is a bad business," Patterson said as they leaned on the polished oak counter. "And I'm sorry for you, too. To have one of your friends commit such an appalling act, is … I don't know, it's just…" He trailed off unable to find the words.

"What makes it worse is the police have the wrong man," Joe insisted.

Patterson's eyes widened. He looked around the room as if ensuring no one else was listening, but Joe knew better. He was trying to absorb the implications of what he had just heard. He swung his head back and looked into Joe's earnest face.

"The wrong man?"

Joe nodded. "I know George Robson. Even if Jennifer turned him down, he wouldn't have hurt her. It's not his style. He wouldn't even slap her about, let alone kill her. There are problems with the police theories, Tom, but that Dockerty is not going to listen to me, and the only way I can help George is to find the real killer." He chuckled. "I can give them three other suspects without even thinking about it. Maybe even four or five."

"You can?"

Joe nodded. "Dennis Wright, me ... and you."

Patterson's chunky features ran a gamut of emotions from surprise, through to amazement and then worry. "Dennis Wright? You? Me?"

Joe nodded. "She had a blazing argument with Dennis Wright yesterday, and with me, and you admitted in the bar last night that you hit on her and she turned you down."

Patterson tried to smile. "Oh, but that was two years ago, Joe."

"Doesn't matter. There are three men with reasons for ... let's say, attacking her, if not actually killing her, and all three of us had stronger motives than George Robson, because George only wanted one thing; his legover. And if I know George, he had it, which in turn, means he had no reason to kill her. Over and above that, there's that greasy little squirt, Oliver Quinton and the other guy; the beard. Warren Kirkland."

Patterson frowned. "I know Kirkland, but I'm not familiar with Oliver Quinton."

"Count yourself lucky," Joe said. "Nasty piece of work. Short, fat, greasy hair; he was arguing with Wright at the bar and then he and Jennifer were having words on the dance floor."

"Oh, yes. I know whom you mean. I didn't know his name." Patterson chewed his lip agitatedly. "Have you told the police any of this?"

"I tried, but they don't wanna listen. I could have done

89

with getting a look in Jennifer's room, though, but they won't even allow that."

The Chair of the LHS shuddered. "It wasn't pretty, believe me. I was called in to identify her the moment the police got here. It was awful. Her handbag spilled all over the floor, the wine from the bottle mixed with her blood." He shivered again. "A terrible sight."

"Yeah. I'll bet." Joe allowed a diplomatic pause. "So what are they doing with her personal effects?"

"Such as we're allowed to take away, they've been handed to me so that I can pass them on to her children and ex-husband. They've kept some back. The contents of her handbag." Patterson's malleable features meandered into vague puzzlement. "I'll tell you what's odd, Joe. Her laptop is missing. I asked the police about it, but they say they haven't found it, and I think they think she didn't have it with her."

"And did she?" Joe asked.

"Oh yes. Jennifer was a workaholic. Even over the Christmas period, she would find time to do a little work, even if it was only a spot of editing on her latest paper." Patterson gave a wan smile. "We're all the same, us historians. I ended up doing a little work this morning, myself, while I waited for the police to interview me. Jennifer never went anywhere without her laptop. She was a very clever woman, you know. Like all of us, she published the occasional title, but while most of us preferred to buy in illustrations, Jennifer did her own."

"On the computer?" Joe asked, unable to hide a trace of envy in his voice.

"Not all of them, no. She could use computer drawing software, but mainly she did her own pencil sketches. I suppose it was a part of her specialisation, the Middleton Light Railway. There are drawings available on the internet, but not many, so she did her own." Patterson shrugged. "I'm not too worried. I know for a fact that she locked the machine with a password so if the killer has stolen it, he won't get into it."

"You're sure of that?"

Patterson nodded. "Jennifer told no one that password. Not even me. She had it written down somewhere, but she never told anyone where it was, and she also insisted that no one would ever get it."

"Right," Joe said, his brow creasing. Across the room, he noticed Detective Constable Barrett making his way out of the room. "Well, listen, it's nice talking to you, Tom, but I need an infusion of nicotine. If you think of anything that may be important, will you let me know as well as the cops? On the QT?"

"Of course."

With a final nod of thanks, Joe hurried across the room and out into reception.

"Excuse me, sir," said a constable on duty, "but have you given a statement?"

"Yes. Over an hour ago to your boss, Dockerty. He didn't believe me then and he won't believe me now. Besides, I'm only going to the door for a smoke. All right?"

The constable stood back and allowed him to rush out to the front entrance where he found Detective Constable Barrett lighting a cigarette.

"Oh," Joe said. "I expected to find you jumping into a car and heading home."

"Not yet, sir," Barrett yawned. "No Christmas for me until everyone in the hotel has been interviewed."

"I hate Christmas, so it wouldn't bother me," Joe admitted. "Does it trouble you?"

Barrett took a deep drag on his cigarette and nodded. "I have a wife and daughter, Mr Murray. I'd rather be home than messing about here, but..." He shrugged. "It goes with the territory."

A dull silence fell. The air hung with the tang of coming snow again. The temperature hovered just above freezing point and the grey skies threatened an imminent shower. Further along the broad street, Joe could see few people. A group of young men turning into a restaurant, one or two other individuals treading warily on the slippery pavements, but in the main, the residents of Leeds had elected to spend Christmas indoors.

He flipped the cap of his Zippo and struck the wheel, putting a light to his cigarette. "I was just talking to old Tom Patterson, the Chair of the LHS. We're all pretty cut up about this business."

"Murder is like that, sir," Barrett ventured. "I may be young but I've done a few already, and it's never pleasant."

"No, no. Course not. I've investigated a few myself." Joe puffed on his cigarette. "Your boss doesn't like me, does he?"

"Making snide remarks about his wife didn't exactly endear you to him." Barrett laughed. "He's a good man, sir. Dedicated, you know. He goes by the book because that's the only way we can be sure of not missing anything. He won't brook interference from anyone who is not connected to the police or directly involved with the case. Privately, he does speak highly of you, though. You're well known, even here in Leeds."

"But not for my steak and kidney pies."

Barrett frowned and Joe elected not to explain.

"So your boss doesn't like interference? Even when he's wrong?"

Again the young detective laughed. "You say he's wrong."

"About George? Yes, I believe he's wrong, but that's not what I'm talking about. Patterson just told me that he can't find Jennifer Hardy's laptop. He also hinted that you, or your boss, think she never had it with her. Patterson says different. She never goes anywhere without it, and if he says that, you should be looking for it."

The humour left Barrett's features. "You think it may tell us something?"

"Indirectly, yes," Joe replied and took another pull on his cigarette. "See, if Jennifer had that laptop but it's not there now, where is it? In other words, what price the killer took it? And if that's so, did you find it in George's room? And if you didn't, what price George isn't the killer? You're a good

92

cop, young Ike, and I've no doubt your boss is, too, but sometimes, you policemen run on rails so straight that you can't see the wood for the trees." He paused to let the mixed metaphors sink in. "People are creatures of habit, and if Jennifer Hardy took her laptop everywhere with her, then she also brought it here. George Robson is a creature of habit, too. No way would he steal a laptop because he isn't a thief, and he'd have no use for it himself. He doesn't need the money, so he wouldn't be looking to sell it. If he killed her, he would have legged it hell for leather out of that room, and he wouldn't have hung around to nick a computer he doesn't need." Joe shivered in the chill and took a final drag on his cigarette before crushing it out on the wall-mounted stubber. "Think about it, son."

He turned back into the hotel, and just as suddenly paused, turned and came back out. "One other thing, Ike. Patterson tells me the contents of Jennifer Hardy's handbag were spilled all over the floor."

Barrett tutted. "That's right, Mr Murray, they were."

"What's your thinking on that?"

The young officer shrugged. "We believe she was reaching into the bag for the eyeliner pencil and the piece of paper to draw that little sketch we found."

"You mean Dockerty believes that?" Joe pressed.

"It's a working theory, sir. No more."

"But if someone stole her laptop it means he was in the room long enough to see her do that and..." Joe left the suggestion hanging in the air.

Barrett sighed. "I take your point, sir, and I'll mention it to Chief Inspector Dockerty."

Joe grinned. "Good lad. You'll make a sound detective one of these days. Was there anything unusual about the contents? Anything missing, for example?"

"If it was missing, how would we know?" Barrett countered.

Joe laughed this time. "I'll tell you something, Ike. I was married for ten years of sheer hell. I hated almost every minute of it and I was glad when it was over. But even so, I got to know about the kind of junk a woman carries in her handbag. You say you're married and yet you're telling me you don't?"

"Oh, right. I see what you mean. No, there was nothing unusual. Everything was there as far as I can remember. The usual rubbish: makeup, eyeliners, even a can of hairspray."

"Mobile phone, diary, address book?"

Barrett frowned. "The phone was there, certainly. The chief insisted I pick it up and check the call logs. I found that photograph on it before I bagged it up after the forensic men had finished photographing the scene. But I don't recall seeing a diary or an address book."

Joe smiled. "So where did she get the piece of paper to draw her little clue on?"

Chapter Seven

Chief Inspector Dockerty glowered thunder at Joe. "It's less than two hours since we last spoke and you've done exactly what I asked you not to do."

Seated in the manager's office where he had been 90 minutes earlier, Joe maintained an air of implacable calm.

Dockerty, his features drawn, tired, was anything but. "I do not need amateur Sherlocks shoving their bloody oar into what is, as far as I'm concerned, a simple case of shenanigans gone wrong."

"I couldn't agree more."

Joe's apparent acquiescence threw Dockerty. "What?"

"I said, I couldn't agree more," Joe repeated. "You don't need an amateur like me sticking his nose into an open and shut case. The trouble is, you don't have an open and shut case. You have something more complex and you won't admit it."

Dockerty heaved out a frustrated sigh. Resting his forearms on the desk, leaning his considerable weight on them, he demanded, "I suppose you know who killed Jennifer Hardy, do you?"

"No. Unlike you, I don't. Y'see, Dockerty, that's one of the differences between us. I don't know who killed her, but you've already persuaded yourself that it was George, and that's blinding you to other possibilities. I don't think it's him, but my belief is based on nothing more than personal knowledge of the man, and I'm ready to admit, I could be wrong. You're not."

Dockerty opened his mouth to protest, but Joe talked right over him.

"Another difference is, I ask questions of myself,

whereas you ask them of other people."

"In that case, you should ask yourself about the penalties for attempting to pervert the course of justice," the Chief Inspector warned. "You asked Constable Barrett about certain matters, and knowledge of those matters may prejudice a trial." He glared at his subordinate. "And he should have known better than to give you answers."

Joe dropped his pretence at calm civility and launched a full frontal attack. "I asked Ike questions that any good defence lawyer would ask. I'm simply trying to save you and the taxpayers a hell of a lot of time and money on an investigation that started on the wrong foot and is heading in the wrong direction."

The Chief Inspector exhaled again, louder this time, and when he spoke, his voice chewed spit. "What do I have to do to get through to you?"

"That's a question I could ask of you, Dockerty. As far as I'm concerned, all you have to do is tell me what I need to know," Joe urged. "Accept my help in the spirit in which it's offered. I'm here to help, not embarrass you."

"And I keep saying, I don't need your help."

"And I think you do. Let's take a simple example. Have you had the post mortem result yet?"

"Yes. The pathologist rang his preliminary report through about twenty minutes ago, but it didn't tell us anything we didn't already know. Jennifer Hardy died from the blow to her head."

"Had she had sex?"

Dockerty nodded.

"And was her partner George Robson?"

"It's too early to say," the Chief Inspector countered.

"Bull," Joe retorted. "A full DNA analysis will take two to three days, but you can get enough from early samples to identify George. Was it him?"

"Yessssss." The word came out as a hiss.

Joe shrugged. "There you are, y'see. George had had her. Why, then, did he kill her?"

"We don't know," Dockerty responded, "because he

denies everything."

"And it couldn't be that he's telling the truth?"

"At the moment," the Chief Inspector reminded Joe, "we have no other suspects."

"And I gave you three earlier today, including myself. I can also give you two more."

"All right," Dockerty amended his statement, "we have no other suspects who were known to be in her room during the night."

"Show me the photographs of the room," Joe demanded.

"Give me one good reason why I should," Dockerty countered.

"Because she knew her killer and I know it wasn't George. It was someone in one of the rooms on the second floor, which means it was a member of the Leodensian Historical Society, not the Sanford Third Age Club. The way her room was left may give me a clue to that person's identity."

The two police officers exchanged glances. "How do you know it was someone from the second floor?" Dockerty demanded.

Joe explained it the way he had told his two companions earlier, and concluded, "It had to be either a guest from the second floor or a member of the hotel staff. Andy Glenn would have told you of a crew member covered in blood and wine, and he didn't or you would have hauled the suspect in, therefore it had to be a guest, and the only guests on the first and second floors are with the LHS party."

"This is all supposition and I'm not about to release George Robson based on your assumptions."

"I'm not asking you to, but a simple way to sort it out would be to ask whether any of the night staff noticed blood or wine stains on the carpets."

"Mr Glenn never mentioned anything, sir," Barrett reported. "But he did tell me he'd had no reports from the night staff of anything out of the ordinary."

"And we can't ask him anything further until tonight when he comes back on duty, so I still refuse to release

Robson." Dockerty smirked. "Which way are you going to go next, Murray? Are you going to plead that I'm ruining Robson's Christmas?"

Joe shook his head and smiled. "If I had my way, I'd strike Christmas from the calendar, so I don't really care if you're ruining his holiday. George might when he sues for wrongful arrest." A study of Dockerty's face told Joe that the Chief Inspector was not impressed. "Do us all a favour, Dockerty. Let me have a look at the photographs your people took of the crime scene."

Dockerty's features screwed in a mask of fury and frustration. He reached across the desk and snatched the case file from beneath Barrett's arms. Opening it, he pulled out a small folder of photographs and handed them over.

They were monochrome, but Joe found the light balance strong enough to distinguish everything on them. He barely glanced at those showing Jennifer's full body and the close ups of her head wound, putting the pictures to one side.

"I'm not a medico," he explained to Barrett, "and I'm not a ghoul."

He reached a mid shot of Jennifer's outstretched right hand and the handbag items nearby. Two makeup brushes, a compact, a small case of eye-shadow, a few tissues, her mobile telephone, and as Barrett had said, a canister of hairspray. On the edge of the picture, its cover smeared in what Joe imagined would be either wine, blood, or an unpleasant mixture of the two, lay a copy of *Missing Pennies*, the white box containing its barcode, where the ISBN would normally be found, plainly visible. Just beyond the reach of her fingers was the scrap of paper upon which she had drawn her final, cryptic message.

"Curious," he muttered.

"What is?" Dockerty asked.

Joe leaned across the desk, with the photograph held so that he could point out his problem and the Chief Inspector could see.

"The drawing is an inch, maybe less, from her fingers. She put it down and let it go as she died. No problem with that. The paper is a little scrunched up, as if she's been holding it in a dying hand. No problem with that, either. Where's the eyeliner pencil she drew the diagram with?"

"A little further out," Dockerty said, "and near her left hand."

"So she was a southpaw?"

The Chief Inspector shrugged. "Is it important?"

"It could be. I'll check with Patterson," Joe said. "But that's not what I noticed. It's the diagram itself. It's the other way up from the way you showed it to me."

He pointed at the diagram and its altered orientation.

"If it was like that when you found it, how come you showed it to me the other way up?"

"It was the only way it made sense, sir," Barrett said.

"Was it?"

Dockerty suddenly appeared alert to other possibilities. "Are you telling me it could make sense that way up, Murray?" Dockerty demanded.

"Yes, but I'll have to check my facts before I commit myself." Joe drummed his fingers on the desk a moment. "Gimme a pen and a piece of paper, and I'll show you what I mean."

Barrett handed over the implements and Joe scrawled 'p o' on the paper. He showed it to them.

"P, O," he said. "That could mean post office, couldn't it?" Both detectives nodded. Joe flipped the paper over. "Now look at it."

The letters now read, 'o d'.

"O, D," Joe declared. "Overdosed."

"Are you suggesting this was drug related?" Dockerty

demanded.

Joe let out a frustrated sigh. "No. I used those letters because it was the only example I could come up with off the top of my head. What I'm trying to point out is that when you turn the letters p and o upside down, you get o and d, and they mean completely different things. There is no correlation between post office and overdose. So if you turn Jennifer Hardy's last message over, it has nothing to do with sex, and something to do with a church."

"A church?" Barrett was surprised. "Where do you get that from?"

Joe pointed to the photograph and the inverted stick figure on the drawing. "A circle with a cross on top is one of a number of symbols used to denote a church." He looked from one policeman to the other. "Was she religious?"

Dockerty shrugged. "Haven't a clue. Patterson would know. Regardless of what that symbol means, the curved arrows still indicate sexual goings on to me."

"And I told you my interpretation of them earlier." Joe sighed. "The only one who really knows isn't going to tell us, either, because she's dead."

Leaning back, he put the photograph to one side and skimmed through the rest. There were various views of the body and the room in general. A small tray of glasses, one or two still containing liquid, which Joe assumed to be spirits, Jennifer's valise stood alongside the wardrobe, and one picture of the interior of the wardrobe, showing a few items of clothing.

"No laptop," Joe muttered.

"Barrett told me you mentioned that. I still don't see where it's important."

"It's important because it's missing, Dockerty," Joe responded. "Was it stolen? If so, you could be dealing with more than one crime, and you'd have to look at the hotel's night crew. I'm sure Andy Glenn isn't the only member of staff to have a pass key. The cleaners would need one, too."

"Day cleaners, perhaps," Barrett commented. "You couldn't have anyone wandering round the hotel during the night carrying pass keys."

"That's not what I'm saying," Joe advised him. "I meant that there must be more than one pass key. What's the hotel policy on securing them?"

"Pointless exercise, Murray," Dockerty said. "The first people interviewed after Patterson, were the night team, and no one, not one person, was covered in blood or wine. You said yourself that the killer must have been soaked." He frowned. "It's about the only thing we've been able to agree on."

"So you interviewed the night crew and didn't ask whether they'd seen anyone else covered in blood and wine?"

"We didn't need to," Dockerty retorted. "We'd already arrested Robson. And to answer your question, Barrett told you earlier, Glenn had had no reports of anything unusual."

"Straight rails, woods and trees," Joe muttered to Dockerty's puzzlement. "Anyway, I'm not talking about her murder. I'm talking about her missing laptop. Think about it. Glenn goes up to the room, finds her dead. He comes out of there, hurries back down to reception to call you guys. Some chancer working for the hotel is on the second floor carrying a pass key and decides to take a peek. He spots the laptop and presto, it's his … or hers."

"This is assuming she had a laptop."

"Creature of habit," Joe retorted. "I told Barrett about it earlier. She never went anywhere without it."

"It's a low priority at the moment," Dockerty said. "All right, all right, I'll concede you may be right, but I have more important issues to deal with. Like nicking the killer before he strikes again." He glared. "Or getting George Robson to confess."

Joe passed the photographs back and got to his feet. "You keep trying, Dockerty, and in the meantime I'll speak to one or two people. See if I can get some sense out of them."

"You keep me informed, Murray."

Joe smiled crookedly. "Naturally."

***

Emerging from the manager's office, going back to the lounge, he spotted his two friends in the same corner as he had left them when called to see Dockerty. Les Tanner and Sylvia Goodson, and Alec and Julia Staines had joined them and the look of anticipation on their faces when he appeared told him they were waiting for news.

He gave them a wave and was about to cross the floor and join them, when Patterson waylaid him.

"Is everything all right, Joe?"

Joe nodded and indicated a nearby vacant table. "It is now," he said as they took seats. "Dockerty is beginning to see sense and has at least agreed to let me poke around." He took out his tobacco and cigarette papers. "I think you may be able to help me here, Tom."

"Anything," Patterson agreed and gestured at Joe's cigarette. "You can't smoke in here…"

"I know, I know," Joe interrupted. "Why does everyone keep reminding me about the damned no smoking rules?"

Patterson did not appear put out by Joe's abrupt retort. "I was about to suggest, Joe, that we step out to the front entrance and enjoy a cigarette while we talk."

"Oh. I forgot you're a smoker too." Joe rolled his smoke quickly and slipped the tobacco tin back in his pocket. "All right. Let's do that."

As they rose, Sheila made frantic motions for him to join them. Joe shook his head, held up his hand, the fingers outstretched, and mouthed 'five minutes' at her.

After explaining their purpose to the constable on duty at the lounge door, they moved to the outside and shivered in the cold as they lit cigarettes.

"Now," Patterson said, drawing in a luxurious lungful of smoke and letting it out with a hiss, "how can I help, Joe?"

"The cops spend too much of their time investigating the killer and not enough looking at the victim," Joe declared. "I always prefer to look into the victim, first. Especially when I'm convinced the police are wrong, as they are now."

Patterson chuckled. "You're very confident of that."

"It's all about knowing people, Tom. Look at it this way. You spend your life studying historical maps, yeah? I spend my life serving people meals. Those meals and the general appearance of my customers tell me lots about them. The guy who comes into my place with a huge belly ain't gonna be fussed for low fat spread on his sausage sandwich, and the wafer thin chicken is more likely to want a yoghurt and camomile tea than that same sausage sandwich. You understand?"

Patterson nodded and Joe relit his cigarette.

"So I need to know about Jennifer Hardy," Joe went on. "Yeah, I know you've told me some things, but I need to know more."

"For example?"

Joe blew a thin cloud of smoke into the freezing air and looked up and down the street. One or two people wearing their Sunday best could be seen, but few others. Churchgoers, Joe decided, just leaving the Christmas service, perhaps looking for a pub or restaurant that may be open.

He swung his focus back on Patterson. "Last night, you painted a picture of this saintly academic who'd lost out on love and yet a couple of hours later, she jumped into bed with George Robson."

Patterson puffed on his cigarette and frowned. "Do we know that for sure?"

"George has admitted it to the police," Joe said with a nod. He drew on his cigarette again. "The cops have had a preliminary report from the pathologist who also confirmed that she had had sex before she died. Dockerty just told me that, and trust me, when George Robson is on the prowl, there's only one candidate for laying her. George was telling the truth when he admitted it to the police."

Patterson appeared disturbed by Joe's workmanlike candour. "I see," he said and puffed again at his cigarette.

"All I need to know, Tom, is what Jennifer was like in reality. Don't worry about speaking ill of the dead or anything. I'm not about to judge her. Was she a bit, you know, easy with her favours?"

"Good heavens, no." Patterson appeared genuinely shocked. "I've known her a good number of years, Joe, and I can honestly say that she was a faithful and loving wife to her ex-husband, and the only other man with whom she's been involved, to my knowledge at any rate, is Dennis Wright." He took another anxious drag on his cigarette. "On the other hand, I have seen her brush off many a man in the time we've worked together."

"Rudely? Abruptly?" Joe asked. "Or did she let them down gently?"

"I've seen her do both," Patterson confessed. "She was firm yet gentle with me. But she could be curt with others, especially if they were too pushy."

"Like Oliver Quinton and Warren Kirkland?"

"I didn't see the incident," Patterson said, "but the way you described it sounds about right." He tutted. "I warned her about those two months ago. Especially that Quinton. Terrible little man. I've always found him to be completely detestable."

Joe agreed, but was not about to say so. "Last night was completely out of character then?" he asked. "Jumping George, I mean."

Patterson nodded. "I can only assume she had, er, over-imbibed. I told you, she had no head for alcohol. An excess of drink and the seasonal, party thing, coupled to your friend's charm probably turned her head."

Joe frowned and stubbed his cigarette out, wondering idly to himself how he had managed to finish smoking first even though his roll-up needed frequent relighting. Dismissing the speculation as nothing more than that, he said, "I really have a problem with that, Tom."

"I'm sorry?"

"I'm not doubting you," Joe urged, "but it really gives me a headache."

Patterson, too, stubbed out his cigarette. "How so?"

"Well, see, when people behave out of character,

104

something has to spark it. If the fat slob comes into my café and orders a yoghurt and camomile tea instead of the sausage sandwich he usually has, I know that something has prompted him to do that. He coulda been reading about how unhealthy his diet was, he could have had chest pains and got scared of a heart attack, or maybe his wife was nagging him to get some blubber off. Y'see?"

"I do," Patterson agreed.

"So here I am confronted with a woman who's chaste and gives in to being chased." Joe grinned at his witticism. It was only when Patterson did not, that he realised the gag would look better on paper. "I said chaste, y'see: C-H-A-S-T-E. Then I said … Yeah, well, never mind. The thing is, it was out of character for Jennifer to jump George last night, and something must have prompted her to do that."

"I understand that." Patterson fiddled with an expensive-looking, gold cigarette lighter. "Listen, Joe, it's not my place to cast aspersions, but the man you really need to speak to is Dennis Wright."

"You think so?"

Patterson nodded and dropped the lighter in his jacket pocket. "Jennifer and Wright had an affair, so I'm led to believe, when she was in America last year. The argument you overheard in Debenhams yesterday was something to do with that affair. I believe that she took to your friend last night in an attempt to make Wright jealous, and you suggested as much yourself, didn't you? When you were watching them from the bar. Or at least that's how Wright explained it to me when we were talking."

"Did he now?" Joe stroked his chin. "I'll have a word with him. Thanks, Tom." Joe racked his brain. "There is just one other thing, and I don't know whether you'll be able to answer me or not. Was Jennifer given to playing, er, games?"

Patterson frowned. "Games? She used to play badminton when she was younger, but –"

"I don't mean those kinda games," Joe interrupted. "I mean *adult* games."

Patterson blushed. "I'm hardly the man to ask. Dennis Wright, now, he may know, but I shouldn't think he'd be willing to answer. Why do you ask?"

Joe replied with a question. "How did Jennifer introduce George to you?"

"The Director of Leisure Services for Sanford Borough Council. The police later told me he was actually a gardener for your council."

"That's correct," Joe admitted. "George claims Jennifer asked him to pose as the Director of Leisure Services. She promised him a good time if he agreed, and I know George. Anything for a laugh, anything to score another notch on his bedhead. He'd go along with it as long as it wasn't criminal. There's something else, too. Jennifer took a picture of him with her mobile phone, and she asked him to put on this strange pose." Patterson's face coloured again and Joe hurried on to reassure the man. "It was nothing, er, naughty. She made him hold a Julio Iglesias CD."

"Oh, yes. Detective Constable Barrett showed me the image. He was trying to confirm Mr Robson's identity. Curious, isn't it?"

"Not half," Joe agreed. "George couldn't stand Julio Iglesias." More seriously, he went on, "Why would she do that?"

The other shrugged. "I really have no idea, Joe. As I said, the best man to speak to is Dennis Wright. He knew her, in that sense, far better than I."

They turned to enter the hotel, glad of the warmth as they strode along the rich carpets to the lounge.

"Did you mention the laptop to the police?" Patterson asked.

Joe nodded. "I did. They don't think it's too important and it may be that an opportunist thief took it."

"It's important, Joe," Patterson urged. "At least, it is to her family and colleagues. She stored most of her work on there. A man like Dennis Wright won't take too kindly to finding his manuscript coming out under a different title by some plagiarist who got it off that computer."

Joe agreed. "Sure. I take your point. I'll mention it to Dockerty when we meet again."

They parted company in reception. While Patterson returned to the lounge, Joe took the lift to the third floor and his room.

In its promotional literature, which Joe had received back in September, the Regency boasted of 'free wireless internet access in all rooms', and in the light of Jennifer's death, it was time, he decided, to check up on one or two people.

Sitting at the escritoire, he booted up his netbook, and while he waited, he stared sombrely through the windows.

The Headrow and the Town Hall were as devoid of life as Park Row had been when he stood at the entrance with Patterson. A snowplough/gritter rumbled along the road, shifting snow to the gutter and spreading a wake of rock salt across the carriageway, turning the surface from virgin white to a dirty brown as it passed. One or two people trudged the pavements heading for the city centre. Joe assumed them to be bar or restaurant workers. Who else would be plodding along at this hour on Christmas Day?

The netbook beeped to let him know it was ready. Joe double-clicked the internet browser and to his satisfaction, the machine picked up the wireless connection, and took him to his homepage.

He typed 'Dr Dennis Wright' into the search box and a second later had over forty million results.

He picked up a Wiki entry and read through it.

As he anticipated, it was a detailed account a Wright's past and his career to date, his specialisation the history of coinage as far back as Ancient Greece and Turkey, which was generally accepted as the birth of currency.

At the foot of the page, just before the references, were notes on Wright's personal life; his two divorces, both acrimonious, and a brief note on a Florida real estate scam in which he and many other 'investors' had been duped out of millions of dollars. Wright's personal losses were estimated in the region of one hundred thousand dollars.

About to shut down the browser, Joe paused. Dennis

Wright was not the only person Jennifer Hardy had argued with the previous day. He typed Warren Kirkland into the search box and waited.

He picked up a company bio, but nothing other than Kirkland's management skills and his hobbies amongst which were golf and coin collecting.

Satisfied, he typed in Oliver Quinton and again waited.

He did not expect much, and was surprised to find a Wiki page on him. He was even more surprised at what he read there. So surprised, that it caused him to laugh evilly to himself as he shut down both the browser and the computer.

Making his way down to the lounge to rejoin his companions, Joe looked around the room. Not for the first time it struck him that they had divided into their separate camps: the Leodensian Historical Society on one side of the vast room, the Sanford Third Age Club on the other, and in the middle, close to the bar, a sort of no-man's land, where he and Patterson had talked earlier, like opposing commanders trying to negotiate a truce. Under the windows at the far end of the room, police officers were still interviewing individuals, and closer to him, Sheila was waving urgently at him again.

He hurried over. "What? What is it? Have you found something out?"

"No," she replied. "We're sat here waiting to hear what you've learned."

"Yes, come on Joe," said Julia Staines, "We want all the juicy details."

Joe fumed and insinuated himself between Sheila and Brenda. "There's nothing to tell. The cops won't let George go because they're still convinced he killed her."

"Spotted you talking to the enemy," Captain Tanner insisted.

"They're not the enemy," Joe retorted. "They're like us. They've lost one of their friends and so have we … at least we have until Dockerty sees sense and starts looking for the real killer."

"Oh, but Joe," Sylvia Goodson said, "won't you get into

trouble talking to Tom Patterson? The police may think you're colluding on your statements."

"Good point," Alec Staines cheered.

Sheila shook her head. "Joe has already been interviewed and so has Mr Patterson. I think Joe is right. These people are not our enemy."

Brenda scanned the room. "You could have fooled me. This is like Christmas in the Great War, when the troops ceased fire for a day."

"But they played football together," Joe pointed out. "Right now, we're not even talking to one another."

Chapter Eight

The bar opened at 12 noon and people drifted slowly to it. Joe noticed that even here, there was a strict divide between the LHS and STAC members, and where they did speak, it was polite but cursory; pleasantries, not conversation.

With Alec and Julia Staines, Tanner and Sylvia drifting off for more stimulating company amongst the STAC members, Joe secured drinks for himself, Sheila and Brenda and then told them what Tom Patterson had said to him.

They listened to Joe's analysis that something had happened to change Jennifer Hardy, but while Sheila chewed her lip introspectively, Brenda was more forthright.

"There's no way she would do that, no matter what had happened," she declared.

"What do you mean?" Joe asked.

"Listen to the voice of experience," Brenda advised. "Sex is sacrosanct. It is the most intimate thing a man and woman can do together. This Hardy woman might have flirted with George to make Dennis Wright jealous, but no way would she have gone to bed with him unless she was that way inclined."

Joe snapped his head the other way, his eyebrows raised to take in Sheila's opinion.

"Brenda has a point," Sheila confirmed. "Jumping into bed with George is a little extreme, and anyway, how would Dennis Wright know about it? He can't be jealous if he doesn't know, can he?"

"She could have planned to tell him this morning."

"Even so," Brenda interjected, "she didn't have to actually do it. If she wanted to make Dennis Wright jealous, all she had to do was what she did. Flirt with George last night, and then *tell* Wright they'd done it this morning. She didn't really have to go through with it. Wright could have lost his temper, threatened George or whatever, George would have denied it, but that wouldn't wash with a jealous man."

"Or woman," Sheila pointed out.

"Or woman," Brenda agreed. "Wright would still believe they had. So, if George really had her last night, then it's because she was the kind of woman who lets her knickers down. Obviously, we're assuming that they did actually do it, that George isn't lying about it to beef up his reputation."

Joe gawped. "Beef up his reputation? He's been charged with murder, for crying out loud. Who's he trying to impress? Lucrezia Borgia?"

"So we assume that George did the business with her?" Brenda said.

"Joe told us that the police have DNA," Sheila reminded her. "It may be too early for a perfect match, but it will be enough to say yes or no."

"For my money that makes her a proper trollop," Brenda declared.

Sheila tittered. "Now there's a word I haven't heard in many a year."

"Well, let's forget about language," Joe suggested. "Let's concentrate on getting George out of this mess." He mulled over his thoughts for a moment. "What's with this picture business and getting George to pose as the Leisure Services boss?"

"Good question," Sheila agreed, but offered no explanations.

Brenda, too, was at a loss. "Telling everyone he was Director of Leisure Services could have been snobbery. She was a hoity-toity little slag and couldn't bear the thought of anyone thinking she'd screw a common grafter like George."

"I like your description," Joe chuckled. "Hoity-toity slag. All right, so what about the picture."

Again Brenda shrugged. "I don't know. Usually it's men

who want pictures, and they want them in the nuddy, not fully dressed…" she trailed off and blushed under the amazed stares of her companions. "I'm not speaking from experience," she floundered. "It's only what other people tell me."

"Yeah, go on. We'll give you the benefit of the doubt. So what was Jennifer playing at with George?"

Brenda shrugged. "Every time I open my mouth, I put my foot in it, so I'd better shut up."

"Make a nice change," Joe commented. He spotted Dennis Wright making for the bar. "Maybe it's time I talked to someone who knew her a bit better. I'll bring fresh drinks on the way back."

He crossed the floor and stood alongside Wright who was waiting for service.

"Bad business," Joe said.

Wright looked down from his superior height with an expression that indicated he had only just realised Joe was there. "What? Oh, you mean Jennifer? Or do you mean your buddy getting caught out?"

The American accent with British overtones grated on Joe, but not as much as the conviction in Wright's final words. "Don't believe all you've been told. George didn't kill her."

Wright ordered a scotch and Joe placed his order with the second barman.

"You're sure of that?" Wright asked, half turning to lean on the bar and face Joe.

"Never been surer," Joe replied. "Listen, do you have time to talk?"

"What about?" Wright demanded.

"About what?" Joe corrected him. "I thought you was supposed to be educated."

Wright paid for his drink. "Don't hassle me. I'm not having the best of Christmases. Now what do you want to talk about?"

"Jennifer Hardy. What else?"

"I have nothing to say to you."

"I think you do," Joe said handing over a twenty-pound note for his drinks. "See, I'll carry on asking questions here, there and everywhere until I prove George guilty or innocent, if he's guilty, he'll pay, but if he isn't, I'll get him off."

"If anyone's going to ask me questions, Murray, it'll be the cops, not you." Wright picked up his drink and prepared to leave.

"If you don't talk to me, Wright," Joe advised, "you'll have to answer to those cops, and they're dumber than me. They'll see things in your answers that aren't there, and they may even see guilt in them."

"I'm guilty of nothing," Wright spat back. "And by the way, it's *Doctor* Wright."

Joe purposely raised his eyebrows. "Doctor Wright? Hey, maybe you can tell me how best to deal with my lumbago. I get out of bed some mornings, and it's…"

"Knock it off, Murray. You know what I mean."

Joe glowered. "Then get off your high horse, *Doctor* Wright. My friend is spending Christmas in jail for a crime I know he hasn't committed. By the same token, I don't know that you killed her, but I do know you had a damned good reason to."

Wright looked away and through the far windows at a fresh snow shower. Joe studied his tanned features and realised that Wright's eyes were unfocussed. He may have been staring through the window, but he was looking at something reflected in his mind's eye.

He focussed again, stared down at Joe, and then moved to one of the tables in 'no man's land', nodding to Joe to accompany him.

Once seated opposite one another, Wright sipped at his scotch, then put the glass on the table and toyed with it, turning it round and round through his fingers. "I didn't kill her, Murray. Sure I had problems with her, but I would never murder anyone … or at least not for such trivial reasons."

Joe said nothing. He took a swallow of his beer and

113

waited.

"Jennifer and I go back a long way. Long before I left for America. She was in her second year and I was in my final year when I first met her. That would be, oh, about 1977 or 78. Sometime around there."

"Which university was this?" Joe asked.

"Right here. Leeds." Wright smiled, wistfully. "We had a bit of a thing, then I graduated and took off to Oxford for my masters and from there I did a little teaching before moving to America. That was in 82, and I've been that side of The Pond ever since. We kept in touch for a while, but then she married and the correspondence tapered off until it all but stopped." He sighed. "Then Jennifer joined the Leodensians and a few months later, so did I."

"You were early members?" Joe wanted to know. "Only Tom Patterson told me that Jennifer was one of the leading lights in the LHS."

"And she was, but that's because she still lived here in Leeds. So many of our members live elsewhere these days."

Joe nodded. "Can you tell me what the score was with Jennifer working for you in the States?"

Wright took another mouthful of whisky. "She acted as my researcher and proofreader. Tom tells me you're a writer."

"In a small way," Joe replied. "Cases I've worked on, little puzzles and mysteries I've solved. I write them up, my friends Sheila and Brenda read them for me, and then I have them printed and put them up in my café for my customers to read. I don't sell them … well, I do, but only as e-books. And I don't sell many."

"No disrespect, Murray, but you're not in my league. The kind of work you put out doesn't need to be factually accurate to the nth degree. You could get away with the occasional error. I can't. I'm a historian. An authority. My books are about history. They need to be factually precise. My reputation rides on them. One error could ruin me. So, when I finish a manuscript, I send it to a reader who must have a university degree in history and an interest in the area the book is concerned with. You understand?"

Joe nodded again. "I get the picture."

"The reader checks the facts and suggests any corrections that may be needed. I make those corrections and it goes back to the reader. If he or she is happy, it then goes to the publisher. They edit and send it back, I make corrections and it goes back to the reader. When he or she is happy, then it goes back to the publisher again. The process is slow, time-consuming and expensive, but I cannot afford even the tiniest of mistakes to creep into my work. My reputation is too precious. If I lose that, I lose everything."

"Belt, braces and a long piece of string, huh?"

Wright nodded. "When it came to *Missing Pennies*, I contacted Jennifer because one chapter was concerned with the Leeds pennies. If you're not already aware, two valuable pennies were set into foundations stones in two churches –"

"In Middleton and Hawksworth," Joe interrupted. "I know all about it. My friend, Sheila, told me the tale. Please tell me about Jennifer."

"I invited her to stay with me in Alabama for a few months while the book was completed. You probably guessed that we renewed our affair." A deep frown etched itself into Wright's brow. "But it wasn't enough for Jennifer. She wanted more. She wanted a life over there, a life with me. It's not what I wanted, and that was the argument you heard in Debenhams yesterday."

Joe played with his glass. "I'm not saying I don't believe you, but, you know, that doesn't square with her final words to you. 'Please your damned self. You know what happens next.' That sounded like a threat to me."

"It was a threat, Murray. You see, Jennifer was convinced that the reason I didn't want her was because there was someone else. But that's not so. I'm twice divorced. I'm not interested in settling down again. Not yet. Maybe not ever. I tried it twice and it didn't work, and I don't believe in third time lucky. Jennifer couldn't believe that because of the way we were when she stayed with me. Hot. You know."

"I think I can remember," Joe agreed.

115

"She really believed I had someone else and, of course, you didn't hear the whole conversation," Wright reminded him. "You only caught the bits when Jennifer raised her voice. She threatened to tell my current lover about our past involvement." Wright frowned and played with his glass again. "I put that badly. Jennifer specifically threatened to tell my current girlfriend that Jennifer and I had been lovers on many occasions. And that is what she meant by 'you know what happens next'."

"But if there was no lover to tell..." Joe suggested and left it hanging in the air.

"Which is why I didn't take the threat seriously," Wright agreed with a nod. "Tom Patterson brought all this up last night, in the bar. He spoke with Jennifer when she came back to the hotel yesterday afternoon, and he was worried, but I told him she wouldn't say a word to anyone about anything."

"And now she can't," Joe pointed out.

Wright's tanned features darkened. "That's not what I meant. I meant she wouldn't say anything to anyone because, first, she would never find anyone to say it to, and second, if she started shouting from the rooftops, telling everyone what an asshole I am, she'd drive the final nail in the coffin of her hopes of ever becoming the third Mrs Dennis Wright."

"Sure, sure." Joe hastened to reassure the academic. "Talking of Tom, he was telling me earlier that Jennifer's performance last night was totally out of character. He says she was flirting with my friend, George, just to make you jealous."

"Tom is probably correct," Wright agreed.

"But it didn't bother you, her dancing with George and then sleeping with him?"

"Why should it?" Wright asked, defiantly. "I'd made my position clear many times, not only here in Leeds, but in Alabama and in our email exchanges." Wright finished his drink and slid the glass onto the table. "And anyway, if I was looking for a third wife, Jennifer still wouldn't be in the

116

frame."

Joe's eyebrows rose. "No? I figured her as a good looking woman."

"And she was, but she was also too fond of the bottle. And, she wasn't the most difficult woman to charm into bed."

Again, Joe exhibited surprise. "Now, there you go again. Y'see, that's exactly the opposite of what Tom told me. He said she was almost virginal when it came to men, and she didn't drink."

Wright laughed, a short, sardonic little bark. "Good old Tom, the faithful little puppy." He shook his head wryly. "Don't misunderstand me, Murray. Tom Patterson is everyone's friend, a hell of a nice guy, and he'd do anything to help a pal, but he's had a thing about Jennifer for years. Even before his wife died, he was besotted with her. He looked at Jennifer through spectacles that weren't so much rose-tinted, as totally opaque. If she stripped and put on a live show in this bar, Tom would swear someone had forced her to do it. He couldn't see any wrong in her."

"And you're saying she was no angel?"

"An angel? Hell, no. Her marriage ended about five years back, maybe longer. She caught her husband out in an affair with a junior colleague, and Jennifer couldn't handle it. But she ignored the times he'd caught her out with other men and overlooked it."

"Many?" Joe asked.

"More than a handful," Wright agreed. "And you don't have to take my word for it. Try asking Oliver Quinton." He nodded to the far end of the room from the police interview tables, where Quinton sat alone. "Jennifer had a three-month fling with him. It only ended a few days ago. I don't know for sure, but I think she may have slept with Warren Kirkland, too." Now he gestured to the other side of the room where Kirkland sat with a small beer.

"Did she?" Joe asked. "So jumping George last night wasn't entirely out of character, then?" He was speaking more to himself than Wright, but to his surprise, the academic answered.

"Your buddy wasn't exactly her cup of tea, Murray. He was working class and Jennifer, to put no finer point it, was an intellectual snob. She wouldn't normally hang out with guys like your Robson."

"She introduced him as the Director of Leisure Services in Sanford." Joe smiled. "George says she asked him to do that. And I know George. Anything to get into a pair of pants." He paused a moment. "So there was still this element of making you jealous too?"

"That and the booze. She had hollow legs." Wright stood. "Now, if you'll excuse me, it looks like they're getting ready to call lunch."

"There is just one last thing," Joe insisted.

About to leave, Wright turned and looked down, his face a mask of annoyance. "What?"

"There are a few suspects for this murder," Joe explained, "and they include you and me."

The academic's eyebrows shot up. "You?"

"I had that argument with her in Debenhams and I argued again with her in the bar last night. I can't prove where I was at the time she was murdered." Joe paused to give his final words some emphasis. "Can you?"

A wry smile crossed Wright's lips. "No. I was in my room. Alone. Asleep."

***

Leaving Wright, Joe dropped drinks off with Sheila and Brenda, and then made his way across the room to where Quinton sat alone, nursing a glass of red wine.

"Joe Murray," he introduced himself. "I think we maybe got off on the wrong foot yesterday." He offered his hand. Quinton looked scathingly at it and then shook it lightly, retracting his hand swiftly as if he feared contamination.

"No, we got off on the right foot," Quinton retorted. "You're the nosy parker trying to get that murdering scum off the hook."

"Back off," Joe suggested. "To begin with, George isn't

scum, and secondly, he isn't a murderer either. Like I told the cops, George has no motive for killing Jennifer … but you have."

Quinton blanched, the colour fading from his tanned cheeks. "I don't think I like you, Murray."

"Trust me, it's mutual."

"And I don't think I have anything to say to you." Quinton stood and prepared to walk off.

"Not even about the way you screwed Jennifer senseless in an effort to get hold of the Middleton Penny?" Joe deliberately raised his voice and the exchange attracted the attention of a few people at nearby tables.

Quinton sat down again, his face now suffused with anger. "Speak to me like that again and I'll make you regret the day you were born."

Feigning disinterest, Joe replied, "There are a lot of people who already regret the day I was born, but I'm not one of them, and most are behind bars."

The wealthy collector leaned across the table and lowered his voice. "I can buy and sell you a hundred times over, Murray. I can arrange it so that you, and that crummy little diner you run, just disappear off the face of the earth." He stabbed his finger into the tabletop to emphasise his threat.

Joe grinned and kept his voice down, too. "You'd have every driver from Sanford Brewery chasing you if you tried, and trust me, they're tough cookies. Way tougher than me … or you. Let's cut the crap, Quinton. I know all about you. I checked you out on the internet. Self made millionaire? My eye and Aunt Fanny. You made your fortune the easy way. Won the lottery back in 2004. You're an ex-bank clerk from Sheffield, and the only reason you're staying here this weekend is because you knew Dennis Wright would be here." Joe paused to let his little lecture sink in. "Now why don't you cut the crap and talk to me. Because if you don't, you'll talk to the law when I'm done telling them what I already know."

"You mean what you think you know," Quinton

corrected him.

"I know you argued with Dennis Wright last night, I know you got short shrift from Jennifer Hardy last night while she was dancing and playing the fool with my murdering scum friend. I saw both incidents. I also know you're keen to get your grubby little mitts on the Middleton Penny and I guess that you figured the best way to it is – was – through Jennifer Hardy."

Quinton did not respond.

Joe went on, "Let me paint you a pretty picture. You've been into Jennifer's knickers for some time and it's not because you fancy her, it's because you want the Middleton Penny. So you tried again when you got here yesterday and she told you where to get off. You're not worried because Dennis Wright is here and you can turn the screws on him. Easy enough, considering he has a large black hole where his money used to be. So late last night, you sat in your room and came up with a plan, a means of applying pressure on Wright. You waited until the early hours of this morning and then knocked on Jennifer's door carrying a bottle of wine. A peace offering. She let you in and the moment she turned her back, you killed her. You then planted a note, a cryptic drawing that could conceivably hint at Dennis Wright. The cops buggered the job up and arrested George instead. But you don't give a hoot about that, because you're getting away with it anyway, and it still allows you to say to Dennis Wright, 'she's dead, you're next unless you tell me where the Middleton Penny is and how much it'll cost me'. How does that sound, Quinton?"

"A lot of hot air. Like most of the guests, I was in my room last night, all night. I didn't come out until half past seven this morning."

"Can you prove that?" Joe demanded.

Quinton shook his head. "No. Can you? You had an argument with Jennifer yesterday, too, so rumour has it. She was that kind of woman. Tough as old boots when she wanted to be. She'd argue black was white when she had it on her. You argued in Debenhams, if the tale is to be

120

believed, and you certainly crossed swords in the bar last night. So you tell me, Murray. Did you kill her?"

"No I didn't," Joe admitted. "But I know I didn't kill her. I don't know that you didn't."

"Touché," Quinton retorted. "It seems to me quite simple, but you won't accept it. Your scum friend killed her. He wanted his legover, she told him where to go and he murdered her." Again, Quinton leaned forward. "Let me tell you about Jennifer Hardy. She was a user of men. She would sleep with anyone if it suited her career, if she felt they could help advance her. She was, to put no finer point on the matter, an intellectual snob."

"Wright said the same thing," Joe agreed.

"At least he and I agree on something," Quinton said. Bringing the topic back to the discussion in hand, he went on, "There is no way on God's earth that Jennifer would have let that mate of yours into her bed. And there you have it, Murray. He tried it on, she said no, he killed her."

Joe stroked his chin. "Interesting."

Haunted by suspicion, Quinton sat upright. "What?"

"You see, according to Chief Inspector Dockerty, George and Jennifer did have sex. Semen samples taken from her confirm it. Oh, it's too early for a definite analysis, but the early indications are that the chances of it being someone other than George are lower than your chances of winning the lottery … again." Joe added the rider as he recalled his research into Quinton.

Taken by surprise, the millionaire resorted to bluster. "He must have forced her."

Joe laughed. "George? Meek, mild mannered George, the council gardener, forced a hard arse like Jennifer Hardy? No way. Besides, there are no other signs of violence apart from the blow to her head. If George had raped her, there would be indications, and she would never have turned her back on him afterwards."

"How do you know that she did?" Quinton demanded.

"How did he hit her on the back of the head if she didn't?" Joe countered. "See, Quinton, it seems to me like someone decided George would be a patsy for this killing. A poor sap taking the fall while the real killer goes free. But once you take into account the knowledge that George got what he wanted, any motive he may have had for killing her is gone, so you're forced to look elsewhere. I have a motive. So does Tom Patterson, so does Dennis Wright … and so do you. Which of us has the strongest motive? Right now, I'd say you."

Quinton shook his head then looked wildly round. His eyes swung back to Joe, filled with anger and disbelief, then he half stood, sat again, and twisted his face into one of anguish. "No … look … aw … this is all wrong."

Joe waited. He knew that Quinton would calm down as quickly as he had heated up.

He was right. After a moment or two, Quinton took a sip of his wine, and again leaned over the table. "You have this wrong, Murray. So you know all about me, great. You know I won the lottery. Half share of four million. It's no big secret, anyway. You know I'm a coin collector. I always have been. I suppose it comes from working in a bank. With the lottery win, I could go for rarer, more expensive coins."

"And that's where Jennifer came into your equation?" Joe's question was more of a statement.

Quinton nodded. "I read about her in Collector's Monthly," he explained. "Well-known rag. Anyone and everyone who collects anything from teddy bears to classic cars buys it. They ran a piece on her last year. All about how she was going to America to assist Wright on his new book. The article also went into some detail about the Middleton Penny. It's an old tale. Everyone in the game knows about it. I contacted her by email, asking if she or Wright knew the whereabouts of the penny. I'd be prepared to pay top dollar for it, and there'd be a nice commission in it for her and Wright. She got back to me saying she didn't know where the penny was, but if Wright did, she would let me know. That was it. Until September this year. She got back to me out of the blue, asked if we could meet. Here. In this hotel. I drove up here, she told me she hadn't yet ascertained where the penny was, but she figured Wright knew and she was continuing to press him on my behalf. In the meantime, like you, she'd done her homework on me, knew I was a lottery winner, knew I wasn't married, and before I knew it, *she* was taking *me* to bed."

"And here you are three months later, still looking for the penny," Joe commented.

Again, Quinton nodded. His grip on the wine glass tightened and the knuckles of his hand turned white. For a moment Joe was afraid the glass would shatter under pressure.

Quinton relaxed a little. "We met a few times. Always here. That's how the barman last night came to know me. We always enjoyed a good romp, and she kept promising me that Wright would let her know where to find the penny, and when he did, she would put me onto it."

"But you got cheesed off with the run-around?" Joe suggested.

"I don't know about cheesed off with it," Quinton said. "I didn't even realise she was giving me the run-around. I got some good times out of her. Then a member of staff told me that Wright would be here for the Leodensian Historical Society's Christmas thrash, and I thought it would be a great opportunity for me to see the butcher not the block, as it were. So I booked a room for this weekend, just to make sure I was here."

"And when you spoke to Wright last night, he gave you the rough edge of his tongue."

"And how." Quinton swallowed the last of his wine and played with the glass. "He told me he didn't know what I was talking about, he told me Jennifer had never mentioned it to him and he told me, quite categorically, that like the rest of the world, he hadn't a damned clue where the Middleton Penny was, and even if he did, he wouldn't tell me." He shrugged. "I started to get mad, but for God's sake, have you seen the size of the man? He'd have torn me to pieces. So I had it out with Jennifer when she was dancing with your friend. She told me exactly where I could get off.

Said I'd had what I really wanted and that was that. Never wanted to see or speak to me again. I tell you, I was pretty hacked off."

"Hacked off enough to come down and kill her in the early hours?" Joe asked.

Contrary to his earlier performance, Quinton was not put out by the question. "No. Definitely not. Look, Murray, you must have guessed now that I amount to nothing. It's all bluster with me. I'm not a violent man. I'm not bloody tall enough for a start off. My front, if you want to call it that, comes from money. I bully my way round because I can, because people are in awe of the money. That's all. Like I told you, I went to bed when I left the disco last night, and I didn't move until half past seven this morning."

Joe considered his position. "Tell me about Warren Kirkland. What's the score between you and him?"

"I can buy and sell him," Quinton sneered.

"What is with you and money, huh?" Joe bit the words off. "Your money isn't worth that!" He snapped his fingers. "It doesn't impress anyone, least of all me, because you don't have anything I want. Just tell me what it is with you and Kirkland."

Quinton did not appear fazed by Joe's outburst. "We're competitors. He wants the Middleton Penny, I want the Middleton Penny. I'm prepared to outbid him."

"You want the Middleton Penny just to put one over on him?"

Quinton shook his head. "I want the Middleton Penny because that's what my life is about; owning rare coins. Putting one over on him is simply a bonus."

"Was he screwing Jennifer Hardy, too?"

Now Quinton shrugged. "Possibly. Probably. I don't know, and I don't care. All I know is what I want.

Joe got to his feet. "I'll leave it at that for now, Quinton, but I'll be talking with Dockerty again, and all this will rate a mention."

"Aw, come on, man, I just told you…"

"And I told you," Joe interrupted, "that I don't know who

killed Jennifer. It could be you, it could be Wright, it could be almost anyone in this hotel, but I only know who it isn't. It isn't George Robson."

Chapter Nine

Leaving Quinton, Joe crossed the room to stand before Kirkland.

"Mr Murray. I wondered how long it would take you to get to me." The voice was softer, quieter than Quinton's, less forceful than Wright's.

Putting his beer on the table, Joe sat down. "You're a management consultant. I'm just wondering if you managed to make George look guilty after killing Jennifer Hardy."

Kirkland smiled, his fine, white teeth showing through the black surround of his beard and moustache. "An entertaining, if idiotic idea."

"You think so? You can prove where you were at three thirty this morning?"

"No. No more so than any of a dozen other people in this hotel. You included." Kirkland's face took on a smug set. "I saw that little tête-à-tête in Debenhams yesterday, and I noticed your exchange in the bar last night." He settled himself into his seat. "So tell me, Murray, did you kill her?"

Joe chuckled. "Nice try, but it won't get you anywhere. Quinton already accused me, so did Wright, and so did Tom Patterson, if my guess is correct. I have an alibi, see. My prints are nowhere to be found in her room."

"Neither are mine," Kirkland countered, "but you're the criminologist. You could have worn gloves."

"So could you, so let's stop fannying around. You were in Debenhams yesterday. I saw you there and you've just admitted it. I saw something else, too. When Jennifer stormed out of the place, you followed her. Why?"

Kirkland sat forward again. "I just saw you speaking with Quinton. And now you have to ask me that? Are your

126

powers of deduction slipping, Murray?"

"I know about the Middleton Penny," Joe retorted, "and I know you're in hot competition with Quinton to get your greedy little hands on it. That doesn't tell me why you followed Jennifer out of the café yesterday. See, if she was in possession of the penny, you'd have hassled her here, yesterday morning when you first arrived."

Kirkland's eyebrows rose.

"But you didn't," Joe went on. "Instead, you followed her round Leeds and sat a few tables away in Debenhams. And before you start, let me warn you. Don't pretend it was coincidence. I know coincidences happen all the time in real life, but when two or three people all have the same thing on their minds, it's not coincidence. You must have followed her round the city."

Kirkland did not answer for a long moment. He toyed with his glass of beer, drank some, then toyed with it some more before finally concentrating a candid stare on Joe.

"I take it back, Murray," he said. "I've heard about you. They say you're a wizard detective. When I first saw you and then learned who you were, I thought it was all a joke. You look like a joke." He paused to see if his observation would provoke comment. When it did not, he went on, "I'm a management consultant. I show people how best to manage their businesses, and it's not all about efficiency. I teach them assertiveness, too. A good manager must be in control at all times. A part of that control is appearance. You have to look the part." Kirkland gestured at his impeccable dress, the finely tailored, dark suit, pristine shirt, the tie snuggling beneath his Adam's apple. "You don't."

"I am what I am," Joe responded. "I'm mean, miserable, surly, grumpy, and I run a successful small business without all this haute couture. You spend thousands on your suits and shirts, I spend a hundred pounds on a pair of jeans, trainers and a set of whites. It works for me, your way wouldn't."

"Which is roughly what I was going to say," Kirkland announced. "You don't look the part, but your appearance

127

hides your intuitive grasp of things. You don't look smart, intelligent, but you are."

Ignoring the flattery, Joe demanded, "Why did you follow Jennifer yesterday?"

"The Middleton Penny. What else?" Again he leaned forward, but this time he cast a furtive glance around the bar as if ensuring no one could listen in. "Ask yourself, Murray, why am I here this weekend? I have a wife back home in Northampton. I should be spending Christmas with her, my children and grandchildren. Why did I drive 140 miles to spend the Christmas weekend in this hellhole? Because I want the penny."

"Before Quinton can get his greasy hands on it."

Kirkland dismissed the idea with a flap of the hand and a derisive snort. "Quinton. He's nothing. He's no one. New money and he came by it the easy way. Won the bloody lottery. He's a bully and a snot, but it doesn't wash with me. I want the penny. I'm not interested in putting Quinton in his place." He smiled thinly. "It would be nice to see his face, though, as I walk off with the prize." He drew a breath. "I followed Jennifer in the hope that she might lead me to the penny."

"You're sure she knew where it was?"

The other nodded. "She told me so. I presume she got the information from Dennis Wright."

"Then why didn't you hit on him?" Joe asked.

"I did. His reply amounted to two words and was, let's say, unrepeatable in polite company."

"So you thought Jennifer might be more amenable after she fell out with Wright?"

Kirkland nodded. "Something like that. As it happens, she moved far too quickly for me to catch her up. By the time she made the corner of Briggate and The Headrow, I'd only reached Starbucks." He laughed. "For some reason, she turned round and I'm sure she saw me. I ducked into Starbucks to avoid her."

Once again, Joe fell silent, mulling over his thoughts, calling on his memory for prompts. "Last night in the bar, early on, you approached Jennifer and George on the dance floor. How did she introduce George?"

"She didn't. Not then, anyway. She just told me to go away, using pretty much the same language as Wright had."

"So you didn't know who George was?"

"I had a brief word with her during dinner," Kirkland replied. "While we were queuing up at the carvery. She told me she was dining with the Leisure Services Director from Sanford Borough Council, and she laid special emphasis on the title. I took that to mean that the chap owned the Middleton Penny and he was the one we would be negotiating with." He sighed and shrugged. "Then, this morning, I learned that he wasn't any such person. He was a gardener. No. I take that back. He was murdering gardener."

"George is like me. Working class," Joe retorted, "and he's no murderer. But I think you might be. Especially when you found out he was a gardener. Because that's what she really told you on the dance floor, didn't she?"

Kirkland maintained his defiance. "No she did not. I've told you things as they happened, Murray, and my statement to the police will be no different." He checked his watch. "And now if you don't mind –"

"I do mind," Joe cut him off. "I haven't done with you, yet. You came here this weekend to get your hands on the penny. How did you know it would be here?"

"I don't think it is. Jennifer emailed me and told me she knew who had it and that the owner would be in Leeds over Christmas. She also told me she would be here with the LHS crowd, and it might be to my advantage to show up. So here I am."

"And you trusted her?" Joe demanded.

"She's a distinguished historian with impeccable credentials. What's not to trust?" He maintained his unruffled calm. "This kind of deal, Murray, is often done through a third party. Someone both sides can trust. The buyer turns up with the money, the seller turns up with the item. The intermediary holds the cash while the item is assessed and verified as genuine. The deal is done and each goes their separate ways. It's standard procedure."

"Especially when the item is known to be stolen."

It was an attempt to rile Kirkland, but it failed. Finishing his beer, he said, "I don't think that would count for much, Murray. The coin was stolen over forty years ago."

"Don't give me that," Joe sneered. "There is no statute of limitations in this country, you know. You're a well-known coin collector, you know the story of the Middleton Penny. There may be a reward for it, but if anyone has the right, it's the Diocese of Ripon, the people the penny was stolen from. If you entered into a deal with the current person in possession of that coin, you would be receiving stolen goods. It may not land you in the nick, but you'd be in one hell of a lot of trouble if and when the church decided to press charges. You and the dealer, and the intermediary. So don't kid me."

"It would make an interesting case," Kirkland said with a thoughtful gaze, "but in the grand scheme of things it's hardly a major crime, is it?"

Joe stood up and collected his glass. "It is when it leads to murder."

***

Rejoining Sheila and Brenda, placing fresh drinks on the table, Joe was surprised to see a group of young boys and men enter the room, led by a cleric.

"The choir of St Dominic's," Sheila explained. "They're part of the afternoon entertainment."

Joe tutted. "With a murder scene two floors above us? It's a disgrace."

"Life goes on, Joe," Brenda said, picking up her glass. "Cheers."

"I love hearing choirs at Christmas," Sheila commented and sipped at her gin. "It reminds me of my childhood when all the family would go to a carol service on Christmas Eve. We were never particularly religious but father always insisted that the carols helped us get into the spirit of

Christmas."

"Too commercialised these days," Brenda said with a predictability that Joe found irritating. She stared him out. "You were going to say something, Joe?"

"Yes," he replied. "I think peace and goodwill is overrated, especially when it comes to employees. Besides, my idea of Christmas spirit is half a pint of paraffin to light the space heater."

Putting her glass back on the table, Sheila changed the subject. "So what did you learn from Messrs Wright, Quinton and Kirkland?"

Through a swallow of bitter, Joe told them of his conversations. Both women listened intently, and as Joe completed the tale, Brenda's face opened into a broad grin.

"Told you, didn't I?" she declared. "She was a slapper."

"Brenda! Really," Sheila protested.

"It's not an insult," Brenda insisted. "Joe always says if you tell the truth, it can't be an insult and I'm just telling it like it is … or like it was."

"Her behaviour is irrelevant," Joe intervened before the two women could properly fall out, "unless it was enough to prompt one of those three to kill her."

The two faces stared blankly.

Sheila recovered first. "You don't seriously imagine one of them murdered her in a fit of jealousy?"

"No, I don't, but it's possible."Joe shrugged. "Men have killed women for less. And Patterson says he heard muttered voices in the room before the bottle struck; as if there was some kind of argument going on." He took another drink. "But like I say, I don't think that's what happened."

The women appeared relieved.

"So what do you think, Joe?" Sheila asked.

"I think we're barking up the wrong tree. A little while ago, I said to Tom that you should always look at the victim when you're looking for the murderer, but this time I think I'm looking too closely at her and that is distracting me. I should be looking elsewhere … or at the very least, I should be looking at more than her bed-hopping antics."

"You're the supposed maestro," Brenda declared, "so what's your next move?"

"I'm not sure. The more I think about it, the more I get the feeling that the computer could tell us something."

A stir ran round the lounge. Joe gazed around the room. With the time coming up to one, several groups were already ambling in the direction of the dining room. He took out his tobacco tin and rolled a cigarette.

"I'll just get a quick smoke before we eat. I'll catch you up in the dining room. Save me a seat."

He made his way from the lounge, through reception and out into the bitter afternoon, and was not surprised to find Patterson and Ike Barrett at the door.

In a playful mood, Barrett asked, "have you solved it yet, Mr Murray?"

Joe smiled back. "I reckon I'm closer than you." He lit his cigarette. "Tom, tell me something. Was Jennifer left-handed."

In the act of taking a drag of his cigarette, Patterson paused and frowned. "No. I don't think so, in fact, I'm sure she wasn't."

Joe smiled at Barrett. "See. I told you I was further ahead than you, didn't I?"

The young detective also frowned. "I'm sorry, sir. I don't understand."

"No, I know you don't, but if you'd been listening when I spoke to your boss earlier, you would. Don't worry about it, Ike. When the time's right, I'll explain everything." He puffed on his cigarette. "Have you found the missing laptop yet?"

Barrett shook his head."We don't actually know that there is a missing laptop, Mr Murray."

Joe looked to Patterson again and raised his eyebrows.

"As I said to your superior, Mr Barrett, Jennifer always had her laptop with her."

"May I ask, sir, did you actually *see* her with the laptop?" Barrett asked.

Patterson shrugged. "No, I can't say that I did, but…"

"There you are then," the Detective Constable interrupted. "With all due respect to yourself and Mr Murray, our primary concern is Mrs Hardy's murder, and our efforts are concentrated in that area. As and when we have the full background, we'll look into other matters like a stolen computer."

"Suppose the computer has a direct bearing on her death?" Joe asked.

"Do we know that it does, sir?"

Joe agreed with Barrett. "No, we don't, but you don't know that it doesn't, either. See, Ike, I keep coming back to motive, because in this case it's all-important. Everyone in the hotel was carrying a bottle of complimentary plonk, and there aren't many people kicking around at half past three in the morning. So when we look at means and opportunity, you have a building full of suspects. The only way you can narrow down the field is to look at those who have a motive. George Robson didn't. George Robson had had what he wanted. Now me: I had a motive. I didn't like the woman. What I saw of her, she was arrogant and vicious with it. And she dug me in the back in Debenhams. It hurt. There's a motive for me to kill her. Tom, here, he had a motive."

Patterson's face paled in shock.

Joe ignored it and went on, "Jennifer had rejected him as a potential husband." To Patterson's relief, Joe immediately said, "As far as Tom and I are concerned, the motives are trivial. But Dennis Wright had a motive, too. She threatened to expose him as a love rat. What would that do to his precious reputation? And Oliver Quinton had been going through her like a dose of Epsom salts for months until she gave him the brush-off last night. He's a nasty piece of work, that, and he was blazing when he came off the dance floor last night, so he, too, had a strong motive. Finally, Kirkland. I think he's been giving her one, too." Joe frowned. "But you can't take any of those motives seriously. Wright wasn't even worried about her threats, and Quinton has admitted he used her to try and get hold of the

133

Middleton Penny. Right, Tom?"

Patterson nodded and stubbed out his cigarette. "Right, Joe."

Barrett frowned again. "The Middleton Penny?"

"I'm sure Tom will explain," Joe said. "All these motives appear trivial, some less than others, and I think it has to be something deeper, something much more serious, and what price that something is stored on the hard drive of her computer?"

Barrett, too, crushed out his cigarette. "Interesting theory, Mr Murray, and I'll make sure my boss is made aware of it. If you'll excuse me, gentlemen."

Joe and Patterson followed him with their gaze as he entered the hotel.

"You really are clever, Joe," Patterson complimented him. "I'm a boring academic, but our discipline demands a certain amount of logic and deductive powers, but I would never have been able to put that together."

Joe smiled modestly. "I told you earlier, Tom, it's all about knowing people."

Patterson checked his watch. "Time for lunch, I think. I can tell you this, Joe. Jennifer locked her computer with a password. Like all historians, she was fearfully protective of her work. Whoever stole that computer won't get very far without the password."

"You told me once before," Joe reminded him. "If it was just a common thief, Tom, a password won't matter. He'll sell it on to experts who have ways of getting into the BIOS and bypassing passwords. They can still turn a profit on it."

Patterson looked puzzled. "BIOS?"

"Basic input/output system," Joe translated. "It's the bit of the computer that starts everything up when you switch on."

Patterson laughed. "You're a computer expert, too?"

"No. Just a bit of a nerd."

"Afraid I'm a total duffer with them, myself. I can just about switch the thing on and off." With a rueful shake of the head, Patterson headed into the hotel.

Joe followed him, mulling over his lack of progress so far. He paused at the reception desk. "Can you tell me what happens to the waste bags when they're taken from the rooms?"

The redhead delivered a suspicious gaze. "Is it important, sir?"

Thinking on his feet, he said, "Yeah. It may be. I, er, I lost my mobile phone. Can't find it. I think I may have dropped it in the waste bin under the escritoire in my room and I…"

He trailed off as his mobile trilled in his pocket.

"Excuse me a minute." Joe took the phone from his pocket. He looked at the menu window, and read 'Lee'. Making the connection, he put the phone to his ear. "What do you want, Lee?"

"Just ringing to wish you a Merry Christmas, Uncle Joe."

"What? Oh. Yeah. Same to you and Christine. And young Danny. Is there anything else?"

"No. Only we did really good yesterday. Takings were well up on Friday."

"They would be. It was Christmas Eve. Now, is that it, only I'd like to get to lunch?"

"Okay. See you Tuesday."

Joe cut the connection, dropped the phone in his pocket and gave the receptionist a weak smile.

She looked down her nose at him. "You lost your phone?"

"I meant my camera." He shrugged. "That is, I think I dropped my camera in the waste basket. It was on the escritoire last time I saw it. Will it have been taken away?"

With a face that spelled out her disbelief, the receptionist told him, "All waste goes into the large bins at the back of the hotel, Mr Murray. Normally, that's emptied daily, but today is Christmas, so the refuse vehicle won't come. Would you like me to get a member of staff to search the bins for you?"

"Could I not do it myself?"

"That, sir, would be highly irregular."

"Tell you what I'll do," Joe said, making a point of checking his watch. "I'll get my lunch and then while the choirboys are entertaining the guests, I'll meet one of your guys at the back and give him a hand. How's that?"

"Well. I'm not, er, sure…"

"Good. I'll be back about half past one." He chuckled and it sounded false even to him. "I never did like choirs anyway." He turned and walked off. "At least that last bit is true, Joe," he muttered to himself.

Making his way to the dining room, he found it a hive of barely subdued excitement and chatter. Tables were laid out to seat four, Christmas crackers were set before each place, bottles of red and white wine stood in the centre of each table, and waiters were already delivering soup to those nearest the kitchens.

Sheila waved at him from a table by the windows. Weaving his way through the crowded hall, he settled in with his two companions as a waiter arrived and left three bowls of consommé before them. Picking up his napkin and spoon, Joe gazed solemnly at the empty seat opposite. It reminded him of George Robson, currently languishing in a police cell.

"Made your mind up what's next, boss?" Brenda asked, tucking her napkin into the V of her jumper.

Joe explained his next move to them, and both women were predictably astonished.

"It's Christmas Day, Joe," Sheila scolded. "You're supposed to be relaxing and enjoying yourself."

"And I will, I will," he assured her.

Slurping a spoonful of soup, Brenda ribbed Joe. "You're never happier than when you're scavenging through the dustbins, are you luv?"

"I've never heard anything so ridiculous," Sheila said, spreading her napkin across her knee.

"Logical is what it is," Joe told them, starting work on his soup. "Didn't I tell you we were barking up the wrong tree by looking at Jennifer Hardy's behaviour?"

Breaking open a bread roll, Brenda ate with gusto. "You

136

did, but you didn't hang about to say why the computer was important."

"Yes I did … well, maybe not to you, but I said it to young Ike Barrett. Motive is the only thing that may lead us to the killer. George didn't have one, and we can forget about Wright getting all jealous. Now let's make a few assumptions. Let's assume that what Tom Patterson heard in the early hours was an argument which led to Jennifer's death. Let's also assume that the argument had to do with either history or coins."

Sheila spooned up more soup. "A fair assumption considering you believe the killer was either Dennis Wright, Warren Kirkland or Oliver Quinton."

"Go on, Joe," Brenda invited.

Joe took another few mouthfuls of soup, and pushed the plate away. "When we serve soup at the Lazy Luncheonette, it's soup, not warmed-up dishwater." He dabbed at his mouth with the napkin. "Now, what was I saying? Oh, yeah. Tom has been pestering me because he can't find Jennifer's computer. Suppose that whatever they were arguing over is on that computer?"

"Then the killer probably still has it," Brenda said, tilting her dish forward to pick up the last dregs. "And you're wrong, Joe. That soup was excellent."

"You're wrong, too, Brenda," Joe countered. "On both counts. The soup was crap and the killer has to get rid of the computer because the hotel is swarming with cops. If they don't hang this on George, and instead go for a room-by-room search, he's snookered. So what does he do with it?"

"He hides it." Sheila, too, finished her dish. "Joe, if that computer contains damning evidence, he needs to erase it."

Joe looked around. A party mood had begun to overtake the crowd. People were pulling crackers, donning party hats and playing with toys from the crackers.

Joe eyed the four crackers on their table and picked up the nearest. Playing with it, he said, "Wrong again. Unless you really know your stuff with computers, you can't erase everything. You have to reformat the drive. And who's to say he wants it erasing? Maybe it's something that he wants to use; an idea he's going to steal. See? What you do is get into the computer, do whatever you're going to do with it, and then get rid of it. You throw it away."

Brenda picked up another cracker and offered it to Sheila. They pulled it. With noise picking up around the room, the crack was almost inaudible. Sheila picked a toy frog from the table, and a written joke, while Brenda picked up and put on an orange paper hat.

Reading from the joke, Sheila asked, "What do you get if you cross a vampire with a snowman?"

"Go on," Joe said.

"Frostbite."

Brenda giggled and Joe groaned.

"You were telling us he had to get rid of the computer, Joe." Sheila reminded him.

"He can't afford to be caught with it, so he has to be rid of it. How does he go about that?" Joe asked, and hurried on to answer the question as Brenda offered him a cracker. "The police haven't begun the room-by-room search yet. They're concentrating on the body and grilling George. So on his way to breakfast, our killer carries the computer from his room, already in the bag from his waste bin, and drops it into the larger bins sited at either end of each landing." Joe pulled the cracker.

This time Brenda picked up a toy dinosaur and the joke, and placed a purple paper hat on Joe's crown.

"How do you make an idiot laugh on Boxing Day?" Brenda asked.

They waited for the answer.

"Tell him a joke on Christmas Eve."

Again Sheila and Brenda chuckled at the inane gag. Joe just shook his head.

More soberly, Sheila said, "You're telling us that he just walked calmly out of his room with the evidence in his hands and dropped it in the bin on the landing?"

"Why not?" Joe demanded as Sheila offered him the third cracker. "He's had the machine since half past three in the morning. Plenty of time to do whatever he was going to do. And what's so suspicious about a man walking out of his room with a bagful of garbage and dropping it in a dustbin? No one will challenge him because at that time the police are not even looking for a missing laptop."

They pulled the cracker. Sheila took the green hat and put it on, and commandeered a toy mobile phone, while Joe picked up the gag.

"Father Christmas came home on Christmas Day and apologised to his wife for not getting the turkey. 'I forgot it's Christmas, all the shops were shut'." Joe groaned at the joke himself this time, and tossed the gag aside. "Well?" he asked his two companions.

Brenda frowned. "I don't get that."

"He's Father Christmas, dear," Sheila explained. "How could he forget it's Christmas."

"Never mind the bloody joke," Joe protested. "Concentrate on the case."

Sheila fiddled with her cutlery. "I think you have a point, Joe, but this is a hotel. The bins are emptied daily."

Joe smiled. "Which is exactly what the killer thought." He picked up the appalling gag he had just read out. "Father Christmas wasn't the only one who forgot that today is Christmas; the one time of the year when the hotel bins are not emptied."

Chapter Ten

It was almost two o'clock by the time Joe emerged from the dining hall, his belly full, the desire for an afternoon nap threatening to overtake him.

The meal, he had to admit, was excellent; from the turkey with all the trimmings, through the Christmas pudding, to the cheese, crackers and coffee, it was superb.

"I still say we coulda done it as good at the Lazy Luncheonette," he had said to his companions as they savoured a small glass of wine. But he said it without conviction. Lee, he had no doubt, could have prepared and presented the meal just as well, but the Lazy Luncheonette could never attain the cheerful ambience of the Regency Hotel. He even chose to forego his customary post-lunch cigarette in order to savour the atmosphere, and it was only when the choir of St Dominic's ranged across the front of the dining hall, that he ducked out.

"They'll only come round with the collection box," he grumbled, "and you know my feelings on chuggers."

"Chuggers?" Brenda asked.

"Charity muggers," Sheila translated. "That's how Joe sees them. You go raid the dustbins, Joe. We'll put a half crown in the box on your behalf."

"Half a crown?" Joe asked with mock incredulity. "You give 'em sixpence, in old money, and tell them I'm a poor man." He hurried out of the dining hall as the choir struck up *O Little Town of Bethlehem*.

He first called to his room and changed out of his shirt, cardigan and trousers into his thick jumper and jeans. Then, after standing, shivering and smoking at the front entrance with only a couple of members of the LHS for company, neither of whom were disposed to talk to him, he stepped out onto the snowy pavements and slipped and slithered his way along the front of the Regency, cursing himself for not bringing his coat, and stopped at the gates to the hotel's side yard. They were locked. He could see the large bins and the overflow of black rubbish bags stacked around them just twenty yards inside the compound, but the gates were held by a stout chain and padlock. As he looked in, a security guard stepped from an office on the right.

"Can I help you, sir?" He injected sufficient inflection into the word 'sir' to tell Joe that what he really meant was 'clear off, scum'.

"Er, no, no. That's all right. I'm staying here, see, and I think I threw my camera into the waste bin by accident. In my room. You know. I was wondering about getting it back."

"I see, sir," said the security officer, lending Joe the impression that he did not believe a word. "Well, I would recommend that you have a word in reception and ask them to get someone out to go through the bins."

"I did. And they were, er, uncooperative, shall we say."

The security man came closer to the gates. "Now listen, sunshine, it's Christmas and I'm thinking peace and goodwill to all men, but if you don't bugger off, I'll call the cops."

"No need," Joe said as he turned to retrace his steps. "The place is already swarming with them."

He trudged the pavements again, back into the hotel, kicking the snow from his trainers, and approached reception, where the same redhead he had spoken to before lunch, was on the phone.

"Thank you," she said into the phone, "I'll deal with it." She put the receiver down and gave Joe a thin smile. "Yes, Mr Murray, how can I help you?"

"We talked before lunch about my camera in the bins. I've just been to the gates and your security man wouldn't let me in."

"Yes, I know." She eyed the telephone. "That was him

calling to report some tramp, his description, not mine, who'd been looking for somewhere to doss. Again, his words, not mine."

Joe smarted at the insults. "If I was prone to spending money, I could buy and sell a dozen like him … and you."

"Now look, sir, we're well aware of people who search through rubbish looking for letters and such that contain names and addresses. It's called identity theft, and…"

"Listen to me, lady," Joe interrupted. "A woman was killed here last night, and I think a vital piece of evidence was thrown into those bins."

Alarm spread across her face. "Well, shouldn't you tell the police?"

"I did, but they're like you. Too eager to close the case and hang an innocent man, so they can go home for their Christmas dinner."

"I'm not doing anything of the kind. I am simply…"

"Giving me indigestion is what you're doing," Joe cut in again. "If that thing is left in those bins, the wagon will come for it the day after tomorrow and the real killer may get away with it. Now cut me some slack, will you? Let me get out there and check those bags."

"It really is most irregular," she complained.

"Whereas finding a murdered woman in one of your rooms is a common occurrence, is it?" Racking his brain for an argument, Joe went on, "If I have to get tough with the cops, they'll order all that crap behind your hotel to stay where it is until every bag has been checked. In a day or two it'll start to stink. That's not gonna do much for the Regency's reputation, is it? And you know what the law's like when it comes to searches? They never tidy up after they're done."

Brimming with frustration, the receptionist snatched up the telephone and after a brief, muttered conversation, slammed it down again. Leaning across the counter so she could keep her voice down, she whispered, "Go to the bar. They'll let you out into the rear yard. But, Mr Murray, please try to keep the mess to a minimum."

142

Joe grinned. "No problem. Hey, I'm in the same business as you, and I know how important these things are."

Leaving reception, he hurried past the dining hall door, where the choir were now running through *Hark the Herald Angels Sing*, and entered the lounge bar. He was halfway to the bar when Dockerty called him over. He diverted his course and joined the Chief Inspector and Barrett by the windows where they were gathering together the multitude of statements they had taken.

"Ike and I are leaving any time now but we'll be back first thing tomorrow. Are you any further ahead, Mr Murray?"

"A little," Joe admitted, "but nothing I can put a finger on at the moment. I promised I'd keep you informed, Dockerty, and I will, but I don't want to add more conjecture to that you're already dreaming up against George."

"Yes, well, on that score I've had a word with my colleagues at Millgarth Street and they've concluded their initial interrogation of George Robson. In view of the, shall we say, *thin* evidence against him, I've decided to release him on police bail. The conditions are quite clear. He must return to the Regency and stay here until Tuesday morning, when he will be required to attend the station again. Considering you're the man in charge of the Sanford party, I hope you'll be willing to support us in this move."

The last thing Joe wanted was to be responsible for George, but if he refused, he knew Dockerty would rescind the decision, and there were questions he wanted to ask of George, so he agreed with a vigorous nod of the head. "Sure. No problem. If I have to, I'll bring him to the station myself on Tuesday morning."

"Good." Dockerty reached into his wallet and took out a business card. "It has my mobile number on it," he said. "I'm not particularly on call, but if you turn up anything, ring me."

Joe tucked the card in his back pocket. "I will."

He retraced his steps to the bar and after a brief word

with the staff, and under the puzzled eye of Dockerty and Barrett, he found himself ushered through the back door and out into the bitter cold of the rear yard where the same security officer who had shooed him from the gates, waited for him.

Joe realised instantly that there was more to the yard than he had been able to see from the street. Aside from the two large bins, there were others stood further back, designated for recyclable materials, and a baler for cardboard. There were also additional, smaller bins, which Joe recognised instantly. Kitchen waste. And they were ranged alongside more receptacles for broken glass. Aside from those, there were stacks of galvanised beer barrels, and crates full of empty bottles racked up near the bar exit, alongside CO_2 cylinders, again presumably empty.

The security man raised his cap and scratched his forehead when Joe came out.

"You really are staying here?"

"Yes," Joe replied, "and I'll thank you not to describe me as a tramp. You can't afford to dress as scruffily as me."

"Well, I didn't know, did I? Do you know how many homeless scruffs and alkies we get trying to sneak into the yard, looking for bottles of beer with dregs left in them, or trying to find somewhere to kip for the night?"

"I run a café in Sanford, so I can imagine," Joe told him. "Now, you know what I'm doing?"

"According to the desk, you're gonna root through that lot, looking for summat." He waved at the heap of bags surrounding the bin and Joe's heart sank. The two large bins were overflowing with bags, and they were also stacked, three and four high, on the ground all around the bins.

"I know what I'm looking for," Joe explained. "I don't need to empty any of the bags, but the one that contains the item I'm after."

"Your camera?"

Joe eyed him sourly. "Yeah. Something like that. Now are you gonna stand there all day or are you gonna give me a hand?"

He looked shocked. "Me? Not bloody likely. Sorting through bags of crap isn't in my job description."

"And we wonder why the country's in the state it's in. Clear off and let me get on with it."

With an annoyed shake of the head, Joe began work on the bags. His policy was simple. Starting with the uppermost bags surrounding the bins, he picked them up and judged the weight. If a bag felt heavy, he would shake it, and if it felt like there was an individual item of considerable weight moving around inside it, he would then feel the bag, seeking the shape of a laptop computer.

The process helped eliminate a good proportion of the bags without him having to investigate their contents further, although he had several false alarms, one of which turned out to be nothing more sinister than a broken fan heater, the kind he kept at floor level in his flat above the Lazy Luncheonette.

In less than thirty minutes, he had checked all the bags on the ground and was ready to climb up and start on those in the bins. Wandering further along the yard, he rolled an empty beer barrel to the bins, stood it upright and climbed on it, acutely aware of the security officer watching him through the windows of his tiny office.

Work on the bins was harder. To begin with, the only way Joe could move the upper layers out of the way was to cast them aside, mostly to the ground, from where he would have to pick them up when he was finished. To make matters worse, the afternoon light had begun to fade as heavy cloud swept in threatening more snow, and he was less than halfway down the first bin when the early flakes began to fall. By the time he could see the bottom of that first bin, it was snowing heavily, he was freezing cold and being so short of stature, he struggled to reach the bottom layer, practically tipping himself in the bin each time he reached in.

And it was all to no avail. Although he checked several suspect bags, the computer was not there.

Climbing off the beer barrel, he spent another ten

minutes throwing the bags back into the bin, by which time his back hurt, his icy hands were blue and he was no longer sure whether his nose was still attached to his freezing face.

Moving the barrel over, his teeth chattering, he climbed up and began the process again.

"It's amazing just how much rubbish a few people can create in less than a day," he muttered to the fading light.

The bin emptied rapidly and he began to despair of finding the machine at all. As each bag returned nothing, he became more and more convinced that some sneak thief had entered Jennifer Hardy's room between the night manager finding her and calling the law, and stolen the thing.

And then, just as he was about to give up altogether, he found it. Too heavy for the ordinary detritus of a hotel room, a solid object had settled to the bottom of the bag, and when he felt it, he traced the flat, square outline of a laptop computer, and despite his discomfort, notwithstanding his freezing skin and bones, his face split into a broad grin.

Climbing off the beer barrel, he carefully untied the knot in the neck of the bag, and peered in. It was filled with tissues, scraps of paper, till receipts, empty cigarette packets, and at the bottom, another black bag. Reaching in, Joe pulled it out, put it to one side, and fastened the larger bag back up. He spent another ten minutes throwing the bags back into the bin and then picked up his prize.

Again, carefully picking the knot apart, he peered in. One small, netbook computer, not unlike his, and a small, ornate, hard backed notebook. Jennifer Hardy's diary!

He was tempted to reach in, touch it, as it if it were some religious icon and the mere laying on of hands would solve all his problems. "Fingerprints, Joe," he muttered to himself.

The security officer emerged from his office again. "You done here, sport?"

Joe nodded. "I found what I was looking for," he said.

The other man shook his head. "All I can say is, I hope it was worth it."

Joe smiled wanly. "So do I."

With the clock registering 3:15, Joe entered through the bar and hurried out into the lobby, past the dining room where the guests were now watching the Queen's Christmas message on large screen TVs, and made for the lifts. The cold had permeated his thick, winter clothing and he was still shivering when he let himself into his room. He was eager to get at the computer, but that was not his primary consideration. His jeans and jumper were dirty, and he had an idea he probably stunk to the high heavens, too, but he dismissed the idea of a shower. What he needed was a soak in a hot bath.

Leaving his prize in the wardrobe, he took out clean clothing, and wondering what on earth he would do for something warm to wear on the journey home, he settled into the bath and allowed the hot water to circulate, sink into every pore and thaw him out.

A quarter of an hour later, he climbed out and was towelling off when a knock came on the door. With an irritated cluck, he wrapped the towel around his midriff, padded across the richly carpeted room, and peered through the door viewer to see Brenda on the other side, her busty figure caricatured by the fish-eye lens.

He opened the door.

"There you are," she said, pushing her way past him. She turned and chuckled. "All ready for me, too."

"Knock it off, Brenda," Joe ordered. "What do you want?"

"George is back. The cops dropped him off ten minutes ago. Apparently, you're responsible for him."

"I knew they were releasing him before I raided the dustbins," Joe admitted. "You didn't come up here to tell me that, so what do you want?"

Brenda tapped her foot on the floor. "It's quarter to four, Joe. We wondered where the hell you'd got to."

"The computer took a bit of finding," he told her.

"But you have it?"

147

He nodded.

"Then get yourself dressed, and let's get back down to the bar and enjoy ourselves. There's entertainment on, you know." Brenda perched on the edge of the bed. "Course, there are other ways we could enjoy…"

"I told you once, knock it off." Joe tightened the towel at his waist. "Do you seriously think I could party downstairs while poor George is worrying himself half to death?"

Brenda shrugged. "George is so worried he's sinking pints like his life depends on it. And you can't clear his name. There's just one constable sitting outside Jennifer Hardy's room on the second floor. Now come on, Joe, we're supposed to be having a friendly Christmas together and Sheila and I were worried about you."

Joe picked up his clothing. "Worried about me? You're only worried in case I don't get back to Sanford to pay your wages. Wait there while I get dressed." He made for the bathroom.

"That's not true, Joe, and you know it," he heard Brenda say through the closed door. "We think a great deal of you. In fact, I think so much of you that I'd be prepared to…"

"If I have to tell you one more time to knock it off, I'll be sorting out your P45 come Wednesday." Joe pulled on his trousers and fastened them up. Slipping his shirt on, he emerged from the bathroom and dug into a drawer for clean socks. "What's this entertainment, anyway?" he asked as he sat down to put them on, "*The Sound of Music* or *Star Wars* on the big screens?"

"No, there's some kind of an act on, and the whisper is Santa's going to turn up."

Pressing his stockinged feet into slip-ons, he pulled on his cardigan. "I wonder what he's bringing me?"

"A young blonde?" Brenda cackled.

"I prefer brunettes. Come on."

Sheila had secured them seats at a table shared with George, the Staines and Les Tanner, and drinks were already set out when Joe and Brenda settled in with them.

"So how are you, George?" Alec Staines asked.

148

"Shell shocked," he replied. "I couldn't believe she was dead, and I couldn't believe they thought I'd done it." He turned worried eyes on Joe. "Have you got anywhere, yet?"

Joe shook his head. "Some progress, but nothing definite. Not yet. Don't worry, buddy, I'll get you off." He swung his attention to Tanner. "Hey up, Cap'n, where's Sylvia? Sleeping it off?"

Tanner smiled uncharacteristically on Joe. "You'll find out soon enough, Murray."

"You know, Les, whenever you smile, I'm always reminded of a lion tripping over a lame zebra."

Tanner smiled again and stared pointedly at Joe's thin arms. "There isn't enough meat on you to fill a sandwich, old man. But your wallet would be worth having."

The lights dimmed and a spotlight shone on the stage. An announcer's voice boomed from the speakers. "Ladies and gentlemen, welcome to Christmas afternoon at The Regency Hotel. Here, now, to entertain you with songs from the shows, please welcome, Miss Vicky Orleans."

While Joe wondered where anyone could find such an unimaginative stage name, the 30-something dark-haired singer took the stage and over the next half hour, to pre-recorded backing music, ran through a repertoire of songs from *My Fair Lady, Oklahoma, South Pacific* and *West Side Story*, eventually coming more up to date with numbers from *Cats* and *Phantom of the Opera*.

Outside, darkness descended, snow fell again, and the streets remained deserted, while inside the four star hotel, inured and insulated from the ravages of the elements, the crowd enjoyed themselves, filling up on drink and vibrant entertainment.

Never a great lover of musicals, Joe switched his brain into neutral; his few thoughts centred more on the computer hidden safely in his wardrobe and George Robson chewing agitatedly at his fingernails.

At 4:45, Vicky Orleans brought *Don't Cry for Me Argentina* to a quavering end and took a breath in the warmth of applause.

"Thank you, ladies and gentlemen," she said. "You're very kind. Now, we have a special treat for you. A very special guest and his wife have dropped in to wish you all a merry Christmas. Please put your hands together and welcome Santa and Mrs Claus."

Vicky gestured towards the main entrance and in walked Santa and his wife. The room erupted into spontaneous applause at their arrival, and while Joe readily recognised Sylvia Goodson, dressed as Mrs Claus, her Santa suit exaggerating her weight problems, he could not place the white-bearded man with her.

The absurd couple made their way to the small stage, where Sylvia took the microphone from Vicky.

Holding up her hand for silence, she said, "Ladies and gentlemen of the Leodensian Historical Society and the Sanford Third Age Club, we're united in tragedy today at the terrible loss of a life. But there is something else that unites us. Good fortune. We who have so much at the side of many in this world that have so little. With that in mind, Santa," she gestured at her companion, "has had a change of plan. Usually it is his task to give out gifts to those who have earned them through good and generous behaviour throughout the year."

"That lets out Joe," Alec Staines called out and many people laughed.

Sylvia smiled and more seriously went on, "I have personal reasons to be thankful to my good friend, Joe Murray. As I was saying, it's Santa's joy to give out gifts on Christmas Eve, but on this visit, he is giving nothing. Instead, he will take. As he and I pass amongst you, we would ask you to donate whatever sum you wish, no matter how small or large, for the Save the Children fund. Please, ladies and gentlemen, please let the spirit of Christmas feed your generosity."

To another round of applause, while Vicky began singing *White Christmas*, followed by *Chestnuts Roasting on an Open Fire*, Sylvia and Santa stepped from the stage and began to circle the lounge. Around the table, Sheila and

Brenda took out their purses, the Staines dug into theirs and Tanner brought out his wallet. Joe reached into his pocket and felt around the coins and notes.

"You can do better than loose change, Joe," Sheila urged.

"And how do you know I'm looking for change?" he asked as Santa made the table nearby.

"We know you," Tanner said.

"What did Sylvia mean she had personal reason to thank you, Joe?" Julia Staines asked.

"Joe cleared her name over the death of Kim Lowe early this year," Tanner explained. "We're hoping he can do the same for you, George."

"I'll do it," Joe promised.

"And there we were thinking he never cares about anything other than money," Alec Staines chuckled.

Joe had stopped listening. He was intent on the bearded face at the next table, his mind working to remove the beard and place the face beneath it.

"Thank you," Santa said to the occupants of the next table as they threw notes into the sack, and Joe recognised the voice of Tom Patterson coming from beneath the whiskers.

Joe felt a secret admiration for his opposite number from the LHS. Patterson had done a good job of hiding himself behind the beard, but he needed no makeup to complete the picture. As he came to their table, his sack held forward and open, his cheeks were rosy from the heat of his getup, sweat poured from his brow.

"Thank you," Patterson said as Alec Staines dropped a ten-pound note in. Brenda and Sheila put in five pounds each, Tanner dropped in ten and Joe, much to the surprise of his fellow members, did not draw change from his trouser pocket, but his wallet.

Taking out a twenty, he dropped it into the sack.

"Thank you," Patterson said.

"You're welcome," Joe replied. "By the way, Tom, well done on the disguise. I knew Santa wasn't one of my members, but I'd never have guessed it was you."

Patterson blushed under the beard. "Kind of you to say so, Joe."

He moved on and Joe took in the stares around him. "What?" he asked.

"You," Sheila said. "Twenty pounds? Christmas spirit getting to you, is it, Joe?"

He shook his head. "Sylvia said it was the Save the Children Fund and I'm hoping they'll save one for me. I could just about eat a whole one." He smiled and the table laughed. "Besides," he pressed home his advantage, "it's tax deductible and I'll probably stop it out of your wages." Without leaving Brenda or Sheila time to argue, he turned to Tanner. "So when did Sylvia and Patterson dream this one up?"

"About two months ago," Tanner explained. "Shortly after you announced the venue in your STAC newsletter. You know what Sylvia is like when it comes to charity. When she learned that the LHS would be sharing the hotel with us, she wrote to Patterson and put the suggestion to him. He agreed and I think it went rather well, don't you?"

"A novel twist on the Christmas theme, Les," Sheila agreed as Vicky led a further round of applause for Santa and Mrs Claus.

While the singer went into the second half of her act, Sylvia and Patterson left the room, to return a quarter of an hour later, when Sylvia handed Tanner her red costume and sat with him to drink a small sherry.

"Well organised, Sylvia," Joe congratulated her. "But who'd have thought old Tom Patterson had that much go in him?"

"I don't understand, Joe?" Sylvia said. "From all I've heard, he does quite a bit for charity, and has done ever since his wife died."

Joe nodded and polished off a half of bitter. "I can see him going round with the collecting tin," he said, "but I'd never have backed him to dress as Santa. Whenever I've spoken to the man, he seems to be the sort of dry and reserved kind. You know."

"Never judge a book by its cover, Joe," Sheila reminded him. "Look at you. Who would have expected you to put twenty pounds into the hat?"

"Oh, but that's nothing new," Sylvia said and Joe silently urged her to shut up. Sylvia did not see his frantic gestures. "As you know, I collect for Sanford Hospital children's ward every December, and Joe always gives me fifty pounds. Don't you Joe?"

He tutted while Sheila stared in amazement. "We are talking about the same Joe?" Sheila asked.

"Never judge a book by its cover," Joe echoed.

"Well, I must say, Joe, you had us all fooled," Alec Staines commented. "You're the last man I'd back to give to children's charities."

"I think I understand," Brenda said, and dug into her bag for a tissue to dry her eyes.

Joe said nothing. Sheila took his hand and he knew that *she* suddenly understood.

But Joe was not thinking about the fact that he had never had children, or that Brenda was crying for the same reason.

There was something else; something trying to force its way through the general feeling of good cheer; something trying to beat down the noise of Vicky Orleans squawking her way through a medley from *Oliver*. It was something someone had said; something that had just happened; something he knew was important; something he knew he was missing.

Vicky left the stage at five thirty and people began to drift from the room.

"Don't forget that dinner is seven thirty to eight o'clock," Sheila said.

"Cabaret nine until ten," Brenda said with relish. "And it's disco and karaoke from ten onwards. It's gonna be a lively night."

"Stay put, George," Joe said, "I need to talk to you before we get any rest."

153

Chapter Eleven

As the room emptied, Joe refreshed their drinks and he and George sat alone at the table.

"I don't need all the gory details, George," Joe said, "but tell me how you came to meet Jennifer and what happened from there."

"There's nowt to tell, Joe," George said. "Most of our lot were out shopping yesterday afternoon, you, Sheila and Brenda included, but you know me. Christmas isn't much of a scene for me, and there's no one I have to buy prezzies for, so I stuck around here all afternoon watching the football on telly. She came into the bar about half past five, I spotted her and thought, 'hey up, lady, it's your lucky day, George is gonna pull you.' I offered to buy her a drink and she told me to clear off. Ten minutes later, she was talking with some suit at the bar, and after that she came over and apologised."

"Which suit?" Joe wanted to know.

"Search me. Kirkwood or someone. Tall, slim feller, maybe our age. Beard."

"Kirkland," Joe said. "Warren Kirkland. Go on. After that?"

"I did what comes natural to me, Joe," George promised. "You know me with the dollies. I know how to charm 'em and she gave me all the right signals. But I knew she was a bit snooty, like. That's why she asked me to tell everyone I was Director of Leisure Services back home. I went along with it because I knew I was on a promise."

"You *knew* or you were just in with a better than even chance."

"No, Joe, I *knew*. She told me so. She would drop 'em if

154

I pretended to be the Director of Leisure Services. Yeah?"

Joe's eyes widened. "She said it just like that?"

"Well, no, but that's what she meant. I think she actually said, 'do me this favour, George, and you'll find me very grateful' and she put a lot of stress on the word very."

Joe nodded. "But she didn't say why?"

George shook his head. "All she told me was she wanted to put that Kirkland bloke, and another guy, the fat one with the greasy hair, in their place. Kick 'em in the cobblers. My guess was she'd had summat going with them and they were hassling her. Plus, like I said, she was a bit snooty, her being a professor and all that. Happen she wanted them to think she'd cottoned on to a man who really was summat."

"Both Kirkland and Quinton – the one with the greasy hair – approached her while she was dancing with you."

"She told Kirkland to eff off. Just like that. I didn't know these university sorts used that kinda language. She was even worse with the other feller. Gave him both barrels. Told him she'd been using him for months and he was no more than a research project. She also said if he came near her again she'd squash him. I think she was gonna go for the poor sod, but I pulled her back and told him he'd better clear off while he was still in one piece."

"All right." Joe shuffled the information in his brain. "Right, you went back to your room and she took your picture holding a CD. Why?"

George shrugged. "Ask me another. Joe, I was hot for this chick, and when you're nearly there, you don't stop to ask questions. If she'd wanted me to strip and then take a full frontal, I wouldn't have refused."

"And after she took the photo?"

"We had a glass of brandy and ... well, you know. We, er, got down to it." George looked away. "Afterwards, I used the bathroom, dressed, kissed her goodnight and that was it. Next thing I knew, plod was knocking on my door and arresting me."

"All right, George." Again, Joe racked his brain for the information he needed. "Did she mention a penny at all?"

"Joe, you've been married, you know what the bedroom score is. You don't talk about money when you're getting it on."

"So that's where I went wrong." Dropping his sarcasm, Joe clucked impatiently. "I'm not talking money, either. Did she mention the Middleton Penny to you at all, any time during the night?"

George shrugged. "Middleton Penny? What's a Middleton Penny?"

"It doesn't matter," Joe insisted. "Did she mention it?"

"No. I've never heard of it, and she didn't talk about anything to do with Middleton … oh, wait, she did mention some railway that runs from Middleton. She's studied it or summat." George frowned. "Maybe she's a train-spotter or something."

"And maybe you should go back to school and learn some history," Joe countered. "The Middleton Light Railway was the first commercial track in the world."

"Was it? Stevensies Rocket and stuff?"

"Stevenson's Rocket is what…" Joe shook his head. "Don't worry about it, George. In fact, don't worry about anything. I know you're innocent. It's just a case of proving it." He downed his drink. "I'll catch you later… By the way, Brenda's promised she'll look after you tonight."

George's eyes lit. "Yeah? I'd better shave and shower then."

***

On reaching his room, Joe felt waves of fatigue threatening to overtake him and thrust him into sleep. He pushed it aside. A life spent running a workman's café involved early mornings and long hours, and he was no stranger to tiredness. He had a mystery to solve, a friend to vindicate, and sleep could wait.

Itching to get at Jennifer Hardy's computer, he dug into the wardrobe and came out with the thin latex gloves he had begged from Barrett. Joe had worked on so many puzzles

156

and crimes that he was fully aware of the risk of disturbing latent fingerprints.

Taking the bag from the wardrobe, he once again opened it carefully, took out the computer and the diary and a dirty tissue stuck to the diary. He peeled it off and threw it back at the bag, which it missed. Ignoring it, he opened the diary. A list of names and addresses, one or two appointments inked in for the early part of the year, then nothing. Jennifer Hardy was not the kind of woman to use a paper diary, and he was willing to bet that she kept her appointments schedule either on the computer or on her mobile phone.

Opening up the machine, he switched it on. The machine sparked into life, but as it went through the boot routine, the battery warning flashed up.

Joe returned to the wardrobe and took out the power adaptor for his netbook and was delighted to find that it operated Jennifer's just as efficiently. Soon he was confronted with a standard Microsoft admin screen demanding that he log on. He frowned. Password. Tom had told him not once but twice that Jennifer locked the machine up. Where would he find Jennifer's password?

He reached for the diary again. A little obvious, and scarcely secure, but he had no other clue. Thumbing through the pages more slowly this time a sense of irritation and anticipation began to build in him. To her credit she had not written the password down, which meant that if the killer/thief had intended adding or removing something from the machine, he could not have done so without the password, and the chances were that the 'evidence' – Joe could think of no other word – was still there.

But that same lack of a password was annoying. He tried 'Jennifer' and got nowhere. 'Hardy' and 'jhardy' produced the same lack of results. He tried other combinations and all led up a blind alley. Worried that the machine may eventually shut down and lock him out altogether, he sat back in the chair and looked out onto the empty, snowy streets. His lively mind ran back and forth over the events of the last 36 hours and all he had learned of Jennifer Hardy.

With the clock pushing up to 6:15, he despaired of working it out and was ready to hand the machine to the police, when Tom Patterson's words came back to him. *Like all historians, she was fearfully protective of her work.*

Her work.

With the memory of gold glittering in his mind's eye, Joe attacked the keyboard again. His first attempt failed, but when he pressed CAPS LOCK and tried again, the screen burst into life with a picture of the Salamanca, Matthew Murray's engine that had run coal on the Middleton Light Railway from Broom Colliery to the Canal Side.

Delighted at his powers of deduction, Joe looked the desktop screen over.

There were few icons; the standard ones, plus shortcuts to Word and Excel, the documents folder, pictures folder and the Firefox internet browser. Joe double-clicked the latter, hoping the machine would pick up the wireless connection in the room. He was content to learn that it did, and immediately shut the browser down. There was nothing he needed from the internet. Instead, he went in search of Jennifer's emails.

He found Outlook empty, so went back online and there he found her university email and several webmail addresses.

Searching through them, it began to dawn upon him what a mammoth task he had set himself. Jennifer never got rid of anything and there were literally thousands of messages stored on the machine.

He was irritated to find that her university account was locked with a password, but when he tried the one for the machine as a whole, it worked, and he tutted. Keeping the same password for all accounts did not constitute good security, especially when she so blatantly displayed that password for anyone and everyone to see.

Here again, there were over 1800 messages. It was as if the woman had never done any housekeeping on her account.

In order to narrow down the choices, Joe clicked on the

recipients' tab, listing all the messages by name instead of date and scrolled down to those between Jennifer and Dennis Wright, Jennifer and Oliver Quinton, Jennifer and Warren Kirkland.

There were many. Too many to go through individually, so he began to dive into them at random.

Most were from Jennifer to Wright. He had obviously chosen to ignore a good many and when Joe read them, he could understand why. The woman was simply obsessed with the idea of becoming, if not his third wife, then certainly his life partner.

My darling Dennis, she had written in January, *we're so good together that I cannot wait until the day when that togetherness is permanent.*

My love, she had said in April, *my mind drifts back to those wonderful weeks in Alabama, the warm night enhanced by the wrap of your arms around me.*

At first Wright's responses had been gentle, but later they were sterner, rebuking.

Jennifer, he had responded late in May, *will you please stop this. I've made it clear that I am not seeking a permanent relationship with you or anyone. What we had was fantastic, but it ended and I'm fine with that. Why can't you be?*

As the months progressed, she exhibited a clear air of desperation in her messages. In October, she wrote, *Dennis, my love, why do you hurt me like this? You know how much I love you, you know how I long to be with you. Please Dennis, for my sake, for our sakes, I'm asking you to reconsider.*

There were no further replies from Wright, other than one message, sent a week earlier, detailing his flight into Manchester. *I arrive at eight in the morning, and I figure I'll be in Leeds by ten. We can finalise details of the signing tour then.*

Jennifer had written back arranging to meet him at the railway station in Leeds, but Wright had not even acknowledged the email.

There was one other message that interested Joe. Sent by Jennifer, the header read, *I can solve your financial problems.*

Joe opened and read it.

Darling. I have the answer to your financial problems, and all it needs is one or two changes to The Missing Pennies. Get on Skype and we can talk about it.

It was sent, so Joe noted, in August; a month before Quinton claimed he and she met for the first time. Joe could not find a response from Wright.

When he checked the exchanges between her and Quinton, they gave no clue to what Jennifer had meant. They were simple arrangement emails and confirmations. The exchanges were always initiated by Jennifer and Quinton merely replied saying, 'I'll be there.'

He shut down the software and opened up the photograph albums. Here again, he found a lack of housekeeping. Over 3,000 images, and not a single folder.

This time, however, he arranged them in date order.

The first thing he noticed was a good number of illustrations. On checking them, he discovered that some were scanned images that had been enhanced to print standards. Others were not. There was an illustration of a pithead captioned, 'Broom colliery, circa 1850', showing miners trudging to work. They looked nothing like modern miners. Carrying Davy lamps, without hard hats, one or two carried caged birds; they had an air of depressed resignation about them. On checking the file properties, Joe discovered that it had originally been produced on Photoshop.

The more recent images that interested him. There were several of Dennis Wright, all taken on Christmas Eve. Not that Joe needed the date stamp on the picture properties to tell him that. All were taken in Leeds and the presence of so many Christmas decorations on the street and in shop windows, and Santas, all in the background, told him everything he needed to know about the photographs' history.

There was one of them together. Taken, Joe guessed, on

Briggate, Wright had his arm around her shoulder, she had her arm around his waist and they smiled into the camera taking no heed of the bustling crowd, the street entertainers, a Father Christmas amidst a sea of children. If Joe had not read the emails, if he had not talked to Wright the previous day, he would have sworn they were a couple in love.

There was someone else in that photograph. Someone quite familiar. In the background, almost lost amongst the sea of faces and bodies, stood a squat, stout figure, clad in a dark overcoat, his cheeks flushed with either the cold or high blood pressure. Joe knew different. The colour came from anger, and the narrowed stare confirmed it. There was something about Wright and Jennifer, the way they stood, perhaps, their nearness, that infuriated Oliver Quinton.

So not only had Kirkland followed her round Leeds, but Quinton had, too.

He also spotted another photograph that interested him. Not one, but two. Both the same photograph but with a minor difference. In one, George Robson was holding the CD; in the other, he was holding a coin in a presentation case.

Puzzled, he shut down the photograph folder and looked over the desktop icons. Up in the top left corner, next to the recycle bin, he found Adobe Photoshop. He double-clicked the icon. It took an age to open and when it did, he stared blankly at the screen.

He freely admitted that his computer skills were limited to opening and saving word processing files, and downloading photographs from his camera. He, too, had Photoshop on both his computers but he had never been sufficiently interested in image manipulation to bother with it. Now he wished he had. The blank screen was inundated with menus and icons, most of which he did not understand.

Clicking on 'File' he spotted the 'Open' command, and below it, after several other options, he noticed, 'Open Recent'. Hovering the mouse over it produced a fly-out menu listing the last ten files Jennifer had used. The top two took his eye. The first filename, he recognised as the original photograph of George he had just viewed on Windows. The one beneath it was named, *1933coin*. When Joe clicked it, the picture filled the centre of the screen. It was a penny in a presentation case. Joe zoomed in on the date and read '1933'.

He sat back and considered the possibilities.

Kirkland had insisted Jennifer knew where to get hold of the Middleton Penny. It seemed likely that Quinton must have thought so, too, else why follow her on Saturday? Yet here she was actually in possession of that penny. Had she arranged its theft in 1970?

Joe dismissed the idea instantly. She would have been about 12 years of age, and whoever had gone about stealing that coin, would have been well organised. Too well organised for someone who was no more than a child. If she had come across the penny at all, it must have been later in life, but again it seemed unlikely. If she had, why not use it to apply pressure on Dennis Wright? Also, why ask George to pose for a picture so that she could fake him as owning the penny?

The word 'fake' rang round his head and Joe's suspicions swung in a new direction.

It couldn't be. Could it? A photograph of a coin was not the same as a coin. She could have got that picture from anywhere on the web, and used Photoshop to manipulate it.

But why?

He closed down Photoshop and opened up the email package again, this time concentrating on exchanges between her and Kirkland and her and Quinton. Her final message to both men had been the same. *Be at the Regency Hotel, Leeds, over the Christmas weekend. It will be to your advantage.*

Fresh scenarios developing in his mind, Joe turned his attention to the documents folder. Had she written it all down there?

Once again, he found a huge list of works. Scrolling through it, unable to find anything resembling the document he had hoped was there, two items took his interest:

missporig and *misspnew.* Joe intuitively translated *missp* as *Missing Pennies*, and when he opened the files, he found full manuscripts for the book.

After hearing Sheila's tale on the coach, Joe had assumed that the book was a history of the coins buried in the local churches, but he soon realised it was not. Instead, it was a detailed account of valuable coins from all over the world that had gone missing; like the Morgan Silver Dollar and the Double Eagle 20-Dollar gold coin. The Leeds Pennies comprised only one chapter of the book.

Nevertheless, given Jennifer Hardy's and Dennis Wright's connection to the West Yorkshire city, Joe concentrated on that chapter. He read *orig* first, making notes as he went along, and then closed the file down and opened up *new.*

He had not read past the first page of the double-spaced document when a frown crossed his brow. Shrinking the window to half size, he opened *orig* again, shrunk that too, arranging both windows alongside each other, then read the same line on both pages.

In *orig*, he read:

In 1970, during renovation work, the penny encased in the cornerstone at St Cross, Middleton, was stolen.

In *new*, he read:

In 1970, during renovation work, the penny encased in the cornerstone at St Mary's, Hawksworth, was stolen.

Joe sat back in his seat and again stared through the window at the deserted streets.

"Can't get people out spending when the weather's this bad, Joe," he muttered to himself. It was a distraction, a means of taking his mind from the immediate problem, so that a solution might occur to him.

Two different accounts in two different documents. What did it mean? Had Wright made an initial error and had Jennifer spotted and corrected it? Or was there something more sinister to it? And which was the correct account? Joe wished he had paid more attention to Sheila on the bus.

Thoughts of his friend reminded him that she had bought

a copy of the book in Leeds. He dug into his pocket, pulled out his mobile and called her number.

It rang for a long time. He was on the verge of cutting it off when she finally answered. "Joe, what is it? Brenda and I are trying to get ready."

Her complaint reminded Joe that time must be getting on. As he replied, he looked through the window at the grand dome of Leeds town hall, and its clock reading 7:10.

"You bought that book of Dennis's Wright's yesterday."

"Yes I did," Sheila replied. "What of it."

"Could you bring it to dinner? There's something I need to check on."

Sheila was appalled."You're going to read through dinner? Joe, that's the most ignorant…"

"Hang on," he cut her off. "You want to see George cleared of all charges?"

"Well of course I do."

"Then I need to read at the dinner table. Bring the book with you. I'll see you down there in about twenty minutes."

Without waiting to hear more protests from Sheila, Joe cut the connection, tucked the phone in his pocket, and switched off Jennifer's laptop.

Once disconnected from the mains, he replaced it in the bag from which it had come and dropped the diary in with it. Standing up, ready to put both in the wardrobe, he looked down and found the tissue, which had been stuck to the diary, now stuck to his shoe. With a cluck, he removed it and threw it in the waste bin, then left the computer in the wardrobe.

Stripping off his shirt, moving to the bathroom while he washed and shaved, questions rang round his head.

A simple error in a book by a famous academic, a woman besotted with him to the point where she would not take no for an answer, and a hint of darker machinations between the two of them which were not followed up on the computer.

Why had Quinton followed them? If Quinton's relationship with Jennifer was so casual, why did he look so

164

angry in that photograph? Kirkland had followed them, too, but he had been neutral on them. Had Quinton discovered something he didn't like?

It all added up to something, but of all the questions he asked himself, he could come to only one sure conclusion: George Robson was a patsy. He just did not know who had cast him in that role.

Chapter Twelve

In 1970, during renovation work, the penny encased in the cornerstone at St Cross, Middleton, was stolen. Alarmed at the theft, in order to prevent a repetition, the Diocese of Ripon ordered that the penny in the foundations of St Mary's, Hawksworth, be removed and deposited at the bank for safe keeping.

Joe pushed the book to one side, and took another mouthful of veal cutlet.

Through the hum, clatter and chatter of a busy dining room, Sheila insisted, "I do wish you would tell us what all this is about."

Pushing her plate to one side, Brenda took a sip of white wine. "Joe likes to be secretive, don't you, Joe? I think he had a thing about Jennifer Hardy and he's jealous of George."

George laughed. He had showered and shaved, grabbed a little sleep and now looked much happier than he had earlier in the evening. More like his usual self. "Joe couldn't have coped with her, Brenda."

"And I think the wine's going to both your heads already," Joe retorted. To Sheila, he said, "I don't know what it's about, except that I found two versions of this book on Jennifer's computer, and they tell different stories."

"One will have been an early draft," Sheila speculated. "Dennis Wright did tell you that Jennifer was his researcher and editor."

"Reader," Joe corrected. "His reader, not his editor. Yes I thought that too, but the error is so glaring that I'm surprised Wright made it in the first place."

Brenda rubbed her belly, suppressed a burp with an

apology, and looked over to the carvery tables. "To pud or not to pud, that is the question. Whether tis nobler to suffer the slings and arrows of outrageous weight loss, or take arms against a sea of sherry trifle and say sod it."

Sheila smiled and gave Brenda a round of applause. "That's very good."

"I'm sure Shakespeare was talking about appetite when he wrote it, and we can't help our urges, can we?" She whipped her head round on Joe. "And we might be able to help if you told us what you're talking about."

"Go get your trifle, Brenda," Joe ordered, "and bring me a slice of lemon meringue while you're there."

"You want anything, Sheila? George?" Brenda asked.

George declined, but Sheila pushed her plate away and said, "I really couldn't eat another thing." She smiled wickedly. "Bring me a dish of trifle, too, please." Brenda wandered off and Sheila turned her attention to Joe as he finished his meal. "Now, Joe, what's troubling you?"

"This business of the churches here in Leeds. You were telling us the tale on the bus coming here, yesterday, but I wasn't taking too much notice. Tell me again."

"Two George the Fifth pennies were set into stones in two churches. St Mary's at Hawksworth and St Cross at Middleton."

"And one of them got nicked," Joe said. "But which one?"

"Middleton."

"You're sure of that?"

Sheila frowned. "Of course I'm sure." She pointed at the copy of *Missing Pennies* at Joe's elbow. "You've just read it for yourself."

"And that's the problem," Joe replied. "Like I said, there are two versions on Jennifer's laptop. The first tells it the way you just did, but the second tells it the other way round. It says the Hawksworth Penny was stolen and the Middleton one, sold. I can't rely on this book because one version has it wrong and I don't know which one."

"Does all this matter?" George asked.

"It might, it might not," Joe replied.

Sheila's clear brow creased. "Joe's right, George. It's a strange mistake for Wright to make. Anyway, book or no book, you can take it from me, Joe, that it was the Middleton Penny that was stolen. I first heard the tale many years ago." She smiled, shyly. "When I was the secretary at Wakefield Road Comprehensive, a certain, rather dishy history teacher told me all about it."

George laughed again. "And there was me thinking you never had eyes for anyone other than Peter."

Sheila returned the laughter. "Eyes, yes, but imagination … well it is apt to wander, isn't it?" Sheila's face became more serious. "Still, it is a strange mistake for a man like Dennis Wright to make, isn't it?"

"Did he make it?" Joe asked.

"Considering it's his manuscript, I should think…"

"No, no, you're not with me," Joe interrupted as Brenda returned to the table. "The file named missporig had the correct account, but misspnew was wrong."

"Miss who?" Brenda asked placing a slice of lemon meringue before Joe and a dish of trifle in front of Sheila. Keeping the other trifle for herself, she sat down and tucked in.

While working his way through the dessert, Joe repeated the tale he had just told Sheila and George.

"So you were saying it may not have been Dennis Wright?" Sheila asked when he had finished.

Swallowing a mouthful of meringue, shuddering at the tart bite on his tongue, Joe nodded. "Let's assume that missporig means the original Missing Pennies file. In it, the account of the two Leeds' pennies was correct, but it had been altered in misspnew – the rewrite. Who made the change? Since Jennifer was his reader and researcher, it's reasonable to assume she was authorised to make changes to manuscripts."

"And she got it wrong," Sheila murmured. "Mind you, I'd say it was an odd mistake for her to make, too. She was, after all, a history graduate, and she would have checked her facts before making the corrections."

"I'd say you're both missing the obvious," Brenda commented through a mouthful of trifle.

"You shouldn't speak with your mouth full," George warned her.

Brenda grinned. "That's what Colin used to say when…"

"Are you trying to put me off my dinner?" Joe interrupted.

"I was going to say when he was kissing me," Brenda argued.

"Yeah, sure you were. Anyway, what is this obvious that we're missing?"

"This bint was hopelessly in love with Wright, yet he kept giving her the order of the boot, didn't he?" Brenda said. "You told us she was all over him in her emails, but he wasn't buying. George, did she mention Wright to you?"

He shrugged and fiddled with his glass of wine. "Only in passing. Y'know. She told me they'd had a bit of a thing back in the seventies, and struck sparks again when she was in the States last year. I got the impression she was a bit piddled off with him."

"There you are then," Brenda declared.

"Where are we?" Joe asked, completely flummoxed.

"I think I can see where Brenda's heading," Sheila remarked, "but go on, dear."

Brenda swallowed another spoonful of trifle. "Delicious this. Think I might have to go back for seconds."

"Saints preserve me from gluttons. People like you are the reason why I never offer all you can eat for a fiver. You'd bankrupt me." Joe paused for breath. "Never mind the trifle. Tell us what you're on about."

"Yesterday, in Debenhams, we heard Jennifer say, and I quote, 'please your damned self. You know what happens next'. What did she mean by that?"

"Well, according to Wright…"

"We know what Wright says," Brenda declared, cutting Joe off. "She was gonna tell his lover all about them. As if he'd give a toss, and anyway, he claims not to have a lover.

Now think about it, Joe, how do you hurt an academic?"

Joe shrugged. "Wright explained that, too. You kick him where it hurts the most. His reputation."

"Precisely."

Joe threw his hands up. "Well, you've lost me."

Brenda sighed and put down her spoon. "Let's suppose Jennifer has had enough of chasing him, but she's determined to get him back for giving her the order of the boot. How does she do it? She fiddles with his manuscript, changes the churches and boots it off to the publishers, claiming it's a revised edition. If she could get through all the channels, and it's printed, it makes Wright look a complete berk. Even if she can't get it out there, the publisher may doubt Wright's credentials. And what would that do to his prospects for further titles and the professorship?"

Polishing off the last of his meringue, Joe sat back. "I can see what you're getting at, but she couldn't hope to get away with it. Publishers have so many checks and balances in place that the book would never get through, and the first person they would contact would be Wright himself, to verify that he'd authorised the revision."

"True," Sheila agreed, "but perhaps Jennifer only meant to threaten him with it. That alone might be enough for him to respond to her. Dennis Wright cannot afford any hint of scandal right now, Joe, or he'd lose the history chair before he's even landed it. And he already has financial worries, doesn't he? If he lost that post, it would probably aggravate his money problems."

"So he decided to call her bluff," George suggested.

Joe ruminated on the possibility. "I'm missing something here. In fact, I'm missing quite a lot, but on this angle, there's something I'm not taking into account."

All around them, people began to leave their tables and make their way from the dining room to the lounge where the evening's entertainment would be held.

Checking her watch, Sheila finished her wine. "Why don't you just ask Dennis outright?" she suggested.

Joe, too, emptied his glass. "I may just do that. Come on, let's go grab a seat."

Brenda gulped down the dregs of her wine and they followed the exodus into the lounge, where they joined the Staines, Captain Tanner and Sylvia on the table by the rear wall, which they had come to think of as theirs. While they took their seats, George went to the bar.

"News, Murray?" Tanner asked.

"Yes," Joe replied. "It's definitely the last time I go rooting through dustbins on Christmas Day."

Julia Staines grinned at Tanner's obvious impatience. "Joe, are we certain that George didn't do it?" With a cautious glance over her shoulder to ensure George was not on his way back, she said, "I know it's unlikely, but even the mildest of men can turn nasty when they don't get what they want."

Joe cast a mean eye on her husband. "Julia hinting at you, is she Alec?"

"Oh yes," Staines replied. "I can be real narky when I don't get what I want, Joe. I refuse to do the washing up for days at a time."

"Very funny," Joe grunted. "At the risk of boring you all, I repeat: George is innocent. I just can't prove it yet. But have faith. I'll get there."

As the clock moved up to the hour, the lights dimmed, the spotlight beamed on the stage and the announcer's voice boomed around the room.

"Ladies and gentlemen, for your Christmas entertainment, the Regency is proud to present, the versatile Tony Carmichael.

Music burst from the speakers and Carmichael hurried into the room, radio microphone in hand, belting out the chorus to Slade's *Merry Christmas Everybody* as he leapt onto the stage. Dressed in a dinner suit, he danced his way around the small platform as he sang, and he was less than thirty seconds into his act when Joe stood up.

"Excuse me," he said to the table, "but I haven't had my after-dinner smoke."

171

He moved out of the room as fast as Tony Carmichael had moved to the stage, and made his way to the front entrance, where the bitter night greeted him. Hands shaking in the icy cold, he rolled a cigarette and lit it.

"Hello, Joe."

He half turned to find Patterson behind him, taking a cigarette from his pack.

"Hiya, Tom. You found the singer a bit OTT, too, did you?"

Patterson nodded. "Noisy blighter." He fired his lighter between cupped hands and for a brief moment, his face blazed in the reflected glow of the flame, eyes narrowed into an intense mask that reminded Joe of his Santa performance earlier in the day. Joe had long thought that Santa could be easily misinterpreted as sinister.

Joe dismissed the illusion. "Police had anything more to say to you?"

"No. You?"

"Nope, but I did find Jennifer's computer. It was in the rubbish out back."

Patterson's eyes lit again. "You did? Well done, Joe. If you'd like to give it to me, I'll make sure it gets to her family."

Joe shook his head. "I'm sorry, Tom, I can't do that. Y'see, I've already had a look at it and there are certain things which may have a bearing on her murder."

Patterson's features underwent another transformation, registering surprise this time. "You found her password, too?"

"No. She didn't have it written down, but it wasn't difficult to guess. She'd been advertising it for long enough." Without waiting for Patterson to question him further, Joe took the initiative. "Tell me, Tom, if Jennifer was in possession of information that may cast Dennis Wright's, er, professional knowledge in a bad light, how rough would that be for him?"

Patterson drew on his cigarette, the tip glowing in the night. Blowing out the smoke, he replied, "Catastrophic, I should say. But surely you don't suspect Dennis? I know they had their differences, but I've known him a long time. He's not a violent man."

Joe drew on his cigarette, and then stubbed it out. "Neither am I, but how many killers have gone to jail after being described as mild and inoffensive?"

***

Joe returned to the lounge ahead of Patterson, and found Tony Carmichael entertaining the audience with a string of one-liners. He had disposed of the dinner jacket and his bow tie, wore a ridiculous, plastic Elvis 'wig' on his head and was rooting through a set of props in a battered old suitcase.

Sidling around the perimeter of the room, signalling to his friends that he was going for drinks, Joe approached the bar, where Dennis Wright stood, staring moodily into a half empty martini glass.

"Gimme half of bitter, a gin and tonic and Campari and soda," Joe ordered, taking out his wallet.

"Ice and lemon, sir?" asked the barman.

"Yes, but not in the bitter." Joe gave the young man a crumpled smile to show he was only joking. While the barman busied himself preparing the drinks, Joe half turned to Wright. "Still running on Alabama time?"

"Huh?" The academic stirred as if he had only just registered Joe's presence. "What? Oh. I see. You mean jet lag? No. I had plenty of shuteye on the flight over and I've been here 36 hours now." Wright straightened up and looked around. "It's this whole scene. Christmas. Not my thing at all, and it's not the reason I came here."

A ripple of laughter ran round the audience as Carmichael cracked another joke. Joe watched him pulling on a glitter suit over his stage clothes.

"Elvis," he said. "Before my time, and I never really liked him, you know."

"He's a god where I live," Wright commented.

Joe paid the barman, and Carmichael ran into a supposed

emotional rendition of *Lonely This Christmas*. Joe tutted. "This guy doesn't know what he's talking about."

"What?" Wright asked.

Joe picked up his beer, took a sip and waved at Carmichael, now gyrating around the stage as he sang. "This wasn't Elvis Presley. It was Mud. Presley did a cover version on an album, I'm sure, but it was Mud who had the hit with it." He placed his glass on the bar. "The guy hasn't done his homework."

Wright smile thinly. "Why do I get the feeling, Murray, that you're stood with me because you *have* done your homework."

Joe returned the smile. "Very perceptive. And right, Wright." He turned and leaned on the bar, ignoring the show. "We found Jennifer's computer."

"Good. I'm glad. Now you can hand it to her family and make their Christmas complete." Wright stirred his drink and sucked the olive from the cocktail stick. "I assume there are things on it you want to ask me about."

"There are. And if you won't talk to me, you'll have to answer to Dockerty and Barrett in the morning."

"Has anyone ever told you what a pain in the ass you can be?"

Joe nodded. "Plenya people, but I don't care. I like to see puzzles solved, and at the moment, a friend of mine is being held up as the solution to this puzzle, when he isn't. The cops have added one and one and come up with three. Right now, I don't know who killed Jennifer Hardy, because I don't know why she was killed. But you are the biggest suspect. You had the biggest reason to murder her."

Wright's glum features darkened further. A flash of anger crossed his face, and faded just as quickly. "Listen to me very carefully. I did not kill Jennifer Hardy."

"I didn't say you did," Joe replied. "I said you had the biggest motive for killing her." He took another sip of beer while Wright ordered a fresh martini. "I've had a good look through that computer, and I have a problem. It concerns you and her."

"Go on," Wright invited.

Joe watched Carmichael bring the song to a close and begin to throw off the absurd jump suit while acknowledging the applause.

"If you're going to watch the floor show, Murray, why don't you just leave the questions to the cops?"

Wright's words brought Joe back from his surly opinions of Carmichael. "What? Oh. Sorry. What was I saying, now? Oh, yes. In August, Jennifer sent you an email saying she had the solution to your financial worries. She said it involved making a few changes to *Missing Pennies*. You never answered her."

"Because her idea was crazy," Wright replied.

To Joe's irritation, Carmichael ran through a couple of Christmas jokes that were older than most of the audience, and then ran into *I Wish It Could Be Christmas Everyday*.

"This guy needs to learn what it means to put an act together."

"You know, Murray, I just said, if you'd rather be with your friends and watch this jerk, it's fine by me. I don't particularly like talking to you."

Joe swung on him. "Her idea was crazy?" he said, demonstrating that contrary to Wright's opinion, he had been listening. "She never said what the idea was."

"Not in the email, no. She used her university email account, and there was too big a risk of it falling into other hands." Wright straightened up, towering above Joe. "She asked me to contact her on Skype. If you don't know, Skype is…"

"I know what Skype is," Joe interrupted. "I learned all about it earlier this year." He pinned Wright with a meaningful stare. "I talk to my brother on Skype. He lives in Australia." Bringing his lecture to a close, he asked, "What was Jennifer's idea for saving your financial backside?"

Wright took a long time answering. When he did, his response puzzled Joe.

"Have you ever read *The da Vinci Code*?" Wright asked.

175

Despite his mystification, Joe nodded. "Not bad. Bit over-hyped, but a clever piece of detective fiction."

"Leaving aside its literary merits, do you know what that novel did for the Louvre and the Dominican Convent of Santa Maria delle Grazie in Milan? You can buy tickets so see *The Last Supper* online these days. The novel sparked conspiracy theories all over the world and the debate is still raging."

Joe nodded. "And all because the book was a bestseller."

"Precisely," Wright agreed. "That was Jennifer's idea. Run a little speculation in the text of *Missing Pennies*, then hire a ghost-writer to build a novel around the speculation. She was even dating that greaseball, Quinton, to learn as much as she could about coin collectors and the lengths to which they'll go to possess coins."

"Was she now?" Joe lodged the information amongst the other factors in his mind. "She suggested you speculate in *Missing Pennies*. Speculate on what?"

"How much do you know of the George the Fifth pennies?"

"A bit," Joe admitted. "One was stolen, the other was sold."

"Correct," Wright said. "The Middleton Penny was stolen sometime around 1970. The Hawksworth Penny was moved to safe keeping to prevent its theft, and it was later sold at auction. Now suppose the Middleton Penny was stolen to order for a wealthy crook like Quinton? You see, Murray, if you stole that penny and had it in your pocket right now, you couldn't do anything with it. Before decimalisation, you could have spent it over the bar, but that would be tantamount to criminal negligence. There were fewer than ten minted so if you were the thief, you couldn't sell it other than to a numismatist who was prepared to deal on the black market. Someone like Quinton, who, by the way, offered me ten percent of the value last night if I told him where he could get his hands on it. Whoever has that penny can't display it in a museum or even a private gallery. Like the Double Eagle 20-dollar coin, its appearance would

176

cause too many ripples, so the Middleton Penny has value only to collectors and they would have to keep it secret. If you think about it from that angle, you have the basis for a novel."

Joe grunted. "Sounds like a plan to me."

"Well, it didn't to me," Wright countered. "I'm a historian. I don't dabble in fiction. My book, *Missing Pennies* is a factual account of rare and valuable coins from all over the world that have gone missing. I don't speculate on where they are, I don't speculate on whether they were stolen, I don't even speculate on who might own them. I simply state facts. My book is aimed at academics and numismatists: coin collectors and others with an interest in coinage and currency. The book is not going to sell millions of copies, but it will help cement my professional credentials."

"Still," Joe said as Carmichael brought his song to a conclusion, "Jennifer's idea would have been nice, wouldn't it?" He rubbed his thumb and forefinger together. "Make plenty dollar and solve money worry."

Wright sighed and looked away. When he turned back to Joe, there was no mistaking the anger in his eyes. "I don't have money worries. Not that it's anything to do with you or anyone else, but I dropped a packet on a Florida real estate deal. It amounts to about one hundred thousand dollars, but I'm not bankrupt. It was a case of bad judgement on my part. The guy pulling the scam has been arrested, but the investors have already been told they won't get their money back. Most of it is gone, or so well hidden, it might just as well be gone."

Joe sympathised. "That's too bad, Wright. I've known a lot of pain in my life, but none of it is worse than losing a shilling down the drain."

Wright glowered. "Are you taking a rise outta me?"

Joe smiled. "Could be." Before Wright could react, he pressed on. "Quinton followed you and Jennifer round Leeds yesterday."

"He did?" Wright's features registered surprise. If it was

faked, it was convincing.

Joe nodded. "He's on a photograph taken in the city centre yesterday lunchtime. I have to say, Wright, in that photograph, you and Jennifer looked pretty friendly."

"Because I have my arm around her shoulder?" Wright asked and Joe nodded. "It's a professional veneer, Murray. Jennifer wanted a picture of the two of us together, the way we used to be, the way she wanted us to be again. I said no, but she pressed and I figured we have to work on the book tour together, so what the hell. But it was strictly for the cameras."

"The look on Quinton's face tells me he didn't believe that," Joe said. "He was mad as hell. In fact, he looked to me like a man convinced he had just been robbed … or he was about to be robbed."

"Not by me he hadn't."

"Tell me about Quinton."

"I already did," Wright retorted and with another sigh, went on, "The man is rolling in money and he collects rare coins. He got in touch with Jennifer last year when he learned she was coming to Alabama to work with me. He wants the Middleton Penny. He offered me ten percent of its black market value if I could get it for him. The value of the Middleton Penny is estimated at a hundred and fifty thousand dollars."

"So he was prepared to pay you fifteen thousand just to tell him where it was?"

Wright nodded. "Jennifer thought it would be a good idea. I don't like the guy and I told him I wouldn't lead him to it at gunpoint. Besides, as I told her, fifteen grand is chickenfeed at the side of the amount I'd lost on the real estate scam, and it simply wasn't worth it. That's when she started dating the guy and milking him for information. If fifteen grand was nothing, maybe the royalties on a novel would help." He shook his head sadly. "She just didn't get the full picture."

Joe chewed over the information. "So, when she learned that you wouldn't go for it, Jennifer would realise that she'd been sacrificing her, er, well, you know."

"She'd been laying him for nothing?" Wright asked, and when Joe nodded, he agreed. "And she would have been pretty mad over it. That's probably why she chewed him out in the bar last night." He glared. "You're looking for someone mad enough to kill her, Murray, look at Quinton. Not me."

"That's not the way I'm thinking, Wright," Joe confessed. "Y'see, what occurs to me is that Quinton is so obsessed with the Middleton Penny that he may be easy to con."

Wright frowned. "What?"

"Let me tell you how I see it." Joe drank a little beer. "You have a large hole where your money used to be. Oliver Quinton has a lot of money at his disposal and he's desperate to get his grubby little paws on the Middleton Penny. Jennifer, ever eager to become Mrs Dennis Wright, comes up with a little plan. She will lure him and Warren Kirkland into a false sense of security. It'll take time, but she uses her finest manoeuvre, taking her panties off, to suck them in, er, no pun intended. She invites them here for Christmas and they turn up because they know you're here. They've been assured that the owner of the Middleton Penny will be here. Jennifer latches onto George, and I know my pal. He'll do anything for a laugh. She asks George to pose as a coin collector, the man in possession of the Middleton Penny. She even cooks up a picture of him holding what appears to be the penny. The idea is to get Quinton or Kirkland, or both, to her room, and negotiate a price with George. They hand over the money, George gets his legover, and everyone is happy; particularly you, because you have just secured a hundred thousand pounds, or however much for a fake penny." He fixed Wright's eye. "So what went wrong?"

"Nothing," Wright admitted and Joe's heart began to pound. "It was a perfect plan. Except that it didn't happen." The academic shook his head sadly. "Quinton may be slime, and Kirkland may be supercilious, but neither of them are

179

stupid. They know their coins. You couldn't get a fake past either man."

"Not even if you, a world authority, produced it?" Now Joe shook his head, and turned to the bar. "I don't accept that, Wright. If anyone could con Quinton or Kirkland into parting with money for a fake, it's you. But something went astray. Maybe you got cold feet; maybe Jennifer got cold feet. Maybe you decided that you'd rather be in debt than saddled with her for the rest of your life. Whatever it was, it led to Jennifer's death."

"You're nuts. You know that?"

"Maybe. But I will get to the bottom of this," Joe warned. "Tomorrow morning, I have to report my findings to Dockerty in order to get an innocent man set free. There are people in this room with motives for getting rid of Jennifer Hardy, but as far as I can see, Wright, you have the biggest motive." He picked up his drinks as Carmichael ran into his final number of the evening, *O Come All Ye Faithful*, which he sang in Latin. "And if you wanna attack me with a bottle of cheap wine in the early hours of the morning, you'll find me in 306." He marched off, skirting the perimeter of the room once again to return to his friends.

He tucked into his seat as Carmichael closed his show to generous applause.

"Excellent entertainment," Tanner declared.

"Amateur," Joe decided. "Trite and hackneyed."

"Joe, where have you been?" Sheila wanted to know.

"You missed every minute of that act," Brenda grumbled.

"I've been trying to find a killer," Joe replied.

"And have you?" Sylvia asked.

"No," Joe admitted, "but if it helped me miss every minute of that clown's so-called act, it was worth it."

Chapter Thirteen

There was a lull in the proceedings, while Nate Immacyoulate set up his equipment, allowing guests to refresh their drinks. Tanner, Sylvia and the Staines wandered off and Joe took the opportunity to give his friends a rundown on his investigations so far.

"I believe it was either Dennis Wright, Warren Kirkland or Oliver Quinton who killed Jennifer, and they took advantage of you, George, sleeping with her to pin it on you," he concluded.

"It seems likely," Sheila agreed, "but which one?"

"I haven't figured that out yet," Joe admitted. "It seems to me that there was something going on in the background, some kinda plan, and they chose George as the patsy. I think it had something to do with the Middleton Penny." He shrugged. "Whatever it was, it went wrong and Jennifer ended up dead instead of whatever they had planned."

"I don't understand, Joe," Sheila complained. "What kind of scheme could they be hatching?"

Again, he shrugged. "I don't know. Maybe Wright had Quinton or Kirkland, or both, down as a mark ... a mug. They were going to hand him a fake penny, take his money and run. But they needed a clown like you, George, so that the other would have someone to come back on when they rumbled the scam. You told me, George, that Jennifer said, 'you can have what you want, but I need you to do me a favour and pretend to be a big wheel art collector'." He raised his eyebrows for confirmation.

"Not really, Joe," George disagreed. "She asked me to pose as a businessman, not an art collector."

"You haven't seen that doctored photograph," Joe

181

muttered and before they could ask, he went on, "Maybe Quinton or Kirkland rumbled it, waited for you to leave then went back and got into an argument with Jennifer and killed her."

"An interesting idea," Sheila ruminated.

"It would also explain why Wright is so moody," Brenda ventured. "Not only has his scam gone to pot, but he's lost his girlfriend, too, and he can't own up about it because he would be exposed as a potential crook."

"What's your next move, maestro?" Sheila wanted to know.

Joe shook his head. "I'm not sure. I need to speak to Quinton again. And I need to crack the whole thing before Dockerty gets back tomorrow morning, because I'll have to hand over both the computer and the diary by then." He frowned. "I still get the feeling I'm missing something. It's trivial, but important."

"That's you all over, Joe," Brenda ribbed him, "trivial, but important; especially when it comes to paying our wages."

Joe scowled. "Overpaying you, you mean." He scanned the room again, seeking Quinton, and spotted him by the windows exchanging words with Mavis Barker. "I'd better go rescue him," he muttered and picked up his glass.

A blast of music from the wall speakers made Joe cringe. It was followed by a thudding, background beat, and the booming voice of the deejay.

"Good evening, ladies and gennelmen, welcome to the Regency partay here on Christmas Day. This is your resident deejay, Nate Immacyoulate, taking you through to the small hours, so let it all hang out and boogie the night away. We're gonna track back to 1979 and get the show under way with Blondie and *Heart of Glass*."

While the music began and people began to move to the dance floor, Joe manoeuvred himself in the opposite direction until he stood alongside Mavis Barker who was giving Quinton both barrels.

"What's wrong, Mavis?" Joe asked.

"This ignorant little twerp. I went to the bar for a drink and he pinched my seat. And when I complained, do you know what he said to me?"

"Well, not everyone learned proper manners," Joe said. "Why don't you go collar Brenda? She was looking for someone to dance with, and George isn't feeling up to it."

With a final scowl at Quinton, Mavis wandered off and Joe sat down.

"Whatever you want, Murray, forget it. I've nothing more to say to you."

"I think you have," Joe replied. "If only an apology for bad-mouthing one of my members like that."

"She's a –"

"She's a smashing woman, if a bit eccentric," Joe interrupted, "and even if you didn't pinch her seat, there's no call for bad language."

"Bad language? Me? You should have heard the way she spoke to me. Like a bloody trooper." Quinton swirled red wine around his glass. "So, what do you want? Come to accuse me of Jennifer's murder again?"

"Maybe. Maybe not. Tell me again what Jennifer said to you on the dance floor last night. When she lost the plot."

"Any reason why I should?" Quinton asked.

"Because I've just heard a different version," Joe replied, "and if you don't tell me, then I may accuse you of her murder."

Quinton sighed. "I spoke to Wright. He sent me away with a flea in my ear. So I decided to have it out with Jennifer and she did the same. Told me she never wanted to see me again, and I had to get out of her life. That's it."

Joe sipped at his ale and Quinton took a mouthful of wine.

"That doesn't quite square with what I've just been told," Joe said, putting his glass on the table.

"Then whoever told you is lying." Quinton, too, put his glass down, and sat forward. "For the umpteenth time, Murray, I did not kill her."

"And I may or may not believe you," Joe retorted, "but

183

my information tells me you had a powerful motive."

"Not getting my hands on the Middleton Penny may be a disappointment, but still no reason for killing her."

"I'm not talking about the Middleton Penny. I'm talking about you learning just how much Jennifer Hardy used you." Joe forced a cynical laugh, almost buried under the noise of Debbie Harry. "She led you on a proper dance, didn't she? Strung you along for months with the hope of landing the Middleton Penny, when what she was really doing was researching a novel. And when she learned last night that Dennis Wright wasn't interested in a novel set around the Middleton Penny, she took it out on you when you confronted her."

While he spoke, Joe watched the millionaire's features darken, and then settle into a mask of absolute fury, and he knew he had it right.

Like Wright earlier, Quinton took a long time to answer and Joe was prompted to goad him further.

"How did that make you feel, Quinton? Even smaller and more ridiculous than you really are? Blazing mad, like you are right now? Mad enough to go for the throat?"

"Yes," Quinton admitted with a hiss. "You're right. That is exactly how I felt. If I'd had a gun in my hand, I would have shot her where she stood and enjoyed watching her die. But I don't own a gun. Instead, I walked out, snapped at a few of the staff and went back to my room to fume in private. And I didn't leave it again until seven thirty this morning. Now for pity's sake, get off my back, will you?"

"Not until I'm persuaded that you're innocent," Joe warned. "There are a few suspects for this murder, but right now, you and Wright stand out from the pack, and I'm sure one of you did it." Joe chewed his lip as the music faded out.

"Blondie there with *Heart of Glass*." Nate Immacyoulate's voice burst from the speakers. "We're taking your requests for the karaoke right now, so if you wanna get up and do your thing to entertain your fellow party peeps, come up and book your slot. Right now though, it's seventy-nine again and for Sad Café, *Every Day Hurts*."

"This guy needs to go further back before he can interest me," Joe muttered as the music began. Concentrating on Quinton again, he said, "You followed Jennifer and Dennis Wright round Leeds yesterday."

"I most certainly did not," Quinton retorted.

Joe shook his head. "More lies. I spoke to Kirkland earlier because I'd seen him in Debenhams, and he admitted he'd followed them. You've just denied it, yet there's a photograph of them together. It was taken in Leeds yesterday at about 12:30. It's on Jennifer's computer. They looked quite, er, chummy, and anyone could mistake them for a couple in love. The street's crowded, but you're plain enough to see, stood in the background, staring straight at them, and if looks were daggers, you'd have skewered the pair of them."

Blind anger suffused Quinton's features again. "What is this? Big Brother? A man can't go Christmas shopping without being questioned?"

Joe refused to be diverted. "I don't care where you shop, Quinton, and I'm not interested in what you buy. I'm interested in why you followed Jennifer and Wright. And if you won't tell me, we'll see how interested Dockerty is when he turns up tomorrow."

Another frustrated hiss escaped Quinton. "All right, so I followed them. When she left here at about half past ten yesterday morning, I knew she'd be going to meet Wright. He was the only one who hadn't shown up at that time. I wondered whether they might lead me to the Middleton Penny. She stopped some clown and asked him to take the picture for them."

"Which clown?"

"I don't know," Quinton protested. "Just some dork in the street. There was a bit of a debate over it, like Wright was reluctant, but she must have persuaded him eventually. He put his arm round her, she hung onto him, and the passer-by took their picture."

"Made you pretty mad, though, didn't it?" Joe pressed.

"Were you worried that she'd jump Wright instead of you?"

"No," Quinton yelped, causing one or two on nearby tables to look their way. "Mind your own damned business," he snapped at them.

"Do you ever stop to wonder why people don't like you?" Joe demanded.

"I know why they don't like me and I don't care."

Joe let the matter drop. "What persuaded you that they might lead you to the Middleton Penny?"

"I wasn't persuaded of it," Quinton argued. "I just hoped they might. Slide your mind into gear, Murray, and think about it. It's Christmas Eve and they're wandering round the shops in Leeds. Now suppose they suddenly diverted and went into a dingy little backstreet nowhere place. As a coin collector, what would you think?"

"I'm not a coin collector, but I take your point. And did they?"

"Did they what?" Quinton asked.

"Did they visit a dingy little backstreet nowhere place?"

"No. They were in Waterstone's for ages." Quinton's features clouded again. "Wright's book is taking up half the window there. That aside, they just wandered from shop to shop, and that's why I was bloody annoyed, Murray. I wasted an entire morning following them for nothing."

It was close to the account Kirkland had given him, and Joe charitably accepted it. "You lied about something else, too," he pressed. "You told me that you'd learned from a member of the Regency staff that the LHS, Jennifer and Wright would be here this weekend, which is why you turned up. But that wasn't true. I found an email on her computer telling you that turning up would be to your advantage."

Quinton had the look about him of a man refusing to be intimidated. "I didn't see what concern it would be of yours. You were so busy getting your friend off the hook that you'd pick up on anything, so I laid low."

Joe let the matter drop and to the backing of Sad Café, mulled over his thoughts. An idea occurred to him. "Did

186

you meet George at all, yesterday, before the incident on the dance floor?"

Quinton shook his head. "No. Has someone told you that I did?"

"No. It's a theory, that's all." Before Quinton could demand details, Joe asked, "How did Jennifer introduce George?"

"Word for word?" Quinton asked and Joe nodded. "She said, 'this is George Robson. He's the Leisure Services Director for Sanford Borough Council. He does real work'."

Joe chuckled. "Who told you he was a gardener?"

"Can't remember," Quinton said, "but it was all over the hotel by lunchtime." He stared. "It might have been you."

Joe recalled that Dennis Wright had mentioned George's occupation and he accepted Quinton's explanation. "Tell me something. As honestly as you can. Would you describe yourself as gullible?"

"No," Quinton replied, the anger coming back to his face. "Forget about my money for a minute. I spent my working life in a bank, dealing with pains in the backside on the other side of the window. Near on twenty years I was there. I've heard every excuse, every scam in the book. I can smell 'em a mile off. So no, I am not gullible."

"That's work." Joe pointed out. "How about coins? I don't mean can you recognise a fake. I'm talking a sting here."

Quinton's clear brow creased into a deep frown. "Come again."

"All right, let me spell it out. You want the Middleton Penny. How much would you be prepared to pay for it? According to Wright, the market value is estimated at a hundred and fifty thousand US Dollars. Call that a hundred thousand pounds, which squares with what I've been told about its British value. Now if Jennifer, for example, said she could get it for you, but the transaction was, er, shall we say, black market, what would you be willing to go to?"

The other man shrugged and drank more wine. "Subject to negotiation, about seventy thousand. You have to understand, Murray, this is stolen property. If, and I stress if, I were to get hold of it, the transaction would be illegal. I could be jailed for it and so could the seller, and any intermediaries. The penny, therefore, won't go for its legitimate value. It would be a knock down sale."

"And your position in the negotiations? Upper hand or underdog?"

"Upper hand," Quinton replied. "The owner must be a collector or he wouldn't have it, and the only way a collector would let it go is if he needed the money. That gives me the upper hand. Although I'd be willing to go to seventy, I'd expect to get it for a lot less. Maybe fifty."

Joe took the information in and sifted it. Swallowing the remainder of his beer, he stared Quinton in the eye. "So if Jennifer Hardy said to you, 'come to my room. I have the penny, but we can't conduct business in the open', would you have gone?"

Quinton nodded. "Naturally."

"You wouldn't suspect a trap or a rip off?"

"I knew her," Quinton reminded Joe. "I'd slept with her a good few times. I trusted her." He, too, drained his glass. "What is all this, Murray. Is it another theory? Because what you're talking about didn't happen."

"No, I know it didn't," Joe muttered. "I'm simply wondering whether it was supposed to have happened, and if so, why didn't it?"

Sad Café faded out and Joe turned in his seat to look across to the dance floor. Mavis Barker was on the podium bending Nate Immacyoulate's ear and the deejay was nodding his head as she spoke.

"So you still believe I killed her?"

Quinton's question forced Joe to turn back to the discussion. "What? Oh. I dunno. Did you know Kirkland would be here?"

Quinton shook his head. "Not until I arrived."

"How did that make you feel? Mad?"

"Very annoyed," he admitted, "but still not annoyed enough to murder her."

Somewhere in the background, his brain registered Abba coming through the speakers singing *Knowing Me Knowing You,* and he silently congratulated Mavis. Only her pestering of the deejay would lead to Abba.

He recalled his final challenge to Wright less than half an hour previously. Was he really willing to put himself in the firing line to save George Robson? It wouldn't be the first time, he decided.

"I don't know if you killed her or you didn't," he said, "but I'll be passing all this information on to Chief Inspector Dockerty in the morning, so if there's anything you haven't told me that you think you should, you can find me in 306."

Joe ambled back to his table, his turbulent thoughts mulling over the information he had come by.

With Sheila and Brenda taking turns to hit the dance floor, and occasionally taking it on together, and then Mavis Barker trying to drag him up, Joe found concentration on the multi-strand puzzle almost impossible. Matters were not helped when all three women took the karaoke microphones and belted out Abba's *Mamma Mia* in voices that he later described as fit only to call in the pigs.

At just after 11 he noticed Kirkland in the far corner, the one opposite Quinton, and made his way over.

"I've nothing to talk about, Murray," Kirkland said before Joe could open his mouth.

"Oh, but you have, "Joe replied, ignoring the rebuff in Kirkland's tone. "I want to know how you felt when you got here and found Quinton in residence. Angry enough to consider it an act of betrayal and kill Jennifer?"

Kirkland shook his head. "Haven't you learned anything about me? Don't you know I don't get angry? I manage, Murray. I manage people, I manage situations, and I do that by keeping my cool, not losing it. Killing her would not get me the Middleton Penny, and no matter that she had invited that fool to the negotiations, I would not lose my temper."

"I accept that," Joe said over the noise of a pair from the LHS singing *I Got You Babe.* "Killing Jennifer, however,

189

was not a random act. It was calculated to throw suspicion on George Robson. No man who lost his rag could plan so carefully."

With a wry smile, Kirkland shook his head once more. "It still wouldn't get me the Middleton Penny."

"It would if you knew who had it and you knew that it wasn't George. Is that what you were searching for when you emptied the contents of her handbag over the floor?" Joe did not wait for an answer. "You worked it out, didn't you, that Jennifer had the penny. You saw her hit on George after she'd done talking to you at the bar yesterday afternoon. You knew he was one of our party, and when she introduced him later, you knew he wasn't what he claimed to be, and you guessed, quite rightly, that she was putting him up as the owner to mask the real owner's identity. And that real owner could only be her or Dennis Wright. So you came to her room to negotiate in the early hours, she wouldn't have it and when she turned her back, you killed her. Then you looked for the penny, but couldn't find it, so you stole her laptop, thinking she might have left a clue on there. You also took her diary because amongst the other information it may contain would be her password. Only it wasn't in there, was it? So you got rid of the lot, and sat back while the cops took George away. You're stuck here, along with the rest of us, but all you have to do is maintain this implacable front and walk away on Tuesday morning."

Kirkland gave Joe a small round of applause. "Very clever. Very inventive, but completely wrong. I didn't make your friend at all. When she told me he was the Director of Sanford Leisure Services, I took that at face value and I guessed he owned the penny. But I'm like you, Murray. I cover my back. When I returned to my room, I checked on the internet. The Director of Leisure Services is not named George Robson. Offhand I can't remember his name, but it isn't George Robson."

"Cliff Leasowe," Joe said and Kirkland nodded.

"The name rings a bell. So, at one this morning, I knew that Robson was not who he claimed to be, but I still had

190

him marked down as the current owner of the Middleton Penny. It was only when I learned he was a gardener that I struck him off the list and thought about Jennifer herself or, more likely, Dennis Wright."

"There's too much here that I don't buy," Joe said, "but I can't pin it down yet." Kirkland was about to protest, but Joe held up his hand. "All right, all right, I'm not saying you topped her, but I'm not saying you didn't, either. Something was going on in the background here, and I haven't figured out what it is, yet. Did Jennifer ever mention using Quinton as research for a novel based on coin collecting?"

"No. And frankly, if I were into that sort of thing, Quinton would be the last person I'd use as a research model." He grinned. "Unless I needed a villain."

Joe stood up. "I'd better get back to my friends, but I'm warning you, Kirkland, if I find out you're lying, I'll be back. And in case you want to hit me with a bottle of wine, I'm in 306." He turned his back and walked away.

Rejoining his friends, he found George had wandered off and Brenda was quite tipsy. By midnight, Mavis was roaring drunk. Joe knew that when the lounge closed at one, he would have to help Sheila and Brenda get her back to her room.

"You can put her to bed," he warned. "I don't want a reputation like George's … at least, not with Mavis, I don't."

And yet, the ill-fitting pieces of the complex jigsaw haunted his thinking, and refused to produce a clear picture. No matter which angle he approached the puzzle from, the murder of Jennifer Hardy made no sense.

"If Wright and Jennifer really were trying to scam Quinton and Kirkland, then Wright wouldn't have murdered her, but neither would either of the others. They may have been mad if they realised what was going on, but it would also have provided them with the biggest hold they could hope for over both of them. Two respected academics trying to defraud potential buyers? They'd have Wright and Hardy by the short and curlies."

"Could Jennifer have decided to swap sides?" Sheila asked. "That would annoy Dennis Wright sufficiently to want her out of the way."

"Then why did she give Quinton the bum's rush on the dance floor, and why did she brush Kirkland off, and why did she jump George?" Joe demanded. "By that theory, she should have been in bed with Quinton or Kirkland, not George."

"Kiss," Brenda said.

"You should switch to lemonade," Joe told her. "Asking me to kiss means you've had too much Campari."

"No, no," Brenda said impatiently. "KISS. Kay, eye, double-ess. It's an antonym. Keep it simple, stupid, where stupid is you."

Joe clucked. "You mean an acronym. Brenda, what the hell are you on about?"

"You keep complicating matters with theories of scams and fiddles and hoaxes. To me, it's simple; one of them, either Wright or Kickling or Quizzling –"

"Kirkland or Quinton," Sheila corrected.

"Them, an' all. One of 'em got jealous. There was a barney, and he murdered her. Simple as that. KISS." She downed another slug of Campari and soda.

"It still doesn't make sense," Joe argued. "Quinton may be a slimeball, but he's not stupid. He knows Jennifer was leading him on, and Wright just wasn't interested in Jennifer. He could be faking it, but I've seen those emails. They're for real. He even threatened her with the courts in one of them."

"Perhaps then, George really did kill her," Sheila suggested.

"Now you're deserting him."

"No, Joe," she disagreed. "I'm just looking at the facts. Neither Wright, Kirkland nor Quinton have a motive that you can pin down. You're no closer to proving any of your theories than you were this morning. There is nothing to link her death with any of them."

"There's the book," Joe reminded her. "There was something fishy going on there."

Sheila shook her head. "It could have been a simple error on Dennis Wright's part when he first typed up the manuscript. Jennifer noticed it and put it right in the edited version. Whatever the explanation, the book turned out all right when it was published."

Joe had to admit she had a point, but doubts entered his mind immediately. "No. I don't' agree. It was edited the other way round. She made the change. I'm sure she did." He chewed his lip. "There's something about that book. Can't think what it is, though."

Sheila picked up the book and thumbed through the pages. "You publish your own little booklets, Joe, and how many times have you asked Brenda – when she's sober – or me to read through them, to make sure there are no mistakes. And how many times have we turned up mistakes you didn't notice when you were preparing them?"

Joe was not listening. He was staring at the back cover of *Missing Pennies*, and in particular at the white box in the bottom right hand corner, which contained the barcode and the ISBN, mentally comparing it to the photograph he had seen of the book close to Jennifer's Hardy's dead hand. They were different. He knew they were. What was the difference? A white box approximately two and half inches long by an inch high, in it were printed the bar code, usually identifying the ISBN and the price. Jennifer's copy had a bar code and the numbers … there were no numbers. Yes there were, but they were underneath the barcode. A printer's identifier. And that meant…

"It was a proof copy."

"Prove it." Brenda giggled and sank the last of her drink.

Sheila frowned. "What are you talking about, Joe?"

"Jennifer Hardy's book. Dockerty showed me a photograph, remember? The book was visible in the top corner, near her right hand. I could see the barcode, but there was no ISBN."

"ISBN," muttered Brenda and nodded off to sleep.

"Looks like we have two of them to get upstairs," Sheila disapproved. "So you're saying Jennifer's copy of *Missing Pennies* didn't have the ISBN on the back. What about it?"

"ISBN's are expensive," Joe told her. "I know. I looked into it back in the days when I thought about putting my Casebooks out in paperback. You buy them in blocks, and the current price is something like a hundred and twenty pounds for ten. So small guys like me, who write more as a hobby, tend not to bother with them. But a major publishing house, like Wright's, wouldn't dream of skimping on the cost of an ISBN. The only copies you're likely to see of Wright's title without an ISBN are proof copies. Even then, it's iffy. It's more like he had it printed privately."

"And what's so odd about that?" Sheila asked. "He may well have had it privately published before he sent it to his publisher."

"When he's had work put out by them before? No way. And besides that, why would Jennifer have a proof or private copy? The thing is published, it's out there. You bought a copy yesterday. It's for real and for sale. Why didn't she have the real McCoy?"

Sheila remained perplexed. "I see what you're saying, but I don't think there's anything sinister about it. Maybe it was memento."

Joe downed his drink. "Yeah, and maybe it was a huge scam that went wrong."

194

Chapter Fourteen

Getting a brace of drunken women and one half-drunken man upstairs and into their rooms proved at least as difficult as hassling Dockerty and Barrett for information, and like the police officers, all three were every bit as uncooperative.

After leaving a fully dressed Mavis on her bed, it was past 1 a.m. when Joe left Sheila to deal with Brenda, closed the door to his room, and set up his netbook to bring his account of the weekend up to date. He then pored over his notes, seeking that missing something that would tip the scales.

But it refused to show itself. Armed with a pen and sheets of Regency Hotel notepaper, he scrawled idea after idea on them, ran them through exhaustive checks, even going so far as to set some up as flowcharts, and every time, it amounted to nothing.

It had gone two before he climbed into bed for some much needed sleep.

But sleep, when it came, was constantly disturbed by the need for the bathroom and the intervention of strange dreams in which both George Robson and Jennifer Hardy urged him to see the solution staring him in the face. In one dream, the face of Quinton became that of Wright, then Kirkland, then Patterson and finally Brenda urging him to, 'kiss, kiss, kiss'.

Up again by 6:30, tired and irritable, he returned to the escritoire armed with a cup of tea and fresh determination, and ran once again through his copious notes, and yet still he could not see anything in them. Fresh ideas would occur to him, he ran them through exhaustive chains of logic, but not one of them would plug all the gaps.

Putting on his 'forensic' gloves, he switched on Jennifer Hardy's laptop, checked the emails between her and Wright and her and Quinton, but could find nothing fresh in them. He stared for a long time at the photograph of her and Wright. Quinton glowered in the background; shoppers with laden bags, grown men dressed in fancy costumes, kids everywhere, other couples arm in arm – most ignoring the pair completely, and Joe could find no fresh inspiration in it.

He checked the chapter of *misspnew*, the altered version of *Missing Pennies,* and sought clues there, but there was nothing. Comparing it to Sheila's copy, that single altered paragraph was the only change he could find in the book.

With the time coming up to eight, he threw open the curtain and stared out at the city of Leeds and its magnificent town hall. The cloud had cleared overnight and the sky was a crisp, polar blue. The temperature, he guessed, would have dropped, and that picturesque, Christmas card covering would have turned to a lethal sheet of ice. Even as he watched, a young man trudging his way along, presumably going to work, slipped and fell on the far pavement.

Joe turned back from the window, and ran through his notes once again. Nothing. Zero. Zip. Zilch. No matter what he did, he could account for everything bar this, or that or the other. He could not make any theory fit all the facts.

At 8:20, in a fit of rage, he screwed up the many sheets of paper covered in his scrawl, tossed them into the waste bin, then shut both computers down and made for the bathroom. A shower and shave left him feeling less like a zombie, but still blazing with anger and frustration. Taking the waste bag from the bin beneath his escritoire, he came out of the room at 8:45 muttering murderous curses to himself. Furious that he would have to hand over Jennifer's netbook to Dockerty and still leave George in the frame, he hurled the waste bag into the bin at the end of the corridor and caught the lift down to the ground floor.

He was not surprised to find Sheila and Brenda already seated at a table by the windows. Sheila, as always, looked spritely, but Brenda sat, her elbows on the table, head in hands, complaining and ignoring a bowl of corn flakes.

"She's very fragile, Joe," Sheila explained, "and she blames you."

"Typical," Joe responded, tackling his own bowl of cereal. "You were there when I helped her back to your room. I never touched her. Nor Mavis if she comes complaining."

"According to Brenda, if you hadn't spent so much time talking to Wright and Quinton, she wouldn't have drunk so much, so it's your fault she has a hangover."

"Yeah, right. It is thirsty work talking to those two. But why should it make Brenda drink more?"

"It's counteractive," Sheila said. "When you're with us she has more time to wind you up and less time to drink."

Joe grunted. "Where's George? Not done a runner, has he?"

Sheila nodded across the room. "Sat over there with Alec and Julia Staines." She smiled. "Apparently someone whispered to him that Brenda would be looking after him last night."

Joe shrugged. "I was trying to cheer him up."

"Yes, well, she got drunk and he got nothing." Sheila chuckled and studied Joe's deep frown. "Are you any further forward?"

He shook his head, pushed the cereal to one side and pulled a plate of bacon and eggs front and centre. Picking up his knife and fork, he complained, "I've looked at this business seven ways from Sunday, and none of it makes complete sense."

Sheila sipped at a cup of coffee. "Try me."

Joe tucked into the eggs, savouring the cholesterol and dismissed thoughts of the Lazy Luncheonette. "Think about the two books," he suggested. "We haven't seen the book Jennifer Hardy had. It was covered in either blood or wine, so the cops have it. But my memory of it is clear and it tells me it was a proof or a fake copy. Now why would she want it? Let me run a little scam by you. She and Wright are looking to con Quinton and Kirkland out of a lot of money. They rope George in who's game for a laugh if he can have what he wants with Jennifer. He pretends to be the owner of the Middleton Penny, or at least he knows where he can get it and the asking price is a hundred thousand. Nice round figure, Quinton can negotiate. In order to back up the idea, they have this fake book which they claim contains clues to the penny's whereabouts."

"This sounds a little like one of those archaeological thrillers," Sheila commented.

"Yes," Joe agreed, "and Wright mentioned them when I spoke to him yesterday. A complicated trail leading to a genuine treasure. The only difference is, by and large, there are no holes in those kind of novels. This theory has a huge hole in it."

"Such as?" Sheila asked.

"I checked the altered manuscript on Jennifer's computer, and the only change made was the swapping of the two churches."

"Perhaps that is the clue to the whereabouts of the Middleton Penny," Sheila suggested.

Chewing on a rasher of bacon, Joe disagreed. "That makes no sense. And even if it did, why was Jennifer murdered? If Quinton or Kirkland was going to murder her, it would make sense to wait until they had the penny in hand. Likewise Wright. What's the point of killing her on Christmas Eve when the penny is still missing?" He shook his head again. "I've said all along that to identify the killer, we need a motive. We first concentrated too much on Jennifer's behaviour, and now we've concentrated too much on the Middleton Penny. It was not the motive for killing her."

"It could be if Wright and Quinton or Wright and Kirkland had reached a separate deal which cut her out of the equation," Sheila said. "Perhaps Jennifer learned of it and confronted one or other of them. Things got out of hand and either Wright or Quinton or Kirkland killed her."

"You're just complicating the issue even further," Joe

grumbled. "Remember Brenda and KISS? You're not kissing."

"I thought I might be onto something," Sheila complained. "The one angle you've never thought of is more than one killer."

"Yes I have, and it doesn't fit with Tom Patterson's account of the voices he heard in Jennifer's room or the police forensic evidence. Muttered voices, possibly an argument. If there were more than one man in there, he would have noticed and said so. Also, the cops have only George's dabs in the room. This was one man. But which one?" Joe swilled down his bacon with a mouthful of lukewarm tea. "When we serve tea at the Lazy Luncheonette, at least it's hot." He checked his watch. "It's nine o'clock. You can bet that Dockerty and Barrett will be back within the next hour. That, Sheila, is how long we have to get George off the hook."

Across the table, Brenda stirred. "You're both wrong," she grumbled. "Jennifer Hardy was killed because she was too free with her favours."

"You reckon?"

Brenda nodded and took a sip of coffee with a grimace. "She spent Saturday upsetting half of Leeds, then jumped into bed with George. That's why she was done. Someone felt left out and smashed her one over the head." Her stomach heaved. "You got any Alka Seltzer, Joe?"

"Up in my room. Ask reception for some bicarb," he told her. "But before you do that, tell me how you can be so sure."

"Because you just said none of your theories don't make sense is why," Brenda groaned.

Ignoring the uncharacteristic double negative, Joe complained, "Neither does yours."

"Yes it does," Brenda retorted, suppressing a dyspeptic belch. "If she was up to something between Wright and Quinton and Captain Kirk, do you think they'd murder her here? No, no, they'd wait until the weekend was over, follow her home and do her there. If you're going to shine someone on, you don't do it in a hotel full of people. Not even at half past three in the morning. It's too obvious. And you don't chuck her computer away without smashing it to bits first. Not with all that evidence on it."

"I think most of that is nonsense, Brenda," Sheila said. "People have been murdered in posh hotels before."

"Name one," Brenda challenged.

"I, er, well, off hand, I can't, but I'm sure there must have been cases. However, Joe, Brenda does have a point on the matter of the computer. Anyone with sense would have broken it up."

Joe shook his head. "Not when it's just as easy to drop it in the bins. I told you this earlier. The dork just forgot it was Christmas and the bins wouldn't be emptied."

"And I say that, too, is nonsense." Sheila gestured around the room festooned with decorations. "How can anyone forget it's Christmas?"

Joe drummed his fingers on the table and finished his coffee. "Unless they come from somewhere where the bins might be emptied on Christmas Day."

Brenda groaned and leaned her forearms on the table. "I feel bloody rotten."

"Well if you're gonna be sick get it over with today," Joe ordered. "I'll want you both back at the hobs on Tuesday."

"Wednesday," Sheila corrected. "Tuesday is a public holiday, remember. Even the Lazy Luncheonette is shut."

"You know what I meant."

Brenda straightened up. "I'd better go to the ladies." With a flash of irritation, she stared at her sleeve where a paper serviette had attached itself. "Bloody things. Spill a drop of milk on them and they stick like glue."

A smile spread across Joe's wrinkled features, and just as quickly died. His colour drained. Images flashed into his mind. Sheets of paper screwed up, thrown into the waste bin. The bag from the waste bin thrown into the larger receptacle by the lifts.

He leapt to his feet. "Oh my God. I've thrown it away."

"What?" Sheila asked. "What have you thrown away?"

"His wallet," Brenda muttered.

"It doesn't matter." Joe was already leaving. "When Dockerty gets here, tell him not to do anything until I've spoken to him."

"But … Joe …"

"I know who did it," Joe called over his shoulder as he hurried from the room.

***

Getting permission to check the bins again proved tougher this time than it had the previous day. The same receptionist continued to batter at Joe's defences every time he brought up an argument, and ultimately, he had to resort to the nuclear option.

"One of those bags contains evidence that will convict a murderer, and if you let it go to the incinerator, the police are gonna be chasing your head on a block."

After a brief and irritated phone call, similar to the one the previous day, she eyed him sourly. "All right. You can go through. But you'd better get a move on. There's so much rubbish accumulated, we've had to call a private contractor out to shift it, and he's here now."

"Oh, no." Joe hurried through the bar and out into the rear yard, where, as the receptionist promised, he found the refuse vehicle, alarms bleeping, lifting one of the huge containers up and tipping it over.

"Stop," he shouted. "You're destroying evidence."

The driver cupped a hand to his ear. "Wassat, mate? Can't hear you for this noisy bugger." He waved at his truck.

Slipping and slithering on the icy surface, Joe hurried to his side. "Stop it. Stop the machine. You're carrying off evidence of a murder."

The driver grinned. "Too late, mate," he said as the ram in the truck forced its way forward.

"Is that last night's rubbish?" Joe asked, his heart sinking.

201

"How the hell should I know?" the driver demanded. "Christmas, yesterday, weren't it? Got an urgent call first thing this morning and I have to clear this place twice today."

Joe shoulders slumped. "And I let him get away with it."

"Let who get away with what, sport?" the driver asked.

Joe shook his head. "Never mind."

He trudged back to the bar entrance, casting his sullen gaze over the mounds of black bags, many of them covered in ice, others barely frosted over, certain that the bag he wanted would have been thrown on the top of the first bin. He would make the effort, of course, and try a few bags, but he was sure the evidence he needed was gone and he had thrown it away.

As he neared the mound of bags, a cleaner came out through the bar exit carrying two more bags.

Joe's heart lifted. "Where are they from?"

"Ground floor reception, mate," said the man. "Always the last place we do of a morning."

Joe's heart sank again. He watched the cleaner throw the bags onto the heap, their frost-free gloss contrasting with those left here for the last 48 hours. At least, he consoled himself, those were two bags he wouldn't have to search…

His thoughts tumbled to a halt. Frost-free. The bag he wanted had come from the hotel within the last hour. It would not have had time to freeze over.

He whirled and took in the stack of bags. Six floors, two, three bags per floor, and there were many in front of him that had no covering of ice.

Joe tore into them, dragging them down, opened them, checking their contents, feeling for the balls of screwed up paper he had dropped in his waste bin. He did not even bother to fasten the bags up again when he was through with them, but cast them to one side.

His watch read 9:35, the driver of the refuse vehicle had already gone on his way, and the security officer was back in his little office, watching as he had done the previous day. After a couple of false alarms – Joe was not the only man making handwritten notes during the weekend – he finally found the bag. Frantically tearing it open, he dug into it, cast the screwed up sheets to one side, and finally, his face split into a broad grin, he found the tissue. He brought it up to his nose and breathed in. Yes! Definitely! A result!

He headed for the bar entrance.

"Hey," shouted the security officer, hurtling out of his office. "Who's gonna clear up this mess?"

Joe scanned the bags strewn about the yard, some of the contents tipped out in his frenzied search. He beamed at the security man. "For all I care, you can."

Hurrying through reception, Joe bumped into Ike Barrett.

"Ah, Mr Murray. We wanted a word with you. According to Mrs Riley…"

"Tell your boss to scrounge a private room off the hotel," Joe interrupted. "I need a shower and a change of clothes, and I'll see you there in half an hour. I'll need to speak to Dockerty, Tom Patterson, Dennis Wright, Warren Kirkland and Oliver Quinton. And you'd better tell Dockerty to think about releasing George Robson."

"Mr Murray…"

Once again, Joe interrupted. "And while you're at it, ask Tom Patterson to bring Jennifer's personal effects. We're gonna need 'em."

"Sir, I…"

For the third time, Joe cut in. "I know who did it and why," he said and headed for the lift.

Back in his room, he changed his clothing again, relieved that he had brought plenty with him. Then he sat at the escritoire and enjoyed a cup of tea while he prepared everything.

First he set up Jennifer's netbook, called up *misspnew* and checked the document properties. "Gotcha!" His face split into a broad grin. The fatigue was gone, he felt refreshed, almost excited.

He needed a printer. After a brief telephone conversation with reception, he bagged up Jennifer's computer and the other bits he would need, carried his netbook and all his other evidence back to the ground floor and spent a few moments haggling with the same receptionist before the duty manager came out and confirmed that he had given Joe permission to use the hotel's scanner and printer.

Finally, fully prepared, with the time coming up to ten, he allowed a porter to show him along the ground floor to the conference room.

On entering, he scanned the faces. Yes. He was here.

The word rang round his head. *Gotcha!*

Chapter Fifteen

The hotel management had already supplied carafes of water and cups of tea dispensed from large thermos jugs. Joe helped himself to a cup and took his seat next to Sheila, putting his belongings on the floor.

"Where's Brenda?" he asked.

Sheila pulled a face. "Yukky. She's gone back to bed to sleep it off."

"Best thing for her." Joe looked around the table. Dockerty sat directly opposite him, with Ike to his right from Joe's point of view. Next to Ike was Tom Patterson, next to him was Oliver Quinton, and opposite him, on Sheila's right, Kirkland, Dennis Wright and immediately adjacent to Sheila, George. Dockerty had the case file before him, and Tom had two suitcases alongside his seat; Jennifer's personal effects.

"I'm sorry I'm a minute or two late," Joe apologised. "I had to make sure I had everything."

"Well I hope you're not going to keep us long, Mr Murray," Dockerty complained. "Constable Barrett and I have enough to be getting on with as it is."

"Yeah, I know, and most of it is paddling up the wrong backwater."

Dockerty's disgruntled features turned a shade darker. "Now look –"

"You arrested George in a matter of an hour," Joe cut in, "yet he was innocent. I told you he was innocent, I knew all along he was innocent, and some of the information you gave me confirmed my belief. You said Jennifer Hardy had had sex before she was murdered and that the preliminary DNA results indicated her partner was George, yet you still insisted that he killed her. Why? The only thing you could come up with was that she wouldn't let him in again. What a lot of tosh. George is 55 years old, for God's sake. He may be a charmer but he's no superstud."

"Thanks Joe," George grumbled.

"I'm just telling it like it is, mate, and there is at least one member of the Sanford Third Age Club who can confirm that." He glanced weakly at Sheila. "Unfortunately, Brenda is unwell this morning."

"We also later released Mr Robson, sir," Barrett defended himself and his chief. "We recognised that our evidence against him was a little thin."

"You were too hasty," Joe complained, reaching down into his carrier bag. He came out with his netbook and the sheets of A4 he had had printed by the hotel.

"I've investigated a lot of crimes and mysteries in my time," he said, "but I've never had one as puzzling as this. Now you're an experienced detective, Dockerty. You know there are three elements to murder. Means, motive, opportunity. Means brooks no argument in this case, and neither does opportunity, but as usual motive is the hardest to prove. I insist that George had no motive, and the one you attributed to him is rubbish. He'd already had what he wanted from Jennifer and as far as I'm concerned, George is, and always was, innocent."

"Then let's see you prove it," the senior policeman challenged.

"I'm going to," Joe declared. "As I said, this case has been about motive, and if we eliminate George from the list of suspects, who are we left with?" He stared about the table. "Tom Patterson, a man rejected by Jennifer, Dennis Wright, a man hounded by Jennifer, Oliver Quinton and Warren Kirkland a pair of men used by Jennifer, and me, a man verbally abused by Jennifer…"

The two coin collectors immediately protested but a warning glance from Dockerty signalled them to silence and Joe carried on.

"I eliminated myself from the list because I know I didn't

do it, and of the four remaining men, who had the biggest motive for killing her? Well, we'll see about that in a minute or two. First, let's get some nonsense out of the way."

He spread his two sheets of paper on the table. Each had a diagram on it, a computer-generated representation of the drawing Jennifer Hardy had left behind.

"Let's look at this note Jennifer is supposed to have left," Joe went on. "This, Dockerty, is the way you showed it to me. It's a copy of the computer-generated image you prepared."

He indicated the first sheet on which was printed:

"Two lines curling in opposite directions, and the international sign for Venus, the female. Your interpretation? A couple having sex and a woman. It indicated to you that the woman was a victim and that the killer was the man with whom she had had sex. I said at the time that it was a deduction made on the thinnest of pretexts. Why didn't she indicate a man instead of a woman? That would have made more sense, and the sign for a man, the sign for Mars, isn't much harder to draw than this."

"Give us your alternative again," Dockerty invited.

"All right," Joe continued. "This is the way I see it."

He pointed to the second sheet with the drawing inverted along both axes.

"You had the drawing upside down," Joe insisted, "and it was this way when it was found near Jennifer's dying hand. When you turn it this way, the *correct* way, it has an entirely different meaning."

"You're right," Barrett said. "It doesn't mean anything, now. I know you told us about the church thing and how they'd been swapped, but with those two arrows added, it means nothing."

"To you, Ike, no," Joe smiled, "but that's because you're young and you didn't have the kind of education the rest of us did." He swung his attention to the right. "Tom, your speciality is maps. That Venus symbol. Now that I've turned it upside down, what does it say to you?"

"A church, and it's been switched," Patterson said.

"Thank you," Joe replied and smiled at Dockerty. "You see? Tom agrees with my interpretation."

"It still makes no sense," Dockerty complained, "because swapped churches make no sense."

"Yet," Joe responded. "Anyway, I was simply reinforcing my argument." He addressed the whole table again. "There are other cartographers' symbols for churches, but this is one of the oldest and it can still be found on some maps."

"The curves are different on your printout, Murray," Dockerty objected.

"That's because on your original printout they looked less like the ones Jennifer Hardy drew. On the original drawing, each curl had a tiny blob at the end, as if she were trying to draw a tadpole ... or an arrow. You thought it indicated sperm. It's only when you look at the drawing this way up, that the meaning becomes clear and it has nothing to do with sex. It indicates that, as Tom has just said, a church, or churches have been transposed. Swapped."

An air of puzzlement pervaded the room. Dockerty summed it up. "It still makes no sense."

"I repeat, not yet, but it will soon," Joe promised. "For now, let's leave the meaning of the drawing and think about Jennifer's dying moments when, according to you, she produced it."

"Do you believe she didn't?" Dockerty challenged.

"I know damn well she didn't," Joe insisted.

Dockerty's thin smile spread again. "Prove it."

Joe, too, smiled. "I will. Do you have the photographs of the crime scene? The ones you showed me?"

Dockerty held up the case file. "Right here."

"Take out the photograph of the drawing close to Jennifer's hand."

Frowning, the Chief Inspector did so. "Go on."

"Look at it closely," Joe instructed, "and tell us what you see?"

"Her hand, the drawing, some of the contents of her handbag, the bottom edge of a book." Dockerty looked up from the photograph. "I see nothing special."

"No?" Joe asked. "Nothing like a mobile phone, for instance?"

"Oh. Well that's there, obviously," Dockerty objected. "You know damn well it was there, but there's nothing sinister about that, Murray. We all carry them. Even you."

"Correct," Joe agreed. "I asked young Ike about the contents of her handbag, and he assured me there was no sign of a diary, address book or notebook. So the first question I ask is where did she get the scrap of paper to draw her cryptic message? Where did she get the pencil? Now you, Dockerty, told me that the eyeliner pencil was out of the shot, close to her left hand, but although we can't be a hundred percent certain, we don't believe Jennifer was left handed. Am I right about that, Tom?"

Patterson stirred as if surprised to hear his name. "What? Oh. Sorry, Joe. No. She wasn't. I told you yesterday, I'm certain she was right handed."

"Which begs the question," Joe picked up his thread, "why was the drawing near her right hand and the pencil near her left? They would only be that way round if she was a southpaw, which we've just heard, she wasn't. I'll tell you why they were laid the way they were. Because when he put them there, the killer was looking at her from her head, and her arms would have been reversed in his view. He was so hyped up at having just murdered her, that he made his first mistake."

"This is all supposition, Murray," Dockerty protested.

Joe shook his head. "It would be except for the phone. Now, I want you to picture this. Her killer has just smashed a bottle on the back of her head. She's hurt; she's dying; she may or may not have known that. And whether she knew it, was irrelevant. She was in a lot of pain." Joe inflected sufficient incredulity into his next words to let everyone know his opinion. "And she takes a piece of paper she doesn't have and draws a few figures on it?" He paused to let the message sink in. "Get real. If she was still alive, if she could move, she would have picked up her mobile phone and dialled 999."

A hush fell over the room as the implications of Joe's words sank in.

Sheila broke it. "So Jennifer never drew the pictogram?"

Joe shook his head. "It was drawn earlier, maybe as she lay dying, maybe months before. It was planted there by her killer. And once you know that the drawing was part of a pre-planned killing, then it becomes obvious that George didn't kill her because he didn't meet her until Saturday evening."

Dockerty disagreed. "It means nothing of the kind, Murray. For all you know, that doodle could have been in her bag, and Robson just emptied it out when he killed her."

"For the millionth time," George protested, "I didn't kill this bint."

"I'd be grateful if you didn't refer to Jennifer like that," Patterson complained.

Disregarding both men, Joe said to Dockerty, "But

you've never explained why George would even touch her handbag."

"We're working on the theory that he was trying to make it look like a robbery, sir," Barrett chipped in.

George was about to protest again, but Joe beat him to it. "A robbery where nothing was stolen?" Joe asked.

"The laptop was stolen, Joe," Tom Patterson said, and a smug smile crossed Dockerty's face. A smile that said, 'get out of that'.

Joe was not in the least put out. "All right. It seems I have to work a bit harder."

The Chief Inspector got to his feet. "Fine. While you're doing that, Constable Barrett and I have some proper inquiries to make."

"Not so fast," Joe said. "When I said I have to work harder, I meant I have to work harder to persuade you."

Huffing out his breath, Dockerty sat down again.

Confident of his audience, Joe began, "I said earlier we need to look at the possibilities and decide who had the strongest motive for killing Jennifer Hardy: Oliver Quinton, Warren Kirkland or Dennis Wright."

All three men protested vociferously and Dockerty called for order.

"I told you I never left my room," Quinton snapped, determined to have the last word.

"And I told you I didn't care what Jennifer got up to," Wright growled, equally determined to be heard.

"And I think it's time I called my lawyers," Kirkland said, losing his cool for the first time since Joe had met him.

"All three of you have lied to me over the last twenty-four hours," Joe said.

"Regardless of that, I notice you left out Mr Robson," Dockerty challenged.

"Patience, Chief Inspector. I'll get there." Joe grinned. "Let's look at the possibilities, huh?"

He dug into his bag again and came out with his gloves. Slipping them on, he pulled out Jennifer's laptop, hooked it into a floor-level mains socket with his netbook's power

211

cord, and switched on.

"I'm not fond of digging through rubbish," he announced while he waited for the computer to boot up, "but I spent an hour yesterday in the rear yard of this hotel, sorting through bags of crap to find this machine." He held up his gloved hands. "I've worn these all the time, Chief Inspector, so my prints are not on it."

Dockerty nodded his appreciation, and Joe went on.

"The first problem I had was working out Jennifer's password, but when I thought about it, it wasn't too difficult. The killer thought she kept it in her diary." Joe took out the book and laid it on the table next to the computer. "Truth is, she was way smarter than that. The password hung round her neck. That odd date I had to figure out on Saturday night." Joe pushed another sheet of paper onto the table. It contained only one line of characters printed at the very top of the page. MDCCMMLVIII. "Jennifer told me that it only made sense if you took out two of the letters. I did that on Saturday night and it left me with one, seven, five, eight. If I put the two ems back into it, I get one, seven, em, em, five, eight. Seventeen fifty-eight, the year of the Middleton Light Railway and MM, the initials of Matthew Murray, the engineer who built the Salamanca, the first steam engine to bring coal from Broom Colliery to the canal side in Leeds. It was Jennifer's specialist subject. She even has a picture of the Salamanca as her desktop wallpaper. When I typed that code in, I got straight into the computer, and you'd be astonished what I found in there."

"You should have handed it to us," Dockerty complained.

"You'd already gone home," Joe retorted. "And anyway, if I'd given it you this morning, you'd have shoved it to one side and ignored it while you carried on hassling poor George … poor *innocent* George. Anyway, like I was saying, I found tons of stuff on there, including hundreds of emails. Some of them were between Jennifer and Wright, others were between her and Quinton, her and Kirkland."

He sat back as the laptop finally settled into operation. "And now, I'm gonna tell you two stories."

Dockerty sighed again.

Joe ignored him. "The first is all about a greedy, ignorant piece of bile from Sheffield who wanted only one thing to make his life complete: the Middleton Penny."

Quinton leapt to his feet. "I don't have to listen to this. You'll hear from my lawyers." He made a move to leave, but Dockerty's interest had already been caught.

"Stay where you are, Mr Quinton. Let's hear what Murray has to say." He raised his eyebrows at Joe. "Constable Barrett explained something about the Middleton Penny to me. Apparently he got the story from Mr Patterson."

"Quinton wasn't alone in his desire for the penny," Joe said. "Kirkland wanted it too."

"But not badly enough to kill her, Mr Murray." Kirkland appeared to have regained some of his aplomb.

"No? We'll see. Let's turn our attention to Jennifer herself. I've listened to a lot over this last twenty-four hours, but nothing that would adequately explain everything that's happened. Throughout it all, however, I've heard what an angel Jennifer Hardy was, and I've also heard what a slut she could be, especially when she felt a man could help her get whatever she wanted."

Patterson rose. "I'm sorry, Joe, but I can't sit here and listen to this. Jennifer was a –"

"Sit down, Tom," Joe commanded. "This isn't going to be comfortable, but you have to hear it. All of you."

Patterson sat down again and Joe consulted his notes.

"What I didn't hear, what I had to work out for myself, was how big a crook Jennifer Hardy was."

The allegation drew gasps from around the table and this time it was Wright who protested.

"Chief Inspector, do we have to sit here and listen to this?"

"For the time being, yes," Dockerty said, his face set like thunder. "But it had better lead to a solution."

"It does," Joe assured him. "I said Jennifer was a crook. But she wasn't born or educated as such. She led a comparatively honest life, until these last few months, and it was an event during the last year that turned her from a respected historian to a confidence trickster and a thief. I said to Tom yesterday, people are creatures of habit. When those habits change, it's usually because of pressures from elsewhere. What changed Jennifer from a respectable academic into a potential thief was her love for you, Dr Wright. More specifically, her unrequited love for you, a love you didn't want and didn't return."

Wright fumed. "If you're accusing me –"

"I'm accusing you of nothing, yet," Joe cut in. "The only thing you were guilty of was not wanting her, and that's not a crime. You tried to make some kind of amends in the bar last night, when I spoke to you, but I never really believed you."

Joe addressed the room in general.

"Jennifer wanted to become the third Mrs Dennis Wright more than anything else, and she was willing to do anything to get there. Anything. Wright persistently rejected her. He told me that even if he were in the hunt for a third wife, Jennifer would never be a candidate. Too flighty, especially when she'd had a few. Jennifer would never see that. We're all a bit that way inclined. When things don't go as we planned, we will look anywhere for a reason other than at our own shortcomings. She thought of many reasons why Wright didn't want her, including the famous lover who doesn't exist, but eventually, she concluded that the real reason was that he was practically broke. Am I right, Dr Wright?"

The academic appeared uncomfortable. "It was part of her thinking, yes."

"So she came up with a plan to rescue the good doctor," Joe went on. "When her trip to Alabama was first announced, both Quinton and Kirkland latched onto it through routine publicity, and both men got in touch with her." Joe patted the computer. "The emails are still on here,

Dockerty."

He checked his notes again. "They wanted the Middleton Penny, and a chapter of Wright's book, *Missing Pennies*, was devoted to that penny and its partner coin at Hawksworth. Neither Kirkland nor Quinton heard from her for a long time, then suddenly, she emailed, inviting them individually to meet her here, in the Regency. I guess they each met her three or four times between September and the end of November, and each time, she slept with them both." He shot a glance at Kirkland. "Don't deny it. She kept a record of it," he lied.

About to interrupt, Kirkland shut his mouth and Joe silently congratulated himself in the accuracy of his guess.

"Bedding these men was her way of building up their trust for what was to be a massive sting. At the beginning of December, she sent them each a final email telling them it would be to their advantage to come to the Regency over Christmas. Neither man knew about the other."

"How do you know?" Dockerty asked.

"Because when you study her emails – there are literally about two thousand on the machine – you see that Jennifer was quite conversant with email. If she needed to email more than one person at a time, she added the second, third, fourth addresses to the outgoing message. In the case of Kirkland and Quinton, she didn't. The messages are duplicated, but they're addressed as individual posts to each man. But you don't have to take my word for it. Ask the men. Kirkland, Quinton, while you were negotiating with Jennifer, were either of you aware of the other?"

"No," said Kirkland.

Quinton merely shook his head.

"You see?" Joe glanced around the table, satisfied with the worry of the possibly guilty. "The emails end at the beginning of December, so I can only guess at what happened after that. Both men probably rang for more details. Jennifer told them clearly that the Middleton Penny was for sale and it would be in this hotel over Christmas. The timing was crucial. You can't have valuable items like that assessed and verified by experts over the festive period because the bods who do that kind of thing are off work enjoying themselves. Jennifer told them the coin would go to the highest bidder."

"This is utter twaddle," Quinton protested.

"No it isn't," Joe argued. "You told me that you expected the penny to be here. You didn't tell me you'd be carrying a large amount of cash, though, did you?" Quinton fell silent and Joe carried on speaking to Dockerty. "If we want to get technical about it, the Middleton Penny is stolen property. Neither Kirkland nor Quinton could be sure of the legal position, but if anyone has the right to that penny, it's the Diocese of Ripon, the people from whom it was stolen forty years ago. Kirkland and Quinton could feasibly be prosecuted for receiving stolen property. So the entire transaction would be carried out in cash. Kirkland told me that it's not unusual, especially when the coin's true ownership is difficult to pin down. In order to prevent anyone doing a runner, an intermediary – in this case Jennifer – would hold the cash and the coin until it could be verified as genuine. At that point, she would hand the cash, minus experts' fees and her commission, to the owner, and the coin to its new owner." He shot glances at both collectors. "Again, don't take my word for this. Ask them. How much were you carrying Kirkland?"

He coughed to hide his embarrassment. "Er, one, er, one hundred thousand."

"And you, Quinton?" Joe demanded.

"The same," the other replied. "And I was prepared to go higher if I had to. But she never told us it would be a bloody auction. I never even thought about it until I arrived and found him here." He jerked a thumb sideways at Kirkland.

Joe smiled. "She was clever, that woman. Very clever. Quinton told me he'd come in at fifty and be prepared to go to seventy or maybe eighty thousand. Jennifer needed at least a hundred grand. If you work that out at current exchange rates, it comes to about 160,000 dollars; enough to pay off Wright's debts and leave some over to start a new life with her lover in the States. The only way she could up the price was by playing them off against one another."

"There's no way she would have cleaned up a hundred thousand in commission on a deal like this," Kirkland protested. "Even if the price went that high, the best she could hope for would be ten thousand."

"Not if she intended doing a runner with the money," Joe countered and again the room stared in astonishment. Joe turned Jennifer's netbook, a single email open, to face Dockerty. "I found this last night. It's a reservation on a flight from Manchester to New York leaving this morning, a full forty-eight hours before they could have the penny verified as genuine." He pointed at Kirkland and Quinton. "By the time these two saps realised what was going on, she would be the other side of The Pond, through immigration and she'd have disappeared into America."

A loud gasp reached his ears. When he looked, Quinton appeared almost apoplectic with rage.

Dockerty interceded before the coin collector could vent his fury. "This is all a bit naïve, Murray. She couldn't possibly hope to get away with it."

"It's naïve from our point of view, Chief Inspector, but remember, we're trying to reconstruct her efforts. Jennifer had had a long time to iron out all the difficulties. She's the only one who could tell us all the tiny details, and she was a clever woman. She would have found ways and means of getting round it all. The first thing she would need was a mug to play the part of the coin's owner. Members of the LHS were out. They knew her too well and they probably knew the tale of the Middleton Penny, too, so she couldn't use any of them. It had to be someone who didn't know her, someone she had met only recently. Someone like George Robson."

Now it was George's turn to gape. "Me? Why me?"

"Because you hit on her in the bar, George. She knew what you were after, but she also knew you were a bit of a berk. Pliable, manipulable…" Joe frowned. "Is there such a word?"

"I think you mean capable of being manipulated, dear," Sheila said.

"Whatever. George tried his luck, she brushed him off. Ten minutes later, she was back and all over him. She had found her mug."

"Joe…" George began, only to be cut off by his chairman.

"Shut up, George. Jennifer asked George to play the part of Director of Leisure Services for Sanford Borough Council. Why? Kirkland summed it up. A common gardener would not be in possession of the Middleton Penny. That's a measure not only of Kirkland's snobbery, but of Jennifer's too. The Director of Leisure Services is a man who earns a vast salary…" Joe trailed off, suddenly thinking about Cliff Leasowe at Sanford Town Hall. "Yes, and he does bugger all for it."

"Concentrate on the job at hand, Joe," Sheila advised.

"Sorry. Where was I? Oh, yes. The Director of Leisure Services is a man who earns a large salary and he's the kind of well-educated man who just might own the Middleton Penny. Someone she could pass off on Kirkland and Quinton." He leaned forward, pulled the netbook to him, and opened up the photograph folder. "Again, we don't have to take my word for this. Look at the photograph of George." He showed it to the table. "Why have a picture of him holding a CD?"

"You're not making sense," Dockerty pointed out.

Joe hit the forward key on the computer, and the image switched to the doctored example. "Does it make sense now?"

Dockerty's eyes widened. "How the hell…?" he trailed off and looked at Joe.

"Photoshop," Joe said. "I don't know much about it, but I do know that you can pull all sorts of stunts with pictures, and Tom told me Jennifer was quite talented at illustrating her own books. She produced some of those illustrations by computer, and if you check the machine when we're through, you'll find some of her work on the hard drive. She manipulated the original image of George to make it look as if he was holding the Middleton Penny in a presentation case. If you zoom the image in, you'll see that the date on the penny is 1933." He turned his attention to Patterson. "Tom, you brought Jennifer's personal effects. Have you looked through them?"

The other shook his head. "I didn't care to."

Concentrating on Dockerty, Joe said, "If you check, you'll probably find a penny in a presentation case, but it won't be a 1933 penny. She will have altered the date in Photoshop."

To Barrett, Dockerty said, "Do it."

"Yes, sir."

Barrett took the bags off to one side and began going through them.

Leaning across Sheila, George whispered, "This is not making sense, Joe."

"It will as we go on, George," Joe promised. "And it'll completely exonerate you."

"As well as making me look a complete prat."

Joe smiled. "You've always been a complete prat. Especially when some trollop offers to take her knickers off."

George frowned. "Trollop?"

"Brenda remembered the word for us yesterday, George," Sheila assured him.

"Found it!"

Barrett's declaration called them back to the table.

He held a presentation case up. Inside was a British penny, looking to Joe more silver than copper bronze.

"May I?" Quinton asked and Barrett passed him a pair of forensic gloves with the penny. Quinton looked it over, sniffed disdainfully, and handed it to Kirkland.

"A 1938 George the Sixth penny, with mint lustre," Quinton declared.

Kirkland agreed. "Probably uncirculated. Value perhaps five pounds." He handed it back to Barrett."

"And she altered the date using Photoshop?" Dockerty

219

asked.

Joe nodded. "She knew how to use that software, I don't. I imagine changing the eight to a three is pretty easy. Cutting it out then overlaying it on the image of George probably needed a deal more patience, but if she really was an expert, as Tom suggests, she could probably do it in minutes. George left her at two in the morning, she was killed at three thirty, so there was a 90-minute window, which was ample time for her to set up the picture. To boot, there's a photo of the penny in its case on the hard drive."

He paused for breath and marshalled his thoughts.

"I told you we were speculating, and here's the way I see it. Jennifer has introduced Kirkland and Quinton to George. Later, she would have shown them the photograph, and announced that she was prepared to act as an intermediary. She needed cash from them, fifty thousand each, and she would secure the penny from the dealer. They would be able to view the penny today in her room. The highest bidder would take the prize. Both Kirkland and Quinton trusted her implicitly. 'What's not to trust?' Kirkland said when I asked him. This should all have happened yesterday, but of course, it didn't. Had it done so, Jennifer would have been half way to America now and it was the last these two would have seen of their money."

Dockerty shook his head. "There is no way she would get a hundred grand in cash out of the country, Murray."

"I know," Joe agreed. "To get away with it, she needed an ally. Didn't she, Dr Wright?"

Wright appeared flummoxed. "I'm sorry?"

Joe sighed. "Lies, lies and more lies," he whined. "Everyone is lying. All right, let me spell it out. She didn't have a hope in hell of getting the money out of the country, but according to her calculations, she didn't have to. All she had to do was get it to a luggage locker at the railway station here in Leeds, or maybe one at Manchester Airport. Then, once she brought Dennis Wright into her confidence, he could wait until the police, Quinton and Kirkland had stopped looking for her in this country, and pay the money into a bank account for transfer to the USA. The bank would ask questions, obviously, but Dr Wright is a distinguished academic and it would be no surprise to find him carrying a large amount of cash around. He could even pay it into a dozen different accounts with a dozen different banks, as long as it was all transferred out to a single account in the States. What I'm saying, Dockerty, is that there are ways and means of getting around the money laundering once you have an accomplice."

"Murray, I was not an accomplice," Wright protested.

"I know you weren't and that's where Jennifer made her biggest mistake." Concentrating on the Chief Inspector, Joe said, "Jennifer kept everything to herself until the morning of Christmas Eve. She told no one. She had Quinton and Kirkland earmarked as mugs, George would become an innocent dupe, and she was certain that Wright loved her. So certain, that when she met him on Saturday, she told him everything … and he told her he wanted nothing to do with it." Now he stared at Wright again. "Please stop me when I get it wrong, Dr Wright. Jennifer was shocked. She probably pleaded with him that the plan had gone too far for her to stop, but Wright would not budge. He had his reputation to consider, and he would not become mixed up in any kind of criminal act. They trailed the streets of Leeds and she begged and pleaded with him, but he was completely unmoved. He really did not want her as his wife or life partner, and he wasn't interested in ripping off those two for a hundred grand. The argument went on and on for several hours until, in the cafeteria at Debenhams, she finally snapped. 'Please your damned self. You know what happens next'. A threat that I've been trying to make sense of since Saturday afternoon." Joe swung his gaze back to the historian. "Why don't you cut out all the bull, Wright, and tell us what it really meant?"

Wright shook his head and looked down at his trembling hands.

"Dr Wright?" It was Dockerty, encouraging him to answer the question.

Wright looked up and stared at the wall behind Kirkland's head. He took a deep breath and let it out with a hiss. "Murray has it right. She told me soon after she met me at the railway station. I tore her to pieces for it, told her to forget it and she told me it had gone too far for that. She carried on harrying and pressuring me, and then, in Debenhams, I told her why I didn't want her. Because she was a well-educated, but drunken slut. She told me she had a right to expect some return on her emotional investment, I said no, and then she said if I didn't toe the line, she would let Quinton and Kirkland know what was going on, and she would blame me." He sneered at both men. "As if that was some kind of threat. I told her to go ahead, and that's when she lost it."

"But she never told either of them," Joe said.

"No. If she had, both would have come for me in the bar."

Ike Barrett half raised his hand. "I don't want to seem, er, picky, Mr Murray, but you, yourself, pointed out that the photograph of George Robson was taken in the early hours of Christmas morning, almost twelve hours after Dr Wright and Mrs Hardy had their fall out in Debenhams."

"Jennifer," Wright said. "I think she was trying to play hardball. Maybe she decided she would go through with it after all, take the money and run for it. After all, with that kind of cash, she didn't have to go to the States. She could have driven over to Hull and hopped on a Continental Ferry. She'd be in Rotterdam or Zeebrugge by tomorrow morning and by the time either of these dorks raised the alarm, she could be anywhere in Europe. I don't know what she was thinking when she took Robson to her room."

"Yet you lied, Wright," Joe challenged. "I asked you what Jennifer meant when she emailed you with a solution to your financial problems, and you told me that in your Skype conversation she mooted a novel based on the Middleton Penny."

"I was not lying," Wright assured the room. "It's what she said during that conversation. I scotched the idea immediately. I wasn't interested in novels or her. But she never said anything about this kind of scam until I got here the day before yesterday."

Joe rounded on Quinton. "You lied, too. When I put Wright's explanation to you, you said that Jennifer had admitted using you to research a novel."

Quinton began to sweat. "I, er, I was trying to keep the real truth from you, Murray. You'd already said that if I got the Middleton Penny, it may be considered an illegal transaction. Then you mentioned her using me to research some novel and I thought, yeah, it sounds good, so I went along with it. That's all. I swear it."

"Kirkland didn't lie" Joe declared, "and it told me that the other two did."

"This is all very well, Murray," Dockerty said, "but it doesn't tell us who killed Jennifer ... or why."

"I'm getting there," Joe promised. "What I've done so far is given you three men with serious motives for killing her. Did Quinton or Kirkland find out about the fake penny or did Wright set out to protect his precious reputation? Quinton, Kirkland, Wright. Which one murdered her?"

Chapter Sixteen

The room erupted as the three men got to their feet, each protesting his innocence, verbal abuse hurled at Joe, causing George to stand and roll up his sleeves ready to enter the fray if he had to. Threat and counter-threat rang round the room, Joe sat it out, Sheila flapped, pleading for calm, Barrett hovered on the fringes trying to keep men apart, but it was only when Dockerty bellowed for order that a rumbling silence fell.

"I'll say this for you, Murray, you don't half know how to cause trouble," the Chief Inspector commented.

"It's a good job Brenda is ill, or she'd have slapped them all about a bit," Joe replied. Taking up the narrative reins again, he went on, "We have three men with possible motives for killing her. Wright to protect his reputation, Quinton because he'd been made to look a fool and Kirkland because there was always the danger that she would tell his wife that they'd been sleeping together. When it comes to Quinton and Kirkland, we also have to consider the possibility that they believed she had the Middleton Penny in her room. Quinton is especially interesting. Like Kirkland, he followed Wright and Jennifer round Leeds on Saturday, but when I challenged him, he denied it."

"I explained that to you, Murray," Quinton gasped.

"And how do I know that your explanation isn't just a lot of hot air?" Joe demanded. "Imagine this. Quinton approached Wright in the bar on Saturday evening, asking about the Middleton Penny. Wright gave him short shrift, but you began to put two and two together, didn't you, Quinton? You saw her dancing with George Robson, the Executive Director of Leisure Services for Sanford Borough

Council. You watched them go back to her room, and you knew what was happening, didn't you?"

Quinton sweated. "This is ridiculous."

"She was laying George the way she had laid you," Joe went on. "Why? Because a well-connected man like him, the Director of Leisure Services for Sanford Borough Council, was exactly the kind of man who would possess the Middleton Penny. Successful, well heeled, a bob or two behind him, and his job under threat from government policies. And Jennifer was in there screwing him for all she was worth so she could come to a deal which would see you and Kirkland fighting it out, head to head, using your money to knock spots off each other and all to own the Middleton Penny. Then she told you to go to hell when you approached her on the dance floor."

Joe paused to call up the photograph of Wright and Jennifer.

"So you waited, bided your time, and went back to her room in the early hours. You pleaded with her, she told you where to get off again and she made a fatal mistake. She turned her back on you. And that's when you hit her on the head."

"No. I never –"

"Then," Joe pressed on, ignoring Quinton's attempted interruption, "you came up with an idea. All the contact details would be on her computer. You quickly drew the pictogram – neat piece of thinking that – because you knew it would point the finger at George, then you took the computer and her diary and got the hell out before someone, Tom for example, could raise the alarm."

Quinton trembled and shook his head. "It didn't happen, I tell you."

"But you made a mistake, didn't you? The password wasn't in her diary and you didn't have the brains to figure it out for yourself. You also knew that when they let George go, the cops would get to a room-by-room search, so you had to get rid of the computer and the diary. You threw them in your waste bin and when you came out of your room at half past seven the following morning, you dumped them in the bin at the end of the corridor, knowing they would be taken away by the cleaners and they'd be on their way to the rubbish dump by mid-afternoon."

"I tell you it never happened," Quinton shouted.

"And if you need proof of how angry he was, Dockerty, take a look at this."

Joe spun the computer round so everyone could see the photograph filling the screen.

"A photograph of Dennis Wright and Jennifer Hardy taken at lunchtime on Saturday, here in Leeds. But look who's behind them." He pointed at the millionaire. "Oliver Quinton. And look at the fury in his face."

Dockerty and Barrett studied the photograph, then Quinton, and then the photograph again.

The Chief Inspector turned calmly on the suspect. "Well, Mr Quinton? What do you have to say to that?"

"Nonsense. All of it." Sweat poured from under his greasy hairline. "I admit I approached Wright concerning the penny, I admit I went onto the dance floor to speak to Jennifer, I admit I've been sleeping with her for a few months, and yes, when I saw them, when she introduced him, I thought that Robson might be the owner of the penny … until I found out who he really was on Sunday morning. And when she told me where to get off, I thought maybe Kirkland had already cut a deal with her. But I swear I never went anywhere near her room on Saturday night. I was pretty teed off with her, sure, but after the incident on the dance floor, I went to bed. I didn't sleep well because I was so bloody mad at her, but I swear I never left my room."

"Why so angry on that photograph, Mr Quinton?" Barrett asked.

"I always look like that. It gets me what I want. Normally." He pointed at Wright. "When Jennifer and he stopped some bloke in the street and asked him to take a picture, all I could think was they were the two people standing between me and the Middleton Penny."

"Which seems to me to be a pretty good motive for

226

murder," Dockerty said.

"It is," Joe agreed.

Barrett stood and moved behind Quinton.

"But unfortunately, he's telling the truth."

A gasp ran round the table at Joe's declaration.

"What? Murray, just what are you playing at?"

"Calm down, Dockerty. You'll have a heart attack at that rate." Joe pointed at Quinton. "He's worthless and he deserved to suffer like that. Even though he didn't kill Jennifer, he should go to prison for life anyway, just for breathing the same air as me."

"Now look –" Quinton began, but Joe cut him.

"Just shut up. And let this be a lesson to you. Don't you curse at my members again. You're sleaze, Quinton. I may be bad tempered, but I don't treat people with the same contempt as you." Joe concentrated on Dockerty. "There are other factors, Chief Inspector, which I haven't explained yet, and when you take those into account, you realise that however much I'd love Quinton to have done it, however much I think he deserves to go down for life, he can't have. To begin with, I don't think he'd have had the wit to draw that pictogram so quickly. I don't think he even has the brains to think of something like that, never mind think of it so quickly. If it was him, he'd be more likely to steal the computer and the diary and get out quick." He swung his gaze on Kirkland. "But you're more rational. You're a thinker. You could conceivably have come up with it."

Kirkland maintained his air of calm. "You're right. I could. But I didn't. I felt the same way as Quinton, and I, too, suspected that Jennifer may have already reached a deal with him. But I've told you before, Murray, I manage people, I manage situations, and there's no profit in losing your temper. Murdering Jennifer would not get me what I wanted, therefore, much though I may have thought about it, I didn't murder her."

"I know you didn't." Joe returned to addressing the room again. "You see, if you tack this onto Quinton or Kirkland, there are too many things which can't be explained. I've already pointed out that Jennifer didn't draw the pictogram, so it would never have pointed at George. Instead, it would point at someone else; the man who killed her. The whole case had me foxed for a long time. How could I explain everything that went on? I couldn't. It was only when I began to forget about the Middleton Penny and Jennifer's silly little plan that I began to stumble on the truth." Joe's gaze rested on the young constable, still standing behind Quinton. "Ike, in that picture of Jennifer's hand, we can just see the bottom of a book. It's covered in wine or blood or something, but I believe it's a copy of Dr Wright's book, *Missing Pennies*. Do you have it to hand?"

"It's with the other evidence, sir."

"Could you get it, please?"

Barrett looked to his chief for permission. Dockerty hesitated a moment and then nodded. Barrett hurried out of the room and Dockerty glowered. "What is going on here, Murray? You've already accused Quinton and Kirkland of killing her, then said they couldn't have done. Who are you going to blame now? The publisher?"

"All in good time, Chief Inspector. We need that book before I can clear it up, but it's a devious tale." He looked at Dennis Wright. "Seriously devious."

Wright stared back. "Are you trying to say there is something wrong with my account of the two pennies, Mr Murray?"

Joe shrugged. "You're the historian. You tell me."

Wright bristled. "I'm not just a historian, I'm an authority. My account is as accurate as it can be."

"Is it?" Joe smiled evilly. "In that case, you have nothing to worry about, do you?"

Barrett returned with the book sealed in an evidence bag.

"You'll need gloves on, son," Joe told him, "because I'll need you to open that book and read a short section of it."

Frowning, Barrett slipped on a pair of forensic gloves.

"Good lad," Joe congratulated him. "We'll make a professional detective of you, yet. Now will you open the book at page 178 and read the third paragraph down.

Still puzzled, Barrett first checked with his boss, who gave a nod, and then removed the book from the bag, teased open the stained pages and thumbed gently through them until he came to the chapter Joe had asked for.

Clearing his throat, he read, "In 1970, during renovation work, the penny encased in the cornerstone at St Mary's, Hawksworth, was stolen. Alarmed at the theft, in order to prevent a repetition, the Diocese of Ripon ordered that the penny in the foundations of St Cross, Middleton, be removed and deposited at the bank for safe keeping. The second penny was later…"

"Thanks, Ike, we've heard enough." Joe rounded on Wright. "What do you have to say about that, Dr Wright?"

All eyes in the room turned on Wright who shrugged. "It's a printer's error. It must be."

"Wright, Murray," Dockerty exploded, "what the hell are you two talking about?"

"Calm down, Dockerty. I told you once, think of your heart." Joe luxuriated in the satisfaction of the Chief Inspector's raised blood pressure. "The churches have been swapped, haven't they, Dr Wright?"

Wright nodded miserably.

Dockerty's voice was not much above a hiss. "I still don't understand."

"Then let me tell you a story," Joe suggested, "A tale of greed and deception, two churches swapped over." He indicated the book Barrett was carefully putting back into the evidence bag. "In that copy, the churches have been turned around. Sheila told me the tale when we were coming here on Saturday. It was the Middleton Penny that was stolen and the Hawksworth Penny put into safe keeping at the bank. Wright himself verified it yesterday. And that's what Jennifer Hardy's drawing was trying to tell you."

"Even if you're right, I still don't get it," Dockerty argued

"Why doesn't that surprise me? Not twenty minutes ago, I pointed out that yesterday morning you'd read Jennifer's note upside down. It had nothing to do with sex or sperm. It was trying to tell you that the churches had been swapped in that text." Joe gestured at the stained copy in Barrett's hands.

"So what?" Dockerty was on the verge of exploding.

Joe tutted. "All right, Chief Inspector, here's the story. There's a reason Wright wasn't interested in Jennifer's plan to con Kirkland and Quinton. He had his own plans and they would be a lot more lucrative than the lousy hundred thousand Jennifer's scheme could offer, plus his plan didn't need her ... well, it didn't need her alive."

Wright fumed. "Murray –"

"Quiet, Wright," Dockerty ordered. "Go on, Murray."

"When I spoke to Wright yesterday, he was at pains to point out how much he rode on his reputation. His books must be one hundred percent, factually accurate. He cannot afford to make a single mistake. Now, take a distinguished academic," Joe gestured at Wright, "who's up for some professorship in the United States, give him two divorces and a business deal gone sour, and what do you have? A distinguished academic, up for some professorship in the USA, but with a black hole where his money used to be."

"This is nonsense –" Wright began but Joe cut him off.

"Let me finish, Wright, and then you can have your say." Joe paused a moment. "I'm divorced. I know how costly it can be. I guess it'll be even more expensive in the USA. Add to that some business deal going down the pan, and I figure you needed a way out of the hole without digging it any deeper by borrowing. So you prepare a second manuscript, one with the churches the wrong way about."

Wright looked flustered and lost. "I'm sorry, I don't understand any of this."

"You're not on your own," Dockerty complained.

Joe disregarded both. "*Missing Pennies* is already on sale in the States, but it's not doing well. Apart from a few anoraks, who the hell is interested in old coins that have gone missing? You have a deal with a British publisher. It's not worth much, because even here we don't have that many coin nerds. But a deal is a deal, and it'll make you enough for a bacon sandwich or two at the Lazy Luncheonette. Then you think to yourself, suppose the Brit publisher gets the churches the wrong way round. What will that do to your reputation? It'll make you look an idiot. The professorship could go, too. What would you do in that situation, Dr Wright?"

"I don't know what you're talking about," Wright insisted, "and I refuse to sit here and listen to any more of this garbage." He got to his feet.

"Stay where you are, Dr Wright," Dockerty insisted. When Wright sat again, the Chief Inspector swung his gaze back on Joe. "Go on, Mr Murray."

Joe registered the Chief Inspector's sudden politeness and felt gratified by it. "You will sue your publisher for tarnishing your reputation. You'll probably come away with a couple of hundred thousand. The publisher may go bankrupt, but what the hell do you care? You don't live in this country these days so you don't care if a few jobbing printers and a shed load of clerks and editors lose their livelihoods. Back home, however, the publicity surrounding the case will turn the book into a bestseller, and just to add a little custard to the jam roly-poly, you'll be in demand on the lecture tour all over the world. You win on all fronts. My best guess would be a million dollars or more."

"This is total hogwash," Wright protested to Dockerty. "The man's a fantasist."

"Am I?"

Once again, Joe took Jennifer's laptop and opened up the documents folder.

"Two versions of the same file: missporig – Missing Pennies original – and misspnew – Missing Pennies new. When I checked them, orig had the churches the right way round but new had them the wrong way round. How do you explain that, Dr Wright?"

The room waited and Wright did not answer for a long time.

When he did, he was unsure, picking his words carefully. "I – I can't. If Jennifer had any plans to try this on, she

231

never said anything to me."

"And I don't believe that," Joe declared. "Let me tell you what I think happened. Jennifer, we all know, was desperate to become Mrs Dennis Wright, version three, but you weren't interested in a lush whose panties were forever in free-fall."

Patterson clucked. "Really, Joe. The woman has only been gone –"

Joe rounded on him and interrupted. "I'm telling it like it is, Tom, not like you imagine it to be." He swung back on Wright. "The trouble with your little plan is, something may go wrong, and that would expose you as a crook, so you needed a scapegoat. I'm speculating again, but it could be that you mentioned it to Jennifer in passing, maybe when she was shacked up with you in the States. Either way, you needed to shut her up."

Running the gamut of interested and accusing faces, Wright sighed. "I told Murray most of this yesterday. Jennifer was the researcher and proofreader on *Missing Pennies*, and when we first started on the project, last year, she came to America for a couple of months. We were lovers. She wanted more. She wanted a permanent home in the USA. Let's put no finer point on it, she wanted to share my permanent home in the USA. I said no. I'd done the marriage thing twice, and lost out both times. I wasn't interested in getting married a third time and I told her so. She continued to pressure me by email, and after the book deals were signed, I cut her off. My attorneys ensured that she was paid her share of the advance and royalties. When the British publisher picked up the project, I contacted her again. I figured enough time would have elapsed for her to realise there was nothing between us. Judging from her emails, I thought that was the case, and we arranged to meet here, in Leeds, over this Christmas weekend to discuss publicity for the book in England."

"But she hadn't written her hopes off, had she?" Sheila said, and Joe marvelled at her intuitive grasp of the dead woman's feelings.

"No," Wright confessed, "she hadn't. Aside from her idiotic idea for ripping off two coin collectors, she kept up the pressure. The rest of it you already know."

"Twaddle," Joe argued. "It's a persuasive argument, Wright, but it doesn't fit because we all know what happened next. She walked out of the ballroom with George and you put your plan into action. George was the perfect patsy. At three thirty in the morning, you knocked on her door carrying a bottle of wine. A peace offering. Only Jennifer never got to drink it. Instead, you hit her over the head with it. And while she lay dying, you took this computer. You realised she would have locked it with a password, you know the password anyway, but you also took her diary to make it look as though it was the work of a common thief who may want the password. And while the cops began their work and arrested George, you installed that second manuscript on the netbook. Then you realised a slight flaw in your plan, didn't you? Something you'd forgotten about. You couldn't get it back to her room. The cops had sealed it off. So you emailed copies of the manuscript to her university account. That way, if things really hit the fan, you could always blame her." Joe nudged Jennifer's netbook again. "If you check her emails, Dockerty, you'll see that one was sent from a webmail account to her university account at 4:40 this morning."

"This is complete nonsense," Wright protested.

"Is it?" Joe demanded. "You were stuck with the computer, knee deep in dirty floors and cooker hoods with environmental health due to pay a visit. You had to do something. So you dropped the diary and the computer in the refuse sack in your room, and then carried it out onto the landing and dropped it in the bin at the end of the corridor. The cops were too busy to notice, and besides, what's so suspicious about a hotel guest dropping a bag full of rubbish in a bin? The cleaners carried your trash away and you went back to bed confident that by the time the police got around to looking for the laptop, it would be buried under tons of rubbish at the local dump." Joe fingered the laptop again.

"You forgot something else, Wright. It's Christmas. This hotel is one of the largest in Leeds. The bins are emptied every day of the year, but not over the Christmas period. What do you have to say to that, Dr Wright?"

Ike Barrett stood and moved round the table to stand behind Wright, ready to arrest him.

The academic's hands shook as he rested them on the table. He stared down at the polished mahogany then slowly raised his head to drill into Joe's eyes. "You've been very clever, Murray. I can't fault your logic, and working out Jennifer's password the way you did is nothing short of brilliant, putting this together the way you have done is the work of a genius." He paused to lend his next words impact. "But it's all drivel. Yes, I'm twice divorced, yes I had a large business deal go sour last year, but as I told you before, I am still solvent and I still have a reputation as a respected academic. I had no more plans to sue my publisher than I had of conning those two clowns out of their money." He pointed at Kirkland and Quinton. "Finally, I did not kill her."

"I know."

Chapter Seventeen

Joe's announcement drew gasps from the small assembly and once again, the room threatened to erupt, but this time the noise came from both Wright and Dockerty.

The academic's face suffused with colour. "What? You have the temerity to accuse me, put me through seven kinds of hell and then say you knew I was innocent –"

"I'm sorry, Wright, but it was necessary." Joe beamed up at Ike. "You can sit down, son. You won't be arresting our distinguished historian."

At the far end of the table, Dockerty looked fit to burst. "What the hell are you playing at, Murray? First Quinton and Kirkland, and now Wright. There is such a thing as wasting police time, you know, and you just took a big step towards a charge."

"I said I was sorry, Dockerty, but this has been a trying twenty-four hours, and I needed to get all that out of my system. We were never supposed to think of Quinton and Kirkland, but some of the circumstances surrounding this case led me to believe one of them could be the killer. We were, however, supposed to believe that Wright murdered Jennifer. I said at the beginning it was a story, and I meant it. But I didn't write it." He turned his head to the right. "Did I, Tom?"

Patterson's florid features ran the gamut from alarm to confusion to embarrassment to puzzlement. "I'm sorry, Joe, I don't understand."

"The story of Dr Wright murdering Jennifer was a tale we were meant to believe, but like most people, when Tom devised it, he failed to plug all the gaps. Let me tell you what really happened." Joe licked his lips. "Poor Tom

Patterson is a man bereft of his wife, in need of another. He has been enamoured of Jennifer for years, and when he finally plucked up the courage to propose, she rejected him. She was, as Wright has told us, besotted with the idea of life on an American campus, basking in the reflected glory of a twice divorced, but highly respected historian. That angered old Tom, but what made it worse was listening in over the last few months, he learned that Jennifer had been unfaithful to him with Kirkland and Quinton, too. To really rub salt into the wounds, when Wright rejected Jennifer on Christmas Eve, instead of coming to her dear friend for solace, she jumped into bed with a common council gardener from Sanford. The anger must have been growing for months, and when he realised that he could never have her, he decided that no one could. And while he was about it, he would kick this Anglo-American upstart right where it hurt most: in the reputation."

"I don't know where all this is coming from, Joe, but you should be wary of my reputation, never mind Dr Wright's," Patterson warned.

"You over-egged the custard tart, Tom," Joe replied. "That drawing was one hen fruit too far." He whipped his attention to the two police officers. "The symbol he used is an old one for a church. There are more modern ones in use now, but Tom specialises in *old* maps. As I suggested earlier, he drew it before he ever entered the room. Then he went in, hit her with the bottle, and while she lay dying, he put the drawing and the eyeliner pencil near to her hands. But he was standing at her head, looking down her body and he put the drawing and the pencil down the wrong way round. To him, her right hand was the left and vice versa. That was mistake number one, confirmed when he told me she was not left-handed. I suggested to you, Dockerty, that it happened because he was hyped up at having just committed murder, and that's probably true. Having done all that, he then stole her computer and her diary. He needed the computer so he could manipulate the files, and he needed the diary to disappear with it so he could point the finger at Wright the way I just did. He then returned to his room and rang reception to tell them about the noise he'd heard."

Patterson folded his hands on the table and looked down at them.

"While you, Dockerty, started your investigation, he was one room away working on her computer. He probably knew her password in advance, but if not, he will have guessed it when I commented on Jennifer's necklace on Saturday night. He deleted her files of Wright's book, all except for one, *missporig*, and then he made a few changes to page 178 before saving it as *misspnew*. Or maybe he already had a copy which he'd changed and loaded onto the machine from a memory stick, but don't ask how he could have got hold of a copy of the manuscript, because I don't know. As I explained, in Tom's version of Wright's book, the churches are switched round. He couldn't be certain that the computer would be found, so he sent a copy from Jennifer's webmail account to her university account. He knew it would look as if Wright had done it. With that finished, he came out of his room clutching a bag of rubbish, which also contained the computer and diary, and calmly dropped them in the bin at the end of the corridor before taking Jennifer's personal effects from Ike. And that was it. Everything was set up to see Wright facing a murder charge." Joe's accusing stare rested on Dockerty, "But you buggered it up. You misinterpreted the note and arrested George instead of Wright."

Dockerty scowled. "You've made your point, Murray. Go on."

"Tom wasn't worried. He saw a way round the problem immediately. He had Sanford's finest detective staying here. He knew months ago that we would be here because he'd been in contact with Sylvia Goodson to arrange the Santa stunt. My presence fell nicely into his plans. He knew I would follow every lead on the case, and like a good lapdog, I did. The first night we were here, he even tested me. What could I tell about him just by looking at him?

Then, when I spoke to him in the lounge before lunch, yesterday, he was at pains to tell me that he couldn't find her laptop. He knew I would realise what had happened to it and that I would either pressure you into looking for it, or, more likely, spend an hour or two digging through the hotel rubbish to get it back, and once I did, I would follow the false trail he had laid, all the way to Dr Wright."

"Which you did," Ike pointed out. "So what put you on this track?"

"A few things, Ike," Joe declared. "First, Tom made an elementary error. He claimed not to know Quinton's name. A few hours later, he told me he'd warned Jennifer about both Quinton and Kirkland months earlier. Now that may sound like nothing, but it actually indicates a man taking a special interest in the woman. Next, although he claims not to be, Tom really imagines he's up to speed on IT, but in truth, he's like a lot of us. An amateur. Every time you do anything with a document, the properties change." Joe pulled the laptop to him again. "I checked the two manuscript files before I came down here, and it confirmed my suspicions. If you check the document properties, you'll find that *misspnew* was created at 5:30 in the morning on December 25th. Yesterday. It was accessed later, by me, but the machine takes the creation date from the date and time it was either imported to the hard drive or actually created, and the only way Tom could change that would be to change the computer's clock and calendar. Maybe I'm wrong. Maybe Tom did know about the document properties and it was part of his plan to accuse Wright."

"He was taking a risk," Dockerty observed. "If we'd knocked on his door, we may have caught him."

"Caught him doing what? Working on a laptop? It could have been his. You wouldn't have questioned him."

Barrett blushed. "He was working on a laptop, sir," he said to his superior. "He told me he'd decided to do some work because he couldn't sleep."

Dockerty fumed. "And you never mentioned it?"

Barrett was about to plead, but Joe got in first. "I

wouldn't blame Ike, Dockerty. At the time you were not even concerned for a missing computer, and to Ike, to anyone, you included, it would have looked like an academic pottering with one of his university papers."

Taking advantage of the short silence that followed, Wright pointed out, "If all this is true, he must have been planning it for months."

Joe nodded. "I'm sure he was. Do you think he just got angry with you yesterday, Doctor? Jennifer has been chasing you for over a year and Tom has probably sat back seething with anger for over a year. By yesterday, he was furious. But he made too many mistakes, and this time he couldn't know he would be rumbled." Joe reached into his carrier again and came out with a copy of *Missing Pennies*. "This isn't mine. I may be an anorak, but not to that extent. Sheila bought this in Waterstone's, yesterday. Wright even autographed it for her in the bar last night."

Joe flipped through the book to a page he had bookmarked. He held it up and open for them to see.

"Chapter seventeen, The 1933 George the Fifth Pennies," he said, and lay the book on the table before him. "I'll just read paragraph three. 'In 1970, during renovation work, the penny encased in the cornerstone at St Cross, Middleton was stolen. Alarmed at the theft, in order to prevent a repetition, the Diocese of Ripon ordered that the penny in the foundations of St Mary's, Hawksworth, be removed and deposited at the bank for safe keeping'." Joe looked up. "This is the official publisher's volume, and the two churches are correctly identified. That book," he pointed to the evidence bag in front of Barrett, "is a fake."

"Complete tommyrot," Patterson complained.

"Is it?" Joe closed Sheila's copy of the book and slid it across the table to Barrett. "Ike, check the ISBN in the barcode of Sheila's book on the back cover, and compare it to the one on your copy."

Barrett read the 13-digit code and then turned his evidence bag over as instructed. "A barcode," he said to Dockerty, "but no ISBN."

"This is absurd," Patterson protested. "How could anyone afford the expense of having a single book published? The cost would be astronomical. And all for what? Sacrificing the reputation of a fellow academic? The whole thing is absurd."

Joe retorted, "It would be enough to sow the seeds of suspicion in the minds of the police and Wright would be charged with murder. Even if he were acquitted, there would always be those who suspected him. His professorship would be scotched, his reputation called into question. It would be enough to kick him back down the ladder a few rungs. And as for the cost of printing a book, have you ever heard of POD? Print on demand?"

"There are plenty of suppliers online," Barrett confirmed.

Joe nodded. "I could get that book printed for less than a hundred pounds. I publish my own books, but I only ever have one copy of them done; I don't attach an ISBN to them because they're not for sale."

Patterson drew in his breath. "Everything I've heard could apply with equal force to Dr Wright."

Dockerty raised his eyebrows at Joe. "He has a point."

"No he doesn't," Joe disagreed, "The barcode on that fake copy is the printer's code only, but it will identify the printer, and when you and young Ike track it you'll find the printers and even if Tom gave Wright's name and address as the buyer, they'll have a credit card number that will bring you back to Leeds ... Leeds, West Yorkshire, not Leeds, Alabama." Joe took a breath. "But you won't need to go to those extremes. You see, Tom made one final and fatal error." He made one more foray into his carrier bag and came out with the tissue he had rescued from the bins. "Like an idiot, I threw this away this morning, and you almost got away with it, Tom. When you put the computer and diary in the waste bin in your room, you forgot you'd already thrown this in."

"A simple tissue," Patterson objected.

"Yeah. I thought that, too," Joe said. "It was stuck to the diary in the bag where I found the computer. I peeled it off and dropped it in my bin, but it missed and stuck to my shoe. Then, at breakfast this morning, Brenda complained about a napkin sticking like glue to her sleeve, and I realised I'd have to go through bags of rubbish again to find it." He passed it to Barrett. "Check it and you'll find it smells of some kind of solvent."

"What about it?" Barrett asked.

Joe called up the street photo again, and turning the computer so that Dockerty could see it, pointed to the Santa. "Like Quinton, Tom followed Wright and Jennifer round Leeds. Unlike Quinton, Tom did it disguised as Santa, and his motive had nothing to do with pennies. It was pure jealousy. No one would notice another Santa in a town full of them on Christmas Eve, but when he got back to the Regency, Saturday afternoon, he had to remove the beard." He gestured at the tissue. "He used a solvent to get the glue off, but some of the glue stayed on the tissue and that's what stuck it to Jennifer's diary and my shoe. It's also why Tom's face appeared so blotchy when I commented on it in the bar. What I thought was a boozer's blush was a skin reaction to either the glue or the solvent." He eyed Dockerty. "If you get your imaging boys on the photograph and get them to remove the beard, you'll find Tom's face under it." He smiled at Patterson."

Patterson shrugged "So I used tissues and solvent yesterday afternoon after Mrs Goodson and I made our charity collection. There's nothing odd about that."

Joe shook his head. "You're losing the plot again, Tom. I just told you, I salvaged that tissue along with the computer and diary from the bins yesterday afternoon. They were in a smaller bag, the kind that comes from the room. To get to the large bins outside, they had to have been disposed of on Saturday night or early Sunday morning, a good twelve hours before you came to the bar dressed as Santa. That can't be the tissue you used yesterday evening." Joe stared in satisfaction. "Now how are you going to explain that?"

Patterson straightened his shoulders and sat upright, his face filled with defiance. "I am saying nothing until I've

241

spoken to my solicitor."

Dockerty nodded to Barrett. "Caution him and take him in for questioning." While Barrett went into the official caution, the Chief Inspector concentrated on Joe. "I suppose I should say thank you. Without your, er, interference, we'd have been chasing shadows for months and we may have sent the wrong man to prison."

"So what about George?"

Dockerty looked at his watch. "All I can do, Mr Robson, is apologise. We made a mistake, but like all such errors, it was with the intention of clearing up a serious crime."

George smiled charitably. "I suppose I should let it go. The next time you're in Sanford, drop by the Lazy Luncheonette and you can buy me one of Joe's full English breakfasts."

***

Joe set a brandy in front of Sheila and a glass of soda water before Brenda.

"How's George?" Brenda asked with a burp.

"Still a bit miffed," Joe replied, settling in beside the women with a half of bitter. "He missed out on Christmas lunch here, and thanks to you getting drunk, he missed out on scoring again last night. He was thinking of suing the police for wrongful arrest." He grinned at Brenda. "I don't know what he's going to do about you."

"Difficult," Sheila said with pursed lips. She blushed. "I mean the police arresting him, not him and Brenda …" She trailed off and coughed to cover a deeper blush. "Their suspicions were well-founded; at least until they learned that he and Jennifer had already, er, you know."

"Had their oats," Brenda said, smacking her lips. She grinned and in a voice filled with glee, said, "Wait while tonight. I'll persuade him not to sue me."

Keen to change the subject, Sheila asked, "How on earth did you twig it all, Joe?"

"I suspected Tom from the moment he started pushing

me to look for the computer, and when he said he didn't know Quinton's name, and then he did, but I couldn't work out what his motive would be. Whatever it was, I knew I wouldn't find it on the computer. And then I remembered the way I behaved on Saturday night."

"With Jennifer, you mean?" Sheila asked.

"Not just Jennifer. Everyone. I was mean, moody, outright miserable."

"In other words, perfectly normal," Brenda suggested.

Joe grimaced. "All right, all right. So I'm a miserable old git. But why? You all figure it's because I'm so tight with money I need to be working all the time, and even I use that as an excuse, but it's not the truth."

"So what is?" Brenda demanded.

"Jealousy," he replied. "Naked envy. I'd love to be like you, like everyone. Let go, enjoy myself, enjoy Christmas, but I can't. You people can, and I envy that. And when I remembered how I snapped at you on Saturday night, that's when I realised just how potent jealousy can be. Powerful enough to commit murder? I think so. How many women in the past – and men – have been murdered by ex-lovers, husbands, wives? Hundreds, maybe thousands. The moment it hit me, I had Tom's motive. All I had to do then was prove it. The computer and Sheila's copy of Wright's book was almost enough, and the tissue was the clincher."

"Amazing," Sheila gasped.

Joe basked in her praise. "Yeah. I thought it was pretty clever, too."

"I didn't mean your deductions, Joe. I meant I'm amazed at your depth of self-knowledge."

Both women laughed and Joe allowed them a wrinkled grin. "All right, so you got me. But if I hadn't been on the ball, George could have finished up in court, and after he was acquitted, Dennis Wright would have been next, while the real killer got away with it."

"A sad and lonely man," Sheila sighed.

"Who? Joe or Tom Patterson?" Brenda asked. She grinned. "Only teasing, Joe. I know you're sad, but as long as you have us two for company, you'll never be lonely."

"And that poor woman," Brenda clucked.

"Who? Jennifer Hardy? An obsessive," Joe pronounced. "A high class, well-educated tramp and a crook to boot."

Brenda wagged a finger at him. "Never speak ill of the dead, Joe, or you'll end up never knowing how much fun you can have with me."

"I'd rather stay as I am, thanks." Joe nodded towards the door where Dennis Wright had just entered. "Here's another lonely man, and he prefers it that way, too."

Nodding greetings to one or two people he knew, Wright made his way to the trio. In his right hand, he carried a hardcover book. He greeted them with a smile.

"Sheila, Brenda, Joe. I owe you so much."

"We were just saying so," Joe said. "We'll send you a bill." He grinned to show he was only joking.

"If it hadn't been for you, I would have a hard time proving my innocence, especially after the way Patterson doctored Jennifer's computer." His tanned features darkened. "I can't believe how cracked he must have been."

"I think he was seriously unstable, Dr Wright," Sheila observed.

"Please, call me Dennis. And I agree. Patterson was unhinged. Sheila, your copy of *Missing Pennies* got sort of chewed up and dog-eared after all the handling. And you'd had it less than forty-eight hours. Let me make it up to you." He handed over the hardcover. "A first edition from last year. Signed, of course."

Sheila took the book and opened it at the copyright page, and read. *For Sheila, Brenda and Joe with grateful thanks for all your help.* It was signed with a flourish, *Dr Dennis Wright.*

Blushing, Sheila said, "Joe did all the hard work."

"I always do," Joe riposted.

"Joe also said he may be an anorak but not to the extent of reading up on coins. I didn't see the point in giving it to him, but you bought a copy on Saturday so I thought you should have it." Wright beamed on them. "You can always share it between the three of you."

Joe shook his head and took to his tobacco tin. "I'd need a new anorak."

Wright laughed, then eyed the tobacco tin. "I don't think you're allowed to smoke in here, Joe."

"I know, I know. I'm just rolling it up." He spread tobacco across the paper. "There is one thing you can tell us."

"Go on," Wright invited.

"Where is the Middleton Penny?"

Wright shrugged. "The truth is, no one knows. The church was undergoing renovation round about 1970 when it disappeared. It could be that the builder spotted it, put it in his pocket, then handed it over for his bus fare. All we know is it disappeared, and it's never been seen, nor heard of since."

"So Quinton and Kirkland are chasing shadows?" Brenda asked.

"If it keeps them happy, let them chase," Wright said.

On a more practical note, Sheila asked, "What about the funeral arrangements for Jennifer?"

"She has children," Wright told them. "They'll handle the matter. I have, however, arranged a memorial service for her, here in Leeds next Saturday. New Year's Eve. I'd be honoured to see you three there."

"Not a chance," Joe said. "Don't be offended, but I left my café on Christmas Eve. I can't leave it on New Year's Eve, too."

"Ignore him, Dennis," Brenda said. "He'll be there. Won't he, Sheila?"

Sheila fixed her beady eye on her employer. "You can count on it."

Joe puffed out his breath. "You know something, Dennis. All of a sudden I understand why you prefer your new found bachelorhood."

THE END

Thanks for reading this Sanford Third Age Collection title.

Why not read the next?

Murder at the Murder Mystery Weekend

Fantastic Books
Great Authors

CROOKED
CAT

Meet our authors and discover
our exciting range:

- Gripping Thrillers
- Cosy Mysteries
- Romantic Chick-Lit
- Fascinating Historicals
- Exciting Fantasy
- Young Adult and Children's
  Adventures
- Non-Fiction

Visit us at:
www.crookedcatbooks.com

Join us on facebook:
www.facebook.com/crookedcatbooks

Printed in Great Britain
by Amazon